I0762260

A HOPE
and a
FUTURE

DELORES KADING

Bladensburg, MD

Inscript

Published by Inscript Books
a division of Dove Christian Publishers
P.O. Box 611
Bladensburg, MD 20710-0611
www.inscriptpublishing.com

Book Design by Mark Yearnings
ISBN: 978-1-7375177-9-5

This novel is a work of fiction. Names, characters, places, and incidents either are the product of the author's imagination or are used fictitiously. Any resemblance to actual persons, living or dead, events, or locales is entirely coincidental.

Printed in the United States of America

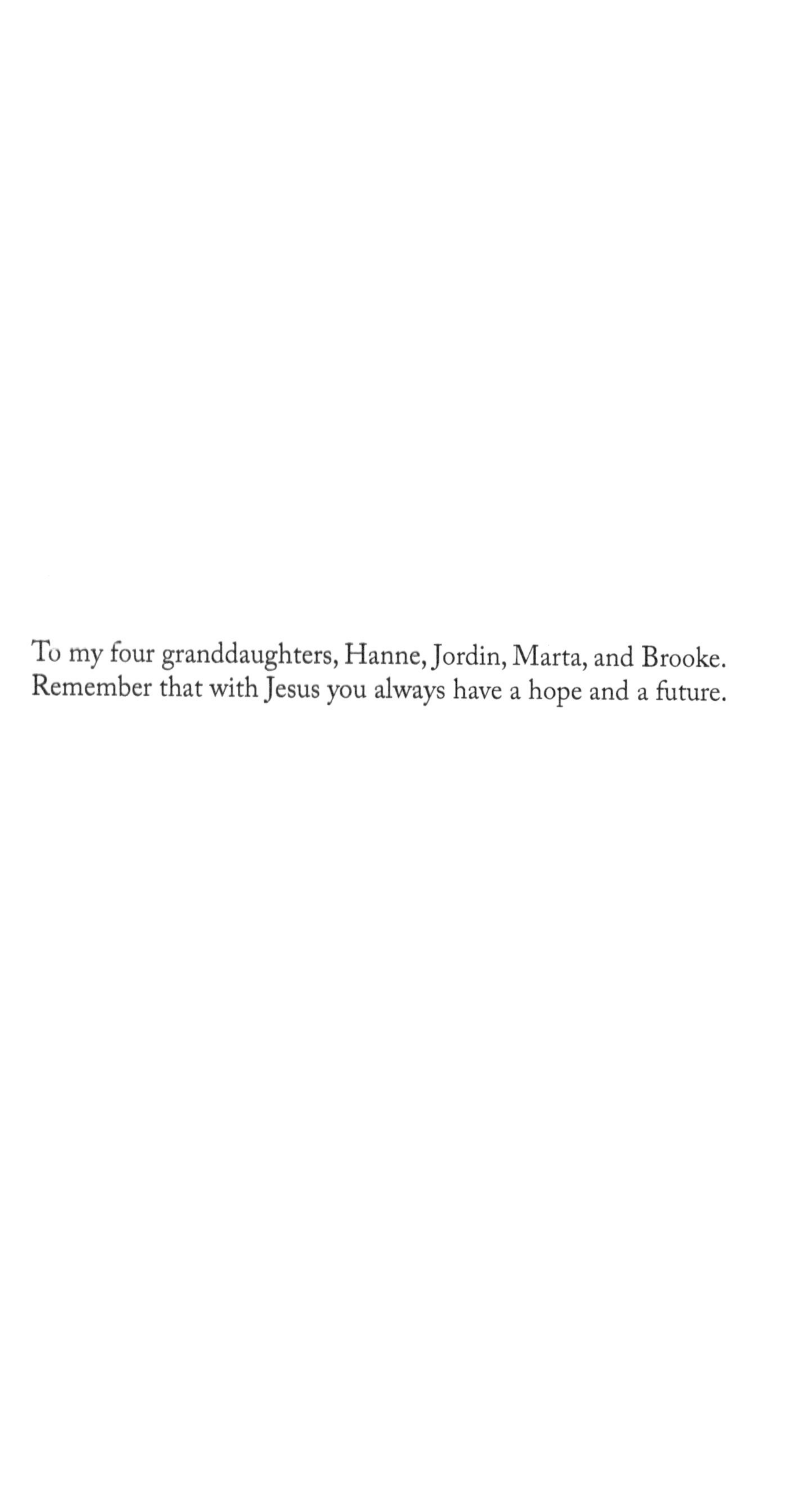

To my four granddaughters, Hanne, Jordin, Marta, and Brooke.
Remember that with Jesus you always have a hope and a future.

Chapter 1

She sat up in bed, drenched with sweat, fighting to catch her breath. The same nightmare—the one she had over and over again—had come to awaken her. She tried to stop the sobs in her throat. Calm down, she told herself, take a deep breath. She looked around the room bathed in the midsummer moonlight. Her dress and undergarments were lying over the trunk, just as she had arranged them last night.

Ruth tried to take comfort in the familiar, her eyes searching out her own things: the writing table and the bench pushed underneath it, a gift from Mother and Daddy on her sixteenth birthday. The small table by the bed with the kerosene lamp centered on a crocheted doily. The doily was her first crocheting project. The chest of drawers in the corner under the sloping ceiling of the small bedroom. The mantel clock ticking loudly in the darkened room. Pink roses, intermingled with green ivy, running up and down the wallpaper.

He had been calling to her in the dream, just like all the other times. Calling to her for help. He was in the barnyard, opening the gate to the pasture. He didn't see the bull behind him…if she had run to him when he first began calling...she could have warned him that the bull was there, that the powerful animal was preparing to charge. But she was looking for the delicate lady slipper flowers...she saw one just out of reach...she would pick that one and then see why he was calling for her. But then it was too late. If she had answered his call right away, she could have told him that the bull was there, that the bull would take his life...

The sobs came again, choking her. She covered her head with the quilt despite the warm night and held her hands over her face as she wept. Karl and Hattie mustn't hear her again. Hattie was dealing with her own grief; her face had become lined, her eyes were swollen, and her cheeks sagged in these past two weeks. Her hands were continually clasped instead of busily working in the kitchen. Karl would not meet her glance; he was seldom in the house. Silence enveloped him, making him seem distant and unapproachable. They could not comfort Ruth; they were dealing with their own grief in their own way. No one could comfort her even if someone tried. Her life was changed forever on that bright June morning when her husband was taken from her by the quick blows from the angry bull's horns. This was the reality, not a nightmare that came to her each night. The bull, the new Holstein bull that Ben was so excited about, had taken his life. The first blow was probably the fatal one, but the bull didn't stop. Rex's frantic barking had brought Ruth running to the barnyard. Ben's body was thrown in the air again and again. It took a while to realize that the screaming she heard was her own.

It was too hot to stay under the covers any longer. Ruth flung them back and lit the lamp on the bedside table. Immediately, the shadows and moonlight retreated from the brightness of the little flame. The large double bed took up much of the room. The trunk, filled with treasures from another life, stood in front of the window. It held things from her childhood home as well as wedding gifts. Embroidered sheets and pillowcases ready when needed for the home she would occupy with Ben. A sheet, hung by a heavy cord, partitioned off a corner of the room to make a closet for Ruth's few dresses and personal possessions. Ben's clothes still hung there as well.

The mantel clock on the chest of drawers, a wedding present from an aunt and uncle in Iowa, showed a little after 2:00. Sleep was out of the question; she might as well get out of bed.

Ruth sat down at the little writing desk in front of one of the room's two windows. The sheer curtain stirred gently with the breeze. She listened to the night sounds—the frogs croaking together in harmony, the June bugs banging on the window screens, a buzzing mosquito attracted to the window by the lamp light.

This window looked out to the backyard with its apple and plum trees and the garden beyond them. It was a tranquil scene. Ruth yearned for the peace of that scene, but it was out of her reach.

The second window looked out to the front of the house toward the barnyard and pasture. During the past two weeks, she tried never to look out that window.

She would write to her mother, she decided. Having a purpose helped settle her agitation and quiet her shaking hands. She found her writing tablet with its delicate thin pages, her pen, the ink bottle. How should she begin?...I am bearing up...everything will work out... Hattie said I can stay here if I like...permanently if I want...but I can't stay here without Ben...I've told Hattie and Karl that...that I have a certificate to teach school...they said they would help me find a school if that's what I want...Karl knows a lot of people, and Thomas, Ben's brother, is on the school board of the town where he lives. He might hear of someone needing a teacher. But I don't want to teach...I don't know what I want. Please tell me what to do...I have no place to go! I don't know who I am without Ben.

Ruth stared at the blank paper. What should she tell her mother? Did she beg for help, ask for some hope to grasp, some future plan to help her meet each day? Her mother could not help her now, living as she did with Ruth's older sister Anna and her husband, Kenneth. Kenneth was a pastor, and he and Anna lived in a large parsonage. Mother was needed there to help with the social obligations of a young pastor's wife. This need was compounded when Anna and Kenneth had twin babies in April. Mother's schedule was more than full. Ruth had received only one letter since Ben's death. Mother had sent a letter of condolence, saying she "hoped everything would work out right given some time."

Ruth got out the letter and reread it again:

"Anna and Kenneth join me in our sadness over Ben's death, but you must be strong."

Mother had gone on to tell of life at the parsonage. The twins were finally sleeping through the night, which was *"such a relief. Anna and I are finally getting caught up on our rest. The babies have such pleasant dispositions, yet they each have their own personalities. They look much alike, but Andy is definitely bigger. Kenneth would like to be of more help, of course, but his responsibilities as pastor keep him more than busy. Anna has turned the duties of cooking and baking over to me. There is no end to the stream of visitors here at the parsonage, some business and some social. Kenneth is so well-liked. People say they can't remember a pastor who settled in as quickly as Kenneth. And everyone says how good it is that I am here. I'm glad I can help out."*

The words blurred as Mother wrote on and on, words flowing over several pages of stationery. "What about me?" Ruth wailed aloud. "I need help, too. Where do I go? Where do I belong?"

Ruth focused on the last paragraph of her mother's letter. *"At least this sad occurrence of Ben's death occurred at the right time of year. You should be able to find a school to teach by this fall. Your father was right in advising you to get a teacher's certificate. Let me know your plans. Love, Mother."*

"My plans? I have no plans," Ruth cried out as sobs again overtook her. Daddy would have helped her. He would have had a plan for her to follow. He'd advise her what to do just as he always had since she was a little girl. He always had plans for her. It was his plan that she become a teacher. That changed with her marriage. Now she must go back to Daddy's plan.

Daddy…. Ben…. she had lost them both. If she wasn't Daddy's little girl or Ben's wife, she didn't know who she was.

Chapter 2

Daddy…the years drifted away…Ruth was playing on the rope swing that hung from a huge old oak tree close to the back porch. The little yard was neat with clipped grass and a small, carefully tended vegetable garden. Flowers of every description followed the picket fence around the yard. Daddy spent most of his time out here when he was not working at the General Merchandise. He loved puttering in the garden or tending the flowers.

Ruth was being reckless on the swing. She was going so high the swing board came within inches of the top of the porch as she sailed backward. If she twisted the swing at just the right time, her feet could kick the porch roof. The impact of the contact with the roof sent the swing and her reeling around from side to side.

"Mercy, Ruth! Be careful. You'll either kick a hole in the roof or fall off and break a leg," her mother admonished as she sat on the porch shelling peas.

"Mother, isn't she ever going to grow up?" Anna sighed as she sat beside her mother stitching a pillowcase.

Anna was thirteen and three years older than Ruth. *She probably wasn't ever ten*, Ruth thought scornfully. She certainly didn't know how to have fun and apparently thought no one else should either. Unfortunately, Mother always seemed to listen to Anna. Anna was the prudent one, the one you could depend on. That's what Mother always said.

"Ruth, you must watch Anna to learn how to be a young lady. It's time you stop running around like an uncivilized hoodlum."

Anna even looked dependable. Her blonde hair was always in place, neatly braided into one long thick braid. Since her thirteenth birthday, she coiled it into a bun at the nape of her neck, giving her a decidedly grownup look. With her blue eyes and small upturned nose, Anna was thought to be the prettier of the two England girls. Not that Ruth wasn't pretty—in fact, they looked much alike. But Ruth's hair never seemed to cooperate with braiding and kept coming undone. Her nose was covered with freckles, and dirt smudges seemed to appear out of nowhere on her face and clothing. Where Anna's blouses stayed neatly tucked into her long skirts, Ruth's tended to hang out of her waist band. Her long stockings sagged above her scuffed shoes. She was small-boned and thin, making her face rather angular while Anna's face was pleasingly round. Mother's eyes lit up when she looked at Anna; she usually sighed when looking at Ruth.

Thinking on these things, Ruth gave a mighty kick against the porch roof so forcefully that she dislodged herself from the swing board seat. Her hands gripped the ropes to keep herself from falling, but her feet hit the ground with a heavy thud.

"All right, Ruth, that's the end of your swinging today," Mother said somewhere between exasperation and concern. "Some time, you are really going to hurt yourself. Just look at you!"

Ruth was a mess. Her hair, undone from her braids, was sticking out at odd angles. A mixture of sweat and dirt made little paths down her cheeks. Her pocket was half torn off her pinafore, and her shoes, after their hard contact with the ground, were covered with dirt that spread up over most of her stockings.

Anna looked her over critically and was about to make a comment when the three of them heard the gate squeak as it opened.

"Daddy's home from the store!" Ruth sang out. Father closed the General Merchandise Store at six o'clock six nights a week unless a last lingering customer held him up with conversation. It took him just a few minutes to walk the short distance from the store to the house. His arrival home was a major event in the daily life of the family, especially for Ruth.

Daddy carried a tall sapling in his long arms. The roots were bound in a burlap sack. The branches surrounded his thin face, tousling his unruly sandy-colored hair.

The mild irritation between the girls and Mother's scolding of Ruth's actions were forgotten.

"Ahh, you ladies are a sight for sore eyes," Daddy said. He paused ever so slightly over his words when he noticed Ruth's appearance. But he smiled at them all through his thick glasses and made no mention of it.

Mother stood up with the pan of peas in her hand. Her round face flushed a little as she gave a knowing look at the tree Father carried.

"Daddy, can I show you what I can do on the swing?" Ruth asked breathlessly, ignoring his struggle with his burden.

"Ruth, you remember what I said," Mother interrupted sharply. "Supper is just about ready anyway."

"No swinging now, Baby Girl," Daddy said, giving her a friendly wink. "But I will need some help after supper. Look what Old Man Simpson brought me to help pay down on his bill—an apple tree. Must be all of five feet tall. Should be ready to bear fruit in a year or two."

"Humph—trees don't put meat and potatoes on our table," Mother fumed. "Whatever happened to paying bills with money?"

Daddy smiled. "You'll change your mind when we have apple pies for dessert and applesauce for breakfast. I thought digging up one of his apple trees was a pretty creative way to pay me."

Mother led the way into the house, letting the screen door slam behind her.

"I'll help you dig a hole for the tree," Ruth offered as Daddy held the door open for his daughters.

"I'll welcome the help," Daddy answered, "But supper first."

"I'll wash the dishes," Anna said with a responsible air. "Mother will want to decide where to plant it."

"What helpful, hard-working girls I have. But let's get to the important things first. What's for supper, Mother?"

***

Happy memories. Daddy always had some project going on in the yard. Ruth and Anna vied for Mother's and Daddy's approval. Sometimes it seemed to Ruth that Anna especially pleased Mother with her helpfulness around the house. But Daddy always seemed to smile when his eyes settled on Ruth. Maybe her tomboyish ways made up for his lack of sons. Ruth had the satisfaction of knowing that she was the apple of her father's eye.

Those happy memories were before the cough started.

It was the summer that Ruth was fourteen when she noticed the change in Daddy. He would come home from the store shortly after 6:00 as always, but he would come wheezing and out of breath. At times he leaned on the gate before opening it. There was no energy for work in the yard now; Ruth tended the garden and flowers. Daddy finished reading the paper before he left the living room for his bed. Worst of all was the cough. Daddy's body would be racked by the harsh dry cough that seemed to never stop. His thin frame became thinner; his face turned pale, and his cheeks became sunken. Then there was the blood on the handkerchiefs that he held to his mouth during coughing attacks.

"Tuberculosis," the doctor said. "Get plenty of rest and fresh air. But as for a cure...well, we hope you have a couple good years yet."

A couple good years to set affairs in order, to plan for the welfare of his family. So much to do, so many decisions to make. Even as his health declined, the family waited for him to make the decisions they faced. Mother lived her days in her usual routine, never fully grasping the situation. She never talked of the future with the girls. It was as if they were all holding their breaths.

The General Merchandise Store had done well over the years. Daddy was good to his customers. He sold at a fair price, and he stood behind his products. Customers would get a good deal on anything from eggs to plow lays, and they knew it. Credit was given to anyone who was down on his luck. It wasn't unusual for Father to work out a swap for farmers needing sugar and coffee but having plenty of garden vegetables to trade.

The England family never wasted a dime, but there was never a time that they had to do without either. Mother always saw to it that she and the girls were dressed in the latest fashions. Mother was a good cook and liked to experiment with new recipes. During the weeks, she would plan and prepare abundant Sunday dinners when friends would often accompany the family home from church. Mother glowed with the compliments showered on her.

Ruth spent more and more time at the store with Daddy. She went directly to the store after school during the school sessions and spent whole days there between school terms. She now did all the ordering, unpacked the crates of merchandise, stocked the shelves, and kept up the ledger. Daddy sat on a chair stuffed with pillows. He stood up when customers came in and visited with them while leaning heavily on the counter. But when customers left, he sagged in the chair and often quickly fell asleep. Ruth tried to anticipate what needed to be done, so Daddy could save his dwindling energy. Despite his health problems, Ruth noticed that Daddy always spoke kindly and respectfully to his customers. They, in turn, always took time to visit, often asking for advice on their own projects. Ruth sometimes wondered if customers came more for the conversation than for supplies. There was no doubt that Daddy was an admired man in the community.

"This town just wouldn't be the same without Howard and Harriet England," Ruth and Anna would hear about their parents. "There isn't anyone in the county that they don't know. And Howard would give a helping hand to anyone who needs it."

The diagnosis brought changes to the family. Much to Anna's delight, it was agreed that Anna could quit school. She had finished her tenth grade and never enjoyed the studying that went with attending school. Her grades showed her priorities. Anna was much too interested in the fashions of her friends and the gossip of which boys liked which girls. She could continue those interests at church functions.

Ruth, however, would continue attending school. She enjoyed the challenge of learning the assignments and writing her thoughts in compositions. She was quick to finish her work and often was asked to help with the younger students. Arrangements were made so Ruth could leave school early to go to the General Merchandise to help her father. The school master was a friend of Howard's and was willing to have her attend school and help at the store.

While Ruth was glad she could make Daddy's work a little easier, she hated working at the store. Working on the books, keeping the ledger up to date, stocking the shelves, and taking inventory were all good, but she dreaded helping the customers. Beyond the briefest interchange of business transactions, she had trouble thinking of anything to say. Pleasantries eluded her; she mixed up her words and could not speak without stammering. Having the doorway of the store darken with a potential customer was enough to bring a flush to her face. Often, she lingered at the back door of the store wishing she could be outside and not deal with store business. Her reticence in talking was noticed; in fact, if Father was home resting as he became weaker, customers would often take a quick look around the store and say they would come back later.

For some time now, Ruth noticed that Tommy, an older boy who lived with his family just outside of town, began hanging around the store when Father took his rest time. "Can I help you with something?" she asked him finally. A deep blush started up his neck and face. Dark hair almost covered his eyes, and he dug his hands into his pockets.

"Naw, I'm just waiting to see if Pa stops here. He might want me to help him load some stuff."

"Well, I haven't seen your pa."

"He might come. I'll just wait around here to see if he does."

"You can wait just as well outside as in here."

He grinned at her. "I like waiting inside better. Then I can talk to you."

"I don't like talking to you. Wait outside."

He slouched out the door. *Why did I talk that way to him?* Ruth wondered. He wasn't hurting anything, wasn't in the way, or even impolite. Her words just seem to abruptly come out of her mouth, even when she meant no harm.

If young men came to the store specifically to talk to Ruth, her conversation seemed so awkward and unfriendly that an invitation to walk her home or a request to visit her some evening never happened. She tried to study Father's art of making conversation, but she never seemed to get the hang of it. "You don't have to say much to have a good conversation," Father reassured her. "Listening to others is more important than talking. Just be sincerely interested in what they're saying, maybe ask a question now and then."

***

It was more than a year after the tuberculosis diagnosis. The family sat at the supper table when Daddy put down his knife and fork and wearily announced, "We can't keep this up. I'm going to sell the store."

Ruth choked on her food, and Mother gasped, "But, Howard, how will we make a living?"

"I can run it for you, Daddy," Ruth spoke up quickly. "You could stay home and rest all the time until you are better. I know how things are done there."

Howard probably knew the store would no longer be a thriving business with Ruth at the helm, but he only smiled and said, "Thank you, Ruth, but I don't want you saddled with such responsibility. I'm too tired to talk more about it, but it's what I must do now while I have the strength."

Finding a new buyer would be no problem, although loyal customers worried about changes coming to their General Merchandise. The business was flourishing, and the store was well maintained.

Ruth spent extra time at the store during the next weeks making notes for whoever would buy the store. Several prospective men came to look over the building and merchandise. Father would come to meet with them and then slowly walk home, exhausted from the exertion.

Ruth had been in the lean-to at the back of the store, counting rakes and garden tools. She entered the building and sat down at the ledger to record the numbers. She realized two men were talking just outside the door of the store.

"This store ain't never goin' to be the same without England in here. People like coming here because of him. He gave a good price and good conversation to boot. Took care of everybody. Old Erickson never paid a cent on his bill for a couple of years after his barn burned. Bet he never got caught up on his bills before he croaked. Yup, you could depend on England to take care of people."

"Yeah, probably took too good a care of his daughters. I don't know how they'll take care of themselves after he's gone. The younger one who works here doesn't seem to know up from down when it comes to working with customers. Those girls are purty enough—they better hope they can find some husbands who'll take care of them like their pa always has."

"I hear Mrs. England won't even admit that England is going to die. I don't think he's got much time left. It's goin' to be plenty hard on that family when he kicks the bucket."

Ruth didn't even try to assist them. She put her head down on the ledger and wept.

Chapter 3

The sale of the store was completed. Howard, however, did not find the peace he expected. The good price he received would dwindle over the coming years. Then what?

"I need to know that my three girls are provided for," he said repeatedly. A familiar gesture was now running his fingers through his hair that seemed to grow grayer and thinner with each passing day.

For Anna, the problem was solving itself. The young preacher, doing his internship at the First Community Church, showed an increasing interest in her. Now almost nightly, Reverend Kenneth Adams came to call on the family after supper. After preliminary comments on the weather and Howard's health, he and Anna would go to the parlor, Howard would retire to bed, and Mother and Ruth would do hand sewing in the kitchen. Mother engrossed herself with knitting or embroidery. Ruth sat close to the kitchen doorway and tried to work on a quilt that never seemed to get closer to completion. She made no secret of the fact that her main goal was overhearing conversations between Anna and Kenneth.

Based on her eavesdropping, Ruth was expecting a wedding for Anna.

"But, what about you, Ruth?" Daddy's forehead creased with worry. "What will become of my Baby Girl and Mother when I'm not here to take care of both of you?"

Ruth didn't want to hear such talk and didn't want to speculate. She couldn't imagine life without Daddy. What would happen to the two of them without Daddy making the decisions for them? Her only work experience besides helping at home were the hours spent at the store before the sale. She certainly had no plans to marry. The young men she had met at the store were as awkward and stilted as she.

"I'll keep house for Mother. I can be a housekeeper for some families in town. Maybe I can enlarge the garden and sell some produce. Or maybe the new owners of the store would like me to keep the books for them." Ruth tried to reassure her father on the rare occasions she was willing to talk of the future with him.

Howard became almost angry with her. "My daughter will not sell produce or clean other people's houses," he said adamantly, even though his passion made him cough. "And the new owners don't need any outside help. I've been talking to the schoolmaster. A normal teacher's training is being offered here in Rolling Valley, starting this summer. I want you to enroll in that. You are a good student, and there's always a demand for teachers. It's a respectable position. You won't have to depend on others."

Ruth didn't want to teach school. While she liked school and loved to read any books she could get her hands on, she had no desire to try to teach children who did not want to be taught. She had had enough of that when she helped the school master with the younger students. She knew they would rather be outside; and as a matter of fact, so would she. Actually, she would have been very willing to sell garden produce or help in people's yards. But all this conversation was too upsetting to both her and Daddy. And Daddy always had a coughing episode when he tried to talk more than a few words. She didn't have the heart to argue. Maybe Daddy would surprise the doctor and get well. Maybe he would live for years, and she wouldn't have to become a teacher.

But Howard wasn't getting well. As the warm days of spring arrived, he did not even have the interest (or perhaps it was the lack of strength) to walk to the backyard to check the garden or flowers. The girls set up a bed on the porch where he spent most of his time. At first, friends and neighbors would drop by for short chats. As he coughed up more blood and fell asleep even during conversations, visitors became infrequent. He spent his days between sitting on a cushioned chair or lying on his bed on the porch.

As Howard's health declined, Mother seemed, more than ever, to lose her grasp on reality. She sat idly rocking on the porch as Howard slept. She let the girls make more of the decisions regarding housekeeping and even in the care of their father. Anna took over the household tasks, and Ruth studied for her final high school exams. She cared for the yard and garden during the long spring evenings.

May of the year 1908 escalated the changes to the England family. Ruth graduated from high school, first in her class of eleven students. Despite his condition, Howard wanted a reception in their home to honor Ruth's achievements.

"Kenneth and I are going to share a secret with our guests tonight," Anna whispered to Ruth as they put sandwiches on platters and filled jugs with lemonade. "Having people over tonight is a good time for our announcement. We haven't even told Mother or Daddy yet. Just pretend like you're surprised."

Ruth had eavesdropped on enough conversations that she didn't need Anna's whispers in her ear.

Later that evening, Howard stood up from his chair, and the small group of friends instantly stopped their quiet visiting. "I'm so glad you could come tonight to recognize Ruth's graduation," he began slowly. "It's an important milestone in the lives of my family." He smiled at Ruth but then coughing racked his thin frame. Kenneth quickly helped him settle back in his chair.

"It certainly is an important milestone," Kenneth spoke up. "At this opportunity, Anna and I would like to announce our engagement. We plan to be married in early August. Mr. England, we hope we have your blessing."

Howard truly was surprised and did not reply. Mother, however, quickly hurried to Kenneth and Anna. "Of course, you have our blessing. We are thrilled to have Anna become a preacher's wife. We will have another occasion to celebrate this summer."

The thought that a funeral may also be observed in the near future occurred to many gathered at the home.

***

The wedding announcement finally awakened Mother out of the stupor that had immobilized her during the last weeks. "My goodness, I have only three months to help Anna sew her trousseau," she said at the breakfast table the next morning. She spoke briskly in a voice she had not used for months. "We must get busy. Anna, right after breakfast dishes, we must sit down and make a list of everything you will need. Material will have to be ordered. The wedding will be held here in the house, naturally. I think we may also need to purchase some new pieces of furniture. Of course, we will check around for the best prices first," she added to Father. Although he had hardly eaten or spoken at breakfast, he looked satisfied to have his wife back to her usual position of event planner in the lives of her family.

"Oh, and Ruth, I am so glad you are done with school. We have so much to do this summer. Do you have special plans?"

"She does," Howard answered for her. He took a deep breath and spoke slowly with great determination not to cough. "Harriet, Ruth is going to enroll in the normal teacher training that starts next week right here in Rolling Valley. The school master and I have been talking about the program, and I've taken care of the cost of the training. Ruth can get a First Grade Studies certificate after six months. If she passes that examination (and of course, she will), she can decide if she wants to continue for another session to get her Second Grade Studies. The training for all the towns in the county is right here in Rolling Valley."

It was the first time Mother had heard these plans. Mother and Anna were pleased that "what to do with Ruth" was taken care of. Ruth had no heart to tell her father she would rather not be a teacher. But, she realized, part of her was relieved to have her future decided for her. She did need a plan.

Howard rested his voice for a bit, then added, "Ruth, a Second Grade Studies certificate doesn't necessarily make you a better teacher, but it would give you more training. You'd get more pay with that certificate." He coughed and paused. "I'd recommend you plan for a Second Grade Studies certificate. But let's get the first session, the First Grade Studies, out of the way first."

Howard's announcement had been more of a surprise to Ruth than Anna's had been the night before. That one had been expected by everyone, except possibly her parents. Howard's long speech tired him. "Girls, please help me to my bed on the porch. I think I'll have a nap. Maybe you can bring me some leftover lemonade after I wake up."

Ruth and Anna took Howard's arms and gently got him settled on his bed. Ruth squeezed back the tears from her eyes as she tenderly tucked a blanket around his bony frame. "Thank you, Daddy, for taking care of things for me," she whispered. She tried to push the thoughts away…will Daddy be here to see if I pass my examination for either certificate?

The England family settled into a summer routine. Howard seemed much relieved to have the future of his girls settled. So much so that for the beginning of the summer, his health improved. He enjoyed sitting on the porch and watching Mother and Anna sew and listening to their wedding plans. When Ruth returned from her Normal Teaching Training studies late in the afternoon, he questioned her on all she was learning.

"You'll be a good teacher," Father told her. She didn't reply. The training was boring; the school was hot. She hoped she would never have to teach.

Howard would get settled for the night right after supper. Anna would entertain Kenneth in the parlor, Mother would continue to sew into the evening, and Ruth would spend some time in the garden and then settle at the kitchen table with her studies. The weeks passed quickly.

After holding his own until after the Independence Day celebration, Howard again began to decline. Ruth was distraught as she watched him struggle to get his breath, to try to stifle his cough. He used a cane all the time now, but even so, he needed assistance to go the short way from the table to the porch. "I have to keep up my strength for Anna's wedding," he told them often. He no longer talked about walking her to the front of the living room where the wedding ceremony would take place. *He's running out of time*, Ruth thought frantically. *How can I buy him a few more weeks?*

"Mother," Ruth implored one morning, "Can I take Daddy to see a doctor in Grand Forks? Maybe he can get some medicine, or something can be done to help him get some strength. Maybe we're not doing all we can for him just doctoring in our little town."

Harriet was startled, which exasperated Ruth. Couldn't Mother see how very frail and weak he was becoming? Did she not realize how much he wanted to be part of the wedding? "What more can a doctor do in Grand Forks than our own Dr. Jelly here in Rolling Valley can do?"

"I'd like to try," Ruth begged. "With the wedding so close, I don't expect you or Anna to go. I can make the trip with him on the train. Please let me try. Maybe we're overlooking something that might help him. Maybe something would give him more strength for the wedding."

Harriet finally reluctantly agreed if Howard was willing. Howard was surprisingly excited about the trip when Harriet and Ruth talked to him about it. "If nothing else, Ruth and I will have an outing. I haven't ridden on a train since I was a kid. We'll have a good time, won't we, Ruth?"

Harriet made an appointment in Grand Forks through Dr. Jelly. "It's not going to do any good, Mrs. England," Dr. Jelly warned her. "The trip is only going to wear him out."

Chapter 4

Ruth was glad she got her way about taking Daddy to Grand Forks, but now that the actual appointment was made, she fought down panicky feelings that washed over her.

Ruth knew from the beginning that neither Mother nor Anna would go along. They both thought the trip was a bad idea. Daddy's condition would make the trip very difficult. Mother's and Anna's days were filled with wedding preparations. Also, Mother explained, "The train tickets will be expensive. Better just two tickets than three or four." Since Howard's illness, she had become obsessively frugal except for wedding expenses. "I'm sure you can manage to get Daddy to Grand Forks by yourself. I know he would enjoy his time with you."

The trip would mean that Ruth and Howard would take the train early in the morning. The ride to Grand Forks would be more than an hour. Then, there were the logistics of getting from the depot to the clinic and back again to catch a returning train late in the afternoon. An exhausting day for anyone. For Daddy, was it even a possibility? Too late now. She had the tickets; this is what she wanted; this is what she got. There would be no backing out.

There wasn't room for Mother and Anna in the buggy, so they said their goodbyes at the house. In an unusual display of affection, Mother clung to her husband for a long moment. Then she handed a basket to Ruth and said briskly, "There is food in here if you get hungry on the train. Ruth, you will have to find some restaurant in Grand Forks for something to eat before returning home." She hurriedly turned to go back into the house, but not before Ruth saw tears in her eyes.

Kenneth took Howard and Ruth to the train depot in his buggy. He helped Howard up the steps of the train car and wished them well. "I better get back to my horse. He's frantic with the noise of the locomotive. I'm afraid he'll break the tie rope and take off. I'll see you tonight."

"We'll be fine," Ruth said in a trembling voice. "Thank you for your help. And thank you for being willing to meet us here again tonight," Ruth called after him as he hurried off to his plunging horse.

As Ruth and her father started for some empty seats, the train suddenly lurched into motion. Howard teetered and was about to fall except for the quick action of a young man who bounded from his seat. He quickly put a firm arm around Howard's waist and guided him to an empty seat.

"That was a quick move, young man," Howard said with a wobbly smile. "You would have had a bigger job getting me up off the floor."

"We would have managed, Sir," the man said with a grin. "Right, Ma'am?" His smile included them both as Ruth and Howard settled in the empty seats. He retook his seat opposite them.

"My name is Ben Gottlieb," he said, stretching out his hand to Howard and then to Ruth. "This is my first train ride, and I am really enjoying it. Never covered so much ground so fast. I'm from close to Twin Oaks. Since it's a very small town, you probably have never heard of it."

"It's been years since I've been on a train. It's a great way to travel. Though I wish I was feeling a little more energetic. My name is Howard England, and this is my daughter, Ruth."

Ruth felt the young man's friendly eyes look closely at her. His eyes were strikingly blue. For some reason, it felt hard to get her breath.

"Is this your first train ride, too, Ma'am?"

"Yes."

For the life of her, she couldn't think of anything else to add. Should she explain why they were on the train, that it was no pleasure trip? But you don't go blurting out personal information to a complete stranger. Ruth's fear of making conversation kept her mouth shut.

"No more 'Sir' and 'Ma'am,' Ben," Howard smiled. "We won't know who you are talking to. Call us Howard and Ruth." He had only finished the sentence before his body was wracked with a coughing spasm. Ben looked on with alarm.

"Can I help you, Sir? I noticed a jug of water at the front of the car. Could I get you a drink?"

They waited until his cough finally subsided enough to allow Howard to answer. "I could use one, thanks. But remember no more 'Sir.'"

"Sorry, Sir…I mean, Howard. I'll get you that water."

The water and the gentle motion of the train seemed to relieve Howard as the eastern North Dakota fields slipped by. The three sat looking out the window. Ben occasionally mentioned things that caught his interest as the train chugged through the countryside.

Ruth was becoming embarrassed about her shyness. She had said only one word since boarding the train. Daddy had coached her in making conversation when she worked at the store. Be interested in what they say…. ask questions…. She surprised herself when she asked, "Why are you making this train trip?" It sounded rather bold when the words came out of her mouth.

Ben laughed. "I've been waiting for somebody to ask me. It's a big deal for me. You see, I farm with my parents—we run a grain and dairy cattle operation. I'll be taking on more of the responsibility of running the farm since the folks are getting older. I've been studying on how to get better milk production. Right now, we have a mixture of cattle breeds, but I've been reading about a Holstein breed. Ever heard of it?"

"I've heard mention of the breed by some of the customers at the store. Can't say I know anything about them, though," Howard replied.

"Well," Ben said, grinning sheepishly, "I'm the man to tell you."

He pulled out a portfolio from a valise at his feet. "The Holsteins are a relatively new breed in this country. They were brought in from Europe—the Netherlands, I think—a little over 50 years ago. They are the highest producers of milk of any breed. Here, I have a picture of a milk cow."

Ben rummaged through the papers in his portfolio and brought out a picture of a black and white milk cow. "She's a beauty, isn't she?" he said as he showed the picture to both Howard and Ruth.

Ruth had not given cows much thought before. She knew her family bought milk from a man who lived up the street. He kept a milk cow in his back yard and brought a pail of fresh milk to the England's doorstep each morning. Ruth had no idea what kind of cow produced the milk—she never even knew there were different breeds of cattle.

But this cow on the picture was definitely nice looking, as far as cows went. "Are they always black and white?" she asked.

"Almost always, but some are red and white.

"My cousin who lives in Reynolds has a neighbor who raises Holsteins. He's very impressed with them. That's why I'm making this trip—to see them and learn more about them. This neighbor has sold quite a number of bulls to farmers in the area."

"How would you ever get an animal back to your farm?" Ruth asked with interest.

"Well, if I would decide to buy a bull, he'd have to ride the train same as me. It would be his first ride, too. And probably his one and only one.

"Uh, oh," Ben stopped talking and nodded toward Howard. "I guess not everyone is as interested in Holsteins as I am. I put your dad to sleep."

"Oh, I'm sure it wasn't because you aren't interesting," Ruth assured him quickly. "He's not in good health and sleeps a lot." She heard Daddy's instructions about conversation in her ears. "I'd like to hear more about these cows."

"Well, when they were first brought to this country, they were in the Eastern part, but now they are becoming more popular throughout the Midwest. I've been hearing more about them with every Association meeting I attend. The breed does have a drawback, though. While Holsteins are top milk producers, their milk is not the highest in butter fat. They also are not so good at putting on fat for good eating. That's why I think it would be good to keep our milking shorthorn cows and keep just a Holstein bull. Combining the two breeds seems like a good way to go."

Ruth studied Ben's face as he talked. His voice was so pleasant, it had almost a musical quality about it. He was boyish in his eagerness to talk about Holsteins, although Ruth guessed he was probably in his mid-20's. His hair was blond and curled a little at his neck. He wore denim pants and a blue short-sleeved shirt that revealed deeply tanned arms and neck. She felt she could never get tired of the sound of his voice, so she tried to think of questions to ask him. She continued to ask him questions about cows, though she really didn't care what he talked about. She remembered how shy she felt when talking to the young men who came into the store. And how awkward they were at making conversation. How different with Ben! He spoke confidently and knowingly. He was so fluent she didn't have to think about making conversation.

Ben continued, "Did you hear that President Taft keeps a Holstein at the White House? She grazes on the White House lawn and provides milk for the first family. Her name is Pauline Wayne."

Ben made everything about cows fascinating even to Ruth, who had never given cows more than a passing thought.

"Wow, I'm sorry to keep talking about my stuff. It's just that you're such a good listener, I'm going on and on and on. Sorry. Guess you've been feeding my ego with your interest. I appreciate that, but I promise not to mention cows again for the rest of the trip."

Howard coughed some in his sleep, then returned to gentle snoring. "I don't mean to pry, and feel free not to answer if you don't care to," Ben said softly, "but is your dad seriously sick?"

Ruth nodded. "We're on our way to see a doctor in Grand Forks. It may be a futile trip."

Ruth told about the diagnosis of tuberculosis and her insistence to try something more. She spoke haltingly at first. But Ben seemed genuinely interested in all she said, and the words came easier. She told him about the close relationship that she shared with her father and then went on to tell him about the store and her family. She couldn't remember talking so much at one time. Ben asked questions that led her to open up and tell more about her life.

"Grand Forks coming up!" the conductor called as he walked through the car.

Ruth couldn't believe the time had gone so quickly.

She gently shook Howard. "Daddy, we're soon to Grand Forks. You need to wake up."

Howard looked a little bewildered at first, then realized where he was. He looked pale and fragile and very tired.

"Are you able to get off the train, Sir?" Ben asked in a concerned voice.

"I can make it. I'll just lean on Ruth here." He stooped over to pick up his small valise at his feet. He grunted and let it sit there.

"But how will you get to the clinic?"

Ruth answered in a worried voice, "Dr. Jelly said there would be buggies for hire. Daddy won't be able to do any walking."

Ben looked at Howard and then at Ruth. "Look," he said quickly. "I'm not on a rigid schedule. It doesn't matter exactly when I show up at my cousin's place, and Pa and Ma don't expect me home on a certain day. I would consider it an honor if I could help you get to the clinic and back to the depot again after your appointment. Would that be okay with you?"

Ruth shook her head quickly. "Oh, we couldn't put you out like that. Daddy, don't you think we can make it by ourselves?"

"You know, Ruth, when someone offers to help, I think maybe we should take it. This young man seems capable to me. I think we'll let him get us to the clinic and back to the train."

Did Ruth see a glimmer of a twinkle in his eye? She wasn't sure. But she knew she was very glad to have Ben's help. And his presence. Yes, he was capable. He would get them to the clinic and back.

The next few hours were a blur in Ruth's mind when she looked back at them. Mostly she was aware of Ben quietly taking charge, of his thinking of needs before the need arose. He hired a rig to get to the clinic and helped them to the waiting room.

Ruth accompanied Howard into the doctor's examination room. The doctor asked them both questions, and he thoroughly listened to Howard's lungs, checked his reflexes, looked into his eyes—all the things their own Dr. Jelly had already done.

"I have no good news for you," the doctor told them both after the examination. "There's no cure for tuberculosis. You've already been told what to do to prolong your strength. I can't stress enough the importance of eating right, getting good rest, and getting a lot of fresh air. Now in this nice weather, sleep with the windows open; sleep outside in an open porch if you can. Enjoy your good days, rest when your body tells you to. I'm sorry I don't have some magic medicine to make you feel good."

"I didn't expect that," Howard said softly. "But my family—especially my daughter here—wanted to make sure all the avenues were tried. My older daughter is getting married, and I want to be part of it. I was willing to make the trip, but I'm not surprised with the result. Thank you for your time."

Ruth felt tears slip down her cheeks as she walked with her father out to the waiting room. For a moment, she felt panic that Ben would not be there; but as they entered, he immediately jumped up from his chair and hurried to Howard's side.

He didn't question the doctor's diagnosis, but looking at Ruth's face, he must have known the news was not good.

"Do you want to sit and rest for a bit before we start back to the depot?" he asked.

"I'd like to rest after I get to the depot, but I'm sure you two are hungry," Howard answered. "I should sit here while you find a place to eat."

"No, let's get you back to the depot first," Ben decided. "You and Ruth can rest there while I find a restaurant. I'll bring some food back for all of us. We have a wait before the train gets in."

Howard went to sleep on the depot bench almost immediately after eating. He was exhausted, but his color was good, and he had eaten the ham sandwich and pickles with surprising vigor.

"I don't know how to thank you," Ruth told Ben. "I realize now I never could have carried out this appointment without your help. What will you do until you catch the next train south again? That won't be until tomorrow."

Ben grinned at her. "I have some books along—besides the Holstein information. And maybe I'll walk back uptown to look around. I can sleep on a bench here at the depot tonight. But are you sure you can get back to Rolling Valley after I help your dad on the train? I could travel back with you and then double back south again."

"Oh, no, please. I couldn't let you do that. I'm sure Daddy will sleep most of the way home. My sister's fiancé will meet us at the train depot in Rolling Valley."

They were quiet for a time. Ben looked as if he was going to speak several times and then changed his mind. They heard the train whistle in the distance. "I'd like to find out how your dad is doing and how things are going with you," he blurted out quickly. "Would you mind if I would write to you?"

His words echoed inside her head. He wants to write? She had been dreading the time of departure. The thought of not seeing Ben again or hearing his voice made her life seem empty even though she had known him for less than a day. "I'd like that," she answered and then paused. "And, of course, I'd like to find out what you thought of the Holsteins that you visited."

Ruth wrote her address on a piece of paper for Ben. "How do you spell your last name?" she asked. "I haven't heard that name before."

"G-o-t-t-l-i-e-b, Gottlieb. It's a very German name, I guess." Ben said. "But I kind of like it. It means 'God's love.'"

Chapter 5

Both Howard and Ruth were exhausted in the days following their trip, but they were glad they had gone.

"It was good to have that time together, Baby Girl," Howard told her. "And I guess getting another doctor's opinion is always good." He stopped to catch his breath. "And, meeting new people is always good, too, huh?" The old familiar look of mischief accompanied his smile.

Ruth did not have a reply, but she always offered to go to the post office to check for mail before Mother or Anna thought to do so. A few days after the trip to Grand Forks, her walk to the post office was rewarded with a letter from Ben. She hid it in her pocket until she could close the door to her bedroom and read it in private. She read the letter slowly, carefully.

Dear Ruth,

I am trusting that the return trip for you and your father went well and without any unpleasant incidents. I hope your father was not too tired after the ordeal. Do you see any improvement in his illness? That certainly is my wish.

I am embarrassed every time I think of our conversation on the train. I do have other interests besides Holstein cattle. I only remember rambling on about cows when I could have talked about many other things. I was afraid that might be the only time I would ever talk to you—I just wanted the time to stand still so our time together would not end. Having you interested in my cow talk just kept me going on and on and on. You are a good listener.

I should have asked you more about yourself. What do you like to do? I know you said you helped in your father's store when he owned it. Do you like to read? I like all kinds of books—I'm especially interested in biographies of people who accomplished things. I do play the violin a little. If you listen real hard, you can tell what song I am playing. Ma plays the organ real well. She plays for church sometimes when the regular lady isn't there to play. We get together with some neighbors once in a while for a sing-along. (I guess in my case, it would be a play-along, since it doesn't work to both sing and play the violin.) Those times are always enjoyable.

I had a pleasant couple days visiting my cousin Daniel. He has two younger brothers whom I hadn't seen for some years. They have become big strong young men. Now those three guys are really into farming. I'm not sure we talked about anything other than crops and animals—yes, especially cows. We went to visit their neighbor who has the Holsteins. They are beautiful animals—the milk cows looked just like the one in the brochure that I showed you. Those neighbors do sell Holstein bulls. I am planning on buying one next spring. They don't have any ready to sell this summer.

All was well here when I returned home. Pa and I started cutting hay, so we are hoping it doesn't rain for the next week or so.

Reading over what I've written makes me feel like I'm babbling again. I am really hoping you will answer this letter. Someday I would like to come to visit you in Rolling Valley if you would be willing to have me come.

Please greet your father from me and give him my best wishes. He is a good man.

Most sincerely yours,

Ben Gottlieb

Ruth read the letter two more times, savoring each word. She hugged the paper to her chest and smiled as tears slid down her cheeks. She couldn't explain the tears even to herself.

***

August was quickly approaching. The days were filled with wedding preparations and care for Howard. He was growing weaker each day, but he was determined to see his older daughter's wedding. But for Ruth, the walk to the post office and the anticipation of another letter from Ben were the highlights of the day. The letters came often, two or three times a week. They were her anchor when Mother and Anna panicked over the bustle of the wedding dress that did not lie just right or the unexpected request of long-lost relatives to stay at the house during the wedding week.

"This is not a free hotel," Mother fumed. "Don't we have enough to do and expenses to cover without providing lodging and meals to people I hardly remember? I'm going to tell them they can put up a tent in the yard, and there is a good restaurant uptown." However, she relented in a calmer moment and wrote the relatives that they could sleep on quilts in the front room.

Late at night, when the household was asleep, Ruth filled pages to Ben. She was amazed at all the things she thought to tell him—she was not much of a conversationalist but putting words on paper was so easy. She told how Daddy was doing, of her concern over his dwindling strength, of trying to get household chores done when the tables and chairs were piled high with fabric and sewing projects. She surprised herself by being rather humorous in her stories. She had not thought of herself as having a good sense of humor. Ben seemed to take delight in her letters. His correspondence became longer and more personal.

"Are you and that young fella from the train still writing back and forth?" Howard asked her one day when he was feeling stronger and sitting in the rocking chair on the porch.

Ruth nodded.

"I'm glad of it," Howard announced. "I like that young man. You may be a farmer's wife yet."

"Daddy," Ruth admonished, "we're just friends exchanging letters." But she could feel the blush rising from her neck to her cheeks.

***

Anna and Kenneth were married at the family home following the Sunday morning church service at the beginning of August. The hot spell was over for the time being; the dresses for the bride, the two bridesmaids, and the flower girl fit perfectly thanks to Mother's skills, and the preacher's words were short. Many friends and relatives crowded into the house after the ceremony. Father's rocking chair was set up in the living room, and he smiled and said a few words to the guests. But most of the time, he slept. Mother and Ruth kept refilling the bowls and platters with cold fried chicken, potato salad, baked beans, glorified rice, rolls, lemonade, and coffee. Anna and Kenneth cut and served the three-tiered wedding cake (that Mother had spent hours baking and decorating) on the porch.

Finally, the exhausting afternoon was over, and guests began to leave. Anna brought down her suitcase, hugged her parents, Ruth, and the few remaining guests, and went off with Kenneth in his buggy. Kenneth had been installed as pastor at the community church in Hoople, a prosperous little town ten miles away. He was already living in the large parsonage. He had taken most of Anna's things there the week before. Her new home, already almost completely furnished, was ready for her.

I wonder what my wedding will be like, Ruth mused as she finally sank into her bed late that night. *Or will I ever even get married?* She had not thought seriously of marriage before. Now how interesting that thoughts of her wedding and thoughts of Ben came at the same time. *Will I ever see him again? How I miss him,* she thought as she fell into an exhausted sleep.

Howard seemed to have been saving his strength to get through the wedding. After Anna and Kenneth were married, he had little strength and lost interest in things around him. He slept nearly all the time.

***

The cooler nights of September reminded them that summer was over. It was too cool to be on the porch, but by then, Howard spent his time in his bed in the bedroom. Mother and Ruth tried to bring him to the table for supper. Within a few days, it became apparent that it was too exhausting for all of them. He took his meals, although mostly untouched, in his bedroom.

"He won't last much longer," Dr. Jelly told the women after one of his visits. "Start thinking of how you will manage after he is gone. Are all his affairs in order?"

Mother looked confused. "What do you mean?"

"I mean you must be prepared to live without your husband. You are fortunate to have Ruth here with you, and Anna is close by. Start thinking of funeral arrangements."

"Funeral arrangements? But I'm still tired out from Anna's wedding celebration last month. I'm not ready."

Dr. Jelly's patience was wearing thin. "You don't have much say in the matter," he retorted sharply. "Now count your blessings that you are not all alone in the world and prepare for the future."

***

The last weeks of Howard's life became fuzzy in Ruth's memory. She finished her Normal Teachers' Training. She had had too many distractions to be first in her class, but she did receive her First Grade

Studies Certificate. That had been Daddy's goal for her, but now he hardly responded when she told him she had completed her training.

Most days found Mother walking slowly from room to room without speaking. She hardly seemed aware of her surroundings. Ruth tried to run the household and prepare food. She did not feel capable, but no one was hungry anyway. A few guests came to call, but she encouraged them to leave after a brief greeting. Anna and Kenneth spent some evenings with them. The demands of housework and the almost complete care of Howard left Ruth drained and exhausted. Spending time in her father's bedroom was her refuge. At times she read to him or talked of who had come to call. He occasionally spoke to her, but he was seldom awake. He slept restlessly with irregular breath and sometimes gasped for breath. Mother would come in, sit down at the bedside for a few minutes, and pat Howard's hand gently. Then she would burst into tears and flee from the room.

Ruth cried, late at night, in the solitude of her own room when she wrote to Ben. Then the tears flowed as she poured out her heart in her letters. She burned some that she felt were too personal or exposed too much of her grief.

Ben's letters, in return, gave her comfort. She always carried the latest one in her pocket and read it dozens of times during the day.

Howard died on October 15 on a cold and rainy day. Ruth thought many times of her last meaningful conversation with him:

"Still getting letters from that young man?"

"I am, Daddy, and I write to him pretty often."

Howard took a deep breath. "I'm glad to hear it. It eases my mind. You and Anna have to take care of Mother. This is hard on her. Guess I've always tried to do things for her and you girls. Maybe that kept all of you from being as strong as you need to be."

His racking cough brought an end to the conversation. They would not have another.

Howard's body lay in his wooden casket in the living room. It seemed like everyone in town came to pay their respects and bring food into the kitchen. Mother sat by the casket repeating the same few sentences to everyone who gazed in the casket and then held her hand. "He looks nice, doesn't he? Thank you for coming. Have some food before you go." Then her eyes went back to linger on the casket.

He does not look nice, Ruth thought with a heavy heart. *He looks dead.* There was nothing there in the coffin that reminded her of the dearest person on earth to her. His skin was drawn tightly over the bones of his face. His hair, now wispy and white, was combed over his forehead. He didn't even resemble the man with the kind smile who called her his "Baby Girl."

Most of the townspeople and relatives had come to call by the day before the funeral. Anna and Kenneth had gone back to their home until the church service the next day. Ruth sat by her mother and held her hand. Neither spoke. Ruth could not look at the casket. In time, they both dozed.

A knock on the door brought Ruth out of her reverie, and she hurried to answer it. She couldn't think of one person who hadn't already been to see them.

"Ben!" Ruth gasped as they faced each other on the threshold. "You came!"

"I got your telegram saying your father had died. I hope it's okay that I came. I came by train this morning. I thought about sending a return telegram saying I planned to come, but I was afraid you'd say I didn't need to."

"I don't think I would have said that!" She felt such relief at seeing Ben. Everything would be okay. He'd help her through this terrible ordeal.

She shyly took his hand and brought him into the living room. "Mother, this is Ben. Remember the man who helped Daddy and me on the train when we went to Grand Forks? He came all the way from Twin Oaks for Daddy's funeral."

Ben studied Howard's body for a minute and then kneeled before Mother's chair. "I'm so sorry for your loss. Your husband was a good man. I'm glad I got to meet him."

"Doesn't he look nice? Thank you for coming. Have some food before you go."

Ruth took Ben into the kitchen. She filled his plate with an enormous amount of food, all brought by caring friends. She surprised herself by feeling starved herself. They sat and ate and talked together. They even laughed some. How good to have him there!

"Will you stay here at our house? Anna's room is empty."

"I've already booked a room at the hotel, and my stuff is there. I'll be at the church tomorrow morning."

Ruth wished Ben could sit with the family at the funeral. She asked Anna about it the first thing in the morning when Anna arrived at the house.

"Sit with the family?" Anna asked in surprise. "Ruth, Kenneth, and I haven't even met this man. I doubt that Mother would recognize him again. He's not part of the family. He can sit anywhere he likes, but not with us."

As it turned out, Ruth didn't see Ben until the funeral was over. The undertaker was at the house early to take the body to the church. Food brought to the house was transported to the church to be eaten there after the burial.

She met Ben at the cemetery as people left to go back to the church.

"Please come back to the church. You will have a chance to meet Anna and Kenneth and some friends. I know there is a lot of food there."

"I'm sorry I don't have time. I need to get my things from the hotel room and get over to the depot to catch the afternoon train. But I'd like to talk more to you when there is a better time. If it's okay with you, perhaps I could come back here again."

"Oh, I'd like you to. Maybe you could come for Thanksgiving. I can't imagine what a holiday will be like without Daddy here."

That's the way it was left. It was just over a month until Thanksgiving.

***

Ruth and her mother struggled through church the following Sunday. As they left the building, Ruth's friend Eliza, who had taken the Normal Teachers' Training with her, caught up with her and patted her shoulder.

"Ruth, I'm so sorry about your father, but I've been dying to ask you.... who was that man who was at the funeral? I saw you talking to him at the cemetery. I think you were holding hands. He was so handsome. I was hoping for an introduction, but he didn't go back to the church after the burial."

Ruth suddenly didn't want to share anything about Ben with Eliza or anyone else. "He's a friend. Just a good friend."

She took her mother's arm and hurried home.

Chapter 6

How much can lives change following a death? Ruth was at a complete loss at how to fill her days after the funeral. Mother wrote letters. After some days of that, she suddenly became obsessively busy. She took all the dishes out of the cupboards and washed them; she washed walls and polished furniture, then polished the pieces again. Before Howard's death, she lived in a daze; now she became a whirlwind of activity. Ruth occasionally helped her, but more often, she just walked. She walked the streets of town and then wandered out on the country roads. The townspeople did not stop to visit. If they wondered about her aimless walking, they didn't ask—they gave her space to be alone.

One afternoon Anna and Kenneth paid a visit. *Anna was blossoming with her role as pastor's wife and hostess of the parsonage*, Ruth thought, as she looked at Anna's rosy cheeks and happy smile. *And me? I'm shrinking. I'm becoming invisible.*

"We'd like to invite you both to have Thanksgiving at our house," Anna announced. "It will be our first Thanksgiving in our own home."

Ruth's head shot up in attention. "Oh, no!" she exclaimed. "It has to be here. Ben is coming. We must have our meal here."

They looked at her in surprise. She had not spoken so passionately in weeks. She realized that while she had been counting the days, she had not told them of Ben's visit.

"Well," Mother considered. "With an outsider coming, we must have our meal here." So, it was decided. Ruth had her way—she could hardly believe it.

Ben arrived by train on Wednesday, the day before Thanksgiving. He would leave again on Sunday. The guest bedroom was immaculate, and the house was filled with wonderful aromas of baking.

Ruth had wanted to meet the train, but Mother refused. "That would be unseemly for a lady," she told Ruth. "And what would the townspeople think? He's been here before; he can find our house again. The weather is perfect for a walk."

Although Mother knew Ben had called at the house before the funeral, she didn't remember meeting him or his attendance at the funeral. True to habit, though, she was a gracious hostess.

Despite the chatter, Howard was the unseen presence at the bountiful Thanksgiving table. Everyone tried to avoid looking at the empty space at the table.

Kenneth told of his pastor's duties that often involved home visits to members of his congregation. "These visits always come with desserts," Kenneth told them, patting his expanding girth. "One of the hazards of the trade."

Ben talked about his family and the farming operation. Again, Ruth thought listening to his voice was like music playing. His voice was soft and expressive. He was a skillful conversationalist. He had them all laughing at his description of a calf getting out of the pasture and the entire family, including his mother in her long skirts, chasing him all the way to the neighbor's farm. When they caught up with the runaway calf, he was calmly nursing from one of the neighbor's cows!

Later, Ruth couldn't remember any details of the conversations that flowed, but she did remember Ben's frequent looks in her direction, the secret smiles he gave her when their eyes met.

Before dessert was served at that Thanksgiving meal, three momentous announcements were made that would change their lives forever. Anna announced that she and Kenneth were expecting a baby, probably due in late April or early May. Kenneth continued with the second announcement: "Managing a parsonage and all the social obligations of a pastor's wife have certainly been keeping Anna's hands full. But," he added quickly, "she's doing a beautiful job. However, now dealing with morning sickness and the prospects of a baby to care for, we'd like to propose that Mother England come to live with us. What do you say, Mother?"

A moment of silence followed. Mother couldn't conceal the pleasure on her face. The prominent role of being co-hostess of a bustling parsonage would be just the sort of role she would love to play.

"Oh, but I couldn't," Mother said reluctantly. "I couldn't leave Ruth here in this house alone."

"Mrs. England, Anna, and Kenneth," Ben interjected immediately. "Ruth and I have our own announcement. Mrs. England, I wish I could also ask your husband—I had great respect for him—but now I ask you for permission to marry Ruth. She and I talked last night, and I believe she is willing." He looked at Ruth. Ruth felt the blush on her cheeks.

"I'm willing," she said shyly and softly. Realizing she sounded tentative, she repeated louder, "I am very willing," and smiled at Ben.

"Ruth hasn't met my family yet, so we would like that to happen before we publicly announce our engagement. I've invited Ruth to visit my home between Christmas and New Year's. Ruth was concerned about leaving you alone, Mrs. England, but that seems to be taken care of. We'd like to be married in late winter or early spring if arrangements can be made by then."

"Then Mother England can sell this house and move into our home," Kenneth said.

Mother was in high spirits. *Probably more because of her new role than for my engagement*, Ruth thought. But that was fine. She could make her new life with Ben without the guilt of leaving Mother alone.

Conversation flew back and forth after that. The house would be put up for sale. Ruth would be needed at home to go through the contents of their house and help with the anticipated sale. Their wedding date would be set after that.

Sunday arrived too soon. Ruth went to the depot with Ben. This time Mother offered no protest. Ruth felt awkward about saying goodbye, but when Ben put his arms around her, she clung to him. She felt she couldn't face life without him.

"We'll soon always be together," Ben reassured her. How she treasured those words. She didn't want to think of being alone.

***

Meeting Ben's family just after the Christmas holiday, selling Ruth's childhood home, and disposing of their possessions were all huge events, but strangely nothing seemed real until late March when she and Ben were married in a simple short ceremony in Ruth's living room that was already mostly empty of furniture. Mother, a very pregnant Anna, Kenneth, and two close friends were present.

My life is starting again, Ruth thought as she sat close to Ben on the train to Twin Oaks. *Not since Daddy died have I felt this loved, this protected. How good to be Ben's wife....*

Chapter 7

While Ben was a thoughtful, loving husband and Ruth rejoiced in the feeling of being cherished by him, adjustments were many. Ruth did her best to settle in as a farm wife. Often, though, she felt like she was acting a part, playing the role of wife and homemaker—and not doing a good job of it, either. She wanted Ben to be proud of her, and she wanted his parents to think highly of her, but most of the time, she had no idea how to become a part of his family.

Hattie ran an efficient household with an established routine. While she was quick to give Ruth room to take over some responsibilities, Ruth was reluctant to try anything beyond the basic, easy jobs. She had done simple tasks in her own home while Daddy was sick, but then no one noticed how things were done. Before the household was preoccupied with Daddy's sickness, Mother had often scolded Ruth about a lack of skill in housekeeping and cooking. Ruth would recall her mother's scorn when she attempted doing things in Ben's home.

She did want to help, though. One of the first mornings after Ruth arrived at the Gottliebs' household as Ben's wife, she entered the kitchen early, determined to be helpful and confident. Ben and Karl were already in the barn doing morning chores. Hattie was at the stove, frying pancakes. Sausage sizzled and browned in another pan, and scrambled eggs were kept warm in a third.

"What can I do to help?" Ruth asked brightly after greeting her mother-in-law.

"Oh, setting the table and making toast would be a great help," Hattie responded cheerfully. "It's such a beautiful morning already even though the sun is hardly up. I believe we will have an early spring. This weather is giving me an itch to start some tomato seeds in containers on the windowsills. I'll try to get that done this afternoon. The bread is there on the counter."

Hattie talked on, mostly about the weather and what dismal weather they had experienced the year before. Ruth's assignment should be easy. *I'll start with the toast*, she decided, pulling a knife with a wide blade out of the cabinet drawer. The knife was dull, tearing and crushing the bread rather than making neat cuts.

"Oh, I'm sorry," Hattie said quickly when she saw the dilemma. "I should have found a better knife for you. Serrated blades are always better for cutting bread. Try this one."

Ruth's cheeks burned. She should have asked before ruining the slices. Now the next step. Toasting the bread by laying it on the top of the woodstove was what her mother did, so she arranged the mangled pieces on the surface of the hot stove. Hattie was in the pantry, dishing jelly and butter and pouring syrup into a pitcher from a crock.

Ruth would need to hurry and set the table. She wondered what plates to use and where were they? Did they use coffee mugs for breakfast, or should she set out the flowered cups they had used for supper the night before? She rummaged through the cupboard, trying to decide which dishes looked familiar, the ones that had been used in previous meals.

Suddenly Ruth smelled the bread burning, just as Hattie returned to the kitchen and pulled the smoking toast pieces from the stovetop.

"It doesn't matter," Hattie assured her. "We don't really need both bread and pancakes. Karl seems to think breakfast has to include toast no matter what. He can put his jelly on the pancakes this morning. It will all go easier tomorrow."

Hattie's kind words did little to make Ruth feel less embarrassed. *I probably would be more help if I stayed out of the way*, she thought. Certainly, that was Mother's opinion. Hearing Ben and Karl enter the house relieved her.

"Hey, Ruth, I've got a surprise to show you. The red roan had her calf last night. A real beauty." Ben pulled her close and planted a kiss on her cheek. Ruth quickly looked to see if Karl and Hattie had noticed. She realized they were putting plates, cups, and silverware on the table. She had forgotten to set it. But now, it didn't matter. Ben was here.

"I'd love to see the calf. What color is it?"

"I'll show you after breakfast. This is the last year for shorthorn calves. Next year we'll have our new Holstein bull. I expect he'll be arriving in a couple months. But right now, nothing is getting between me and that food. It smells great, Ma." If he noticed the smoke in the air or the fact that the table had not been set, he didn't mention it.

Ruth looked forward to going outside after breakfast, not only to see the newborn calf. In the few days she had been here, she found she loved all the animals. Rex, the brown, furry farm dog, accepted her immediately, leaping in joy in front of her and grinning in his dog fashion. It was the time of year for baby animals—eight baby pigs had been born just days before. Ruth never tired of watching them nurse from their huge mother as she lay on her side, grunting contentedly. The babies crawled over each other and pushed their way to the teats, so they could get their share of milk. They squealed in dismay when they were pushed aside by their siblings.

The chickens started up a racket of clucking shortly after daylight. It seemed like they were in a contest to see who could sing the loudest. Ruth peeked into a secluded room in the barn where six brooding hens sat quietly on eggs, patiently waiting to hatch out their own families.

And now the new calf. After breakfast, Ruth happily accompanied Ben to the barn. What a relief to get out of the house and be alone with Ben. The cows turned their inquisitive eyes toward Ruth when she entered and greeted her with gentle moos. Ruth was learning a respect for all the animals on the farm, but she had a special regard for these large, dignified animals. They quietly finished up their ground oats and corn and waited patiently to be let out in the barnyard for hay and water. The pastures would be ready for grazing in a few weeks. The cows had total trust that their needs would be met by their kind caretakers. How important that the farmer is trustworthy, Ruth realized. All the animals depended on him for not only their comfort but their entire existence. It elevated the importance of the farmer's work in Ruth's mind. It was a high and noble calling.

The new calf, born during the night, was darling and already beginning to frisk about on unsteady legs.

Here in the cozy barn with Ben, Ruth could relax. It didn't matter that she was inept at homemaking skills. Ben didn't care. He probably didn't even notice. Hattie was so efficient it would be easier for everyone if she just did it herself. It would be different when they had their own house and Ruth could do things as she wanted to. She would learn to be a good homemaker, but she could do it on her own terms.

She knew the time would come when they were in their own house. Then she would have to learn homemaking skills, but for now, she much preferred being outside. Watching the milking process was one of her favorite activities. The barn was a picture of contentment—the purring of the cats as they finished their milk, Rex sleeping in his corner of straw, the cows relaxed as they were relieved of their milk.

"I think they like to be milked," Ruth observed to Ben.

"Absolutely," he answered. "This is their purpose. I think they're proud to be good producers of milk. People and animals like to be good at their jobs."

Ruth looked at him to see if he was kidding. He looked serious, and the cows did seem to be pleased to be milked.

I wish I felt I was good at my job, Ruth thought. *I'm good at being Ben's shadow, following him around and watching him be good at everything.*

Ruth did not admit to Ben that, as kind and good-hearted as her in-laws were, she felt intimidated by them. Their days were filled with specific jobs to be done, and by nightfall, the tasks were accomplished. Karl and Hattie, and Ben, too, took joy in their work. They greeted each day with enthusiasm and anticipation. Even with busy schedules, they made pleasant conversation with each other. Their home was peaceful. *I just have to learn to be a part of it*, Ruth determined. As she watched the family's confidence in handling many chores, she realized that there were skills that she should have learned growing up in her own home. Finding her place in this family was challenging.

Ben never seemed to notice Ruth's discomfort. If she was inside, he was always overjoyed to see her whenever he entered the house. Ruth realized with a smile that he invented excuses to come in. He'd give her a loving, gentle bear hug and invite her to accompany him on his jobs. He was getting machinery ready for the coming field work and checking the quality of his seeds. Ruth noticed that often Karl would ask Ben's advice on what to plant in certain fields or how warm the soil temperature might be. She saw their roles were shifting. Ben was becoming the decision maker. She felt proud of him. She was happy to be his tag along, and she assisted whenever she could.

One morning in late spring, however, he surprised her.

"Ma said the pie plants are ready to cut," Ben told her enthusiastically.

"Pie plant is my favorite pie. I hope you can work with Ma today to see how to make it."

"Pie plant?" Ruth responded. She could feel her lower lip begin to protrude. "I've never heard of it."

"Well, I've heard some people call it rhubarb. But whatever you call it, the plant is best this time of year. Having that to look forward to for dessert tonight will make this a special day."

"But I was thinking I'd like to help you mend the fence over by the creek," Ruth said reproachfully, pursing her lips. "I heard you tell your pa that you'd work on that today. I thought I'd pack a picnic lunch and go with you. It's such a lovely day; I'd rather not be inside."

After just a second's hesitation, Ben grinned at her. "And, having you spend the day with me sounds like a lot more fun. You make even fixing a fence sound more special than pie plant dessert. Besides, Ma will probably get it made herself. You'll have plenty of time to learn how to make pie. I like your plan better. But remember," he teased, "we do have to work."

It will be so different when we have our own house, Ruth thought, for the thousandth time. Then it would not matter if she didn't know how to do some household task—she could practice with no one judging her but Ben. And she knew he would be pleased by whatever she did.

He would be pleased. Ben was easy to please. But when he had talked to his parents about their approaching marriage during her first visit to Twin Oaks, she had given no thought to what adjustments awaited her. Not only for her, but for Ben and his family, too. She realized now that living in the same house with Karl and Hattie created tension between them. *My fault*, she acknowledged. Marriage certainly involved more than the two people being married. At the time of their engagement, she thought only of becoming Ben's wife. The consequences of coming to live in his home with his parents had not registered before she arrived as his wife.

Ah, yes, Ruth thought, *living here has been full of adjustments. But being Ben's wife has made it all worthwhile. And soon we'll have our own house....*

But their own house never came to be. The bull took that away from her.

Chapter 8

Two months after Ben's death - August 1909

The train had been warm, but now as Ruth looked up and down the railroad platform after getting off at Four Corners, the heat was oppressive. A young husband was hugging his wife and child; an old man leaning heavily on a cane was being helped to a buggy by two young men. That was all. No one resembling a Superintendent of Schools or even a school board member was waiting for her. *Of course, that's understandable*, Ruth told herself, *this is a busy time for field work*. But surely some arrangements could have been made. She tried to quiet the uneasy, queasy feeling in her stomach. She gripped her handbag tightly to quiet her shaking hands.

Charles Olson. That was the name Karl and Hattie had found for her through their older son Thomas. Thomas had heard that the town of Four Corners was looking for a teacher. Four Corners was about forty miles away, but on the railroad line. The superintendent of schools, Charles Olson, would have the authority to hire the teacher.

He was the man Ruth needed to see.

The sun had reached its zenith, and its rays were excruciatingly hot. Sweat trickled down the small of her back and wet the underarms of her dress. She could only imagine what her hair looked like. Right now, those things were unimportant. She had to find someone who knew where she belonged, someone who could help her with accommodations. Being alone here was frightening. She decided her small trunk would have to stay on the platform, and she set out for the main part of town in the next block. She read the names of the half dozen stores as she walked by them—a tavern, a hotel, a restaurant, a bank. "General Dry Goods" was a welcome sight. She would start there. If it was like her father's store, much of the town business would be known within its walls.

The store seemed dark as she stepped out of the hot sun. It was much smaller than her father's place, but the smell of the store hit her hard. The smells were the same as the General Merchandise back home—the odor of leather from the harnesses, baskets of apples, newly-dug potatoes still covered with soil, and the faint odor of kerosene. For a moment, Ruth was so overcome with loneliness for her father she thought the tears would start. She concentrated on her surroundings. Household goods lined the wall behind the high counter, and farm equipment was on the other side. Ruth assumed the man with a dirty gray apron over his huge paunch was the proprietor. He was playing rummy on the counter with an old man in overalls.

"Hello, I'm looking for Charles Olson. I'm the new schoolteacher," she said more loudly than she needed to, directing her remarks to the proprietor. "Do you know if any arrangements have been made for me?" Her voice sounded high-pitched in her ears, like a scared child. The few customers stopped to stare at her.

The proprietor looked up at her in surprise. He didn't look particularly friendly. *Daddy would have smiled at me and made me feel welcome,* Ruth thought.

"The new teacher?" he asked in a puzzled voice. "Humph, that's a new one on me. I'm purty sure the new teacher's been hired for the town school and the country school never opened. There's a lady staying in that house right next to the school where the teachers always live. Ain't that right, Reuben?"

"Yup," the old man in the overalls nodded. "She's been there a couple weeks now. I seen her cleaning out the school building. Looked too uppity to be that dirty, that's what I was thinkin'."

One of the customers, a farmer in a sweat-stained short-sleeved shirt, walked over to join the conversation. "Well, you know why that gal got hired so fast. She's the Superintendent of School's niece—just finished her training. She was going out east to a big school but changed her mind at the last minute. She needed a job, and there aren't many teaching jobs left around here."

Ruth felt panic rising in her chest. "But I understood that I was to be the teacher. I have a letter from Mr. Charles Olson." Why did her voice sound like that? Did she always sound so unpleasant and frightened?

She rummaged through her handbag and brought out a crumpled letter. She read aloud, "We are in need of a teacher. Please come to Four Corners as soon as possible, and we will work out the details." The words now seemed indefinite, certainly far from a binding contract.

By now, a couple customers looked over Ruth's shoulder and read snatches of her letter. "I never did have much time for that Olson fellow," one said. "I don't think you can put much stock in what he says."

The other customer, a heavy-set motherly type, strained her neck to see the letter and said, "I see the date is July 10. I think this niece of his came to town after that. I s'pose that wiped out any other agreements. You know what they say about blood being thicker than water." She patted Ruth's shoulder in sympathy.

The customers looked concerned for her, but no one offered any solutions. She took a deep breath. Surely this would work out okay. There had to be other jobs. She was never that excited about teaching anyway. Something better was certainly available. Maybe she could work here at this store. She knew more about running a store than teaching school. She looked at the faces watching her. She concentrated on making her voice sound mature and confident. "Would there be an opening here at this store?" she asked the proprietor. "I have experience in storekeeping."

"Work here? How do you expect me to make a profit if I pay somebody else to do my work? I ain't never hired no one. Guess I can take care of my own work."

"Do any of you know if anything else is available?" she asked the faces surrounding her. "There must be something…I could help someone with housework. I can clean…or cook." She hoped no one questioned her too closely on her housework skills. "There must be some job."

The customers silently looked at one another in thought. Finally, the motherly woman said, "Well, I know Amos Armstrong needs help. He can't do a thing since he smashed his legs in that wagon accident…"

The woman was interrupted by her husband, who spoke to Ruth. "Ma'am, he needs a man's help. Not a little lady like you. He's got a bunch of cows to milk. Some relative of his is doing the milking now, but I hear that's temporary. The neighbors are doing his harvesting for him."

"Amos is too hard to get along with for anybody to stay and help him for long," the old rummy player said. "All his help will always be temporary."

Ruth listened to the comments about this man with the smashed legs and cows to be milked. Working for him didn't sound like a suitable solution.

"Can you think of anything else?" she asked again. "I don't have much money. I'm going to need something soon." That high-pitched sound was back in her voice again.

Again there was silence. Finally, someone suggested, "Why don't you check at the post office. Maybe they know of something over there."

Ruth thanked the curious customers and crossed the street to the post office. The building was empty except for the woman behind the window.

"Well, Amos Armstrong is really needing someone to milk cows," the post mistress offered in answer to Ruth's question. "But I wouldn't recommend that anyone work for that man. I've never seen anyone who is as crabby as he is. And that was before his accident. But I'm sorry I can't think of any women's jobs for you."

"Well, I know how to milk cows," Ruth replied. "Could you tell me how to get his place?"

Ruth's words surprised even herself. Yes, she had helped Ben with barn chores and had milked cows, but could she take over a milking operation herself?

Maybe she would get a chance to find out, Ruth thought, as she walked along the rutted country dirt road, following the post mistress's reluctant directions. If Amos Armstrong was as hard to get along with as the townspeople said, she probably wouldn't be there more than a week or two anyway, but it would give her some time to earn a little money and look for something else. *And I'm going to find Mr. Charles Olson and tell him how misleading his letter was and what a terrible predicament I'm in,* she thought. But even as she thought it, she knew that confronting him would take more courage than she possessed.

It was less than four miles to Amos Armstrong's farm; the directions were easy to follow. The late afternoon's sun had cooled a bit. The locusts were so noisy they drowned out the birds singing in the few cottonwood trees that lined the road. The time alone gave Ruth a chance to evaluate her situation. She had no job and just over $11.00 in her handbag. That would be enough for a couple days at the hotel and then a train ticket back to Gottlieb's farm. But then what? Karl and Hattie would take her in without question. She knew that. But she couldn't stay there without Ben. She wouldn't feel welcome going to her mother, who had already carved a comfortable niche for herself at the parsonage. Ruth needed a job. Teaching was all she was trained for, but she could do other things...couldn't she? She had helped her father in the store. Ben said she had a way with animals, and even Karl had admitted that she handled the milk cows well, even though he didn't like women doing barn work. Now, if she could convince Mr. Armstrong that she could take care of his livestock, the immediate problem of a job and income would be temporarily taken care of until she found something else. From the comments of the townspeople, he must not be easy to get along with. But Ruth had watched Daddy handle all kinds of customers, and he could deflate anyone's complaints. Surely, she had learned something in working with Daddy. She was a grown woman; she would be able to negotiate a working relationship.

The dirt road turned to the right and the Armstrong driveway angled to the left. The driveway consisted of wagon wheel tracks through tall grass. Weeds grew along both sides. As she entered the yard, she walked by the barn first—its lower walls were made of stone, the upper walls were unpainted and rough. It looked sturdy and would be warm in the winter. Each side had a lean-to, probably to house chickens or young stock. A few brown cows found relief from the late afternoon sun in the barn's shade. The long shadows made the place look forlorn and melancholy. A couple outbuildings for grain or machinery stood beyond the barn. A wooden fence ran from the barn to the back of the house and into the trees. She arrived at the house last. The small house showed obvious signs of neglect. If it had ever been painted, there was no evidence of it. The railing on one side of the steps had broken and still lay where it had fallen, causing Ruth to have to carefully step over it. The windows were streaked with dirt, and one was broken. A few had screens, but they served no purpose since there were large holes in them.

Ruth had a sudden desire to run back to town. She dreaded what she would find inside this house. She stood for a moment on the top step, breathing deeply. She was about to reach out her hand and knock when suddenly the screen door was pushed open, and a large brown and black dog bounded out of the house, barking furiously. She stood frozen as the dog snarled and sniffed at her skirts.

"Brute, shaddup and lay down," a man's loud, raspy voice yelled at the dog from inside the house. The dog obeyed instantly, dropping down on the step landing.

Ruth again raised her hand to knock, this time reaching over the dog's prostrate body. Her heart was pounding.

"Ya think I haven't heard you by now?" the voice said again, this time to Ruth. "Git in here and tell me what you're doing on my place."

Ruth stepped over the threshold and into the kitchen.

Chapter 9

She stood inside the kitchen door. Everything looked dark as her eyes adjusted from the afternoon sunshine outside. A variety of smells assaulted her—all of them unpleasant. Onions, body odor, and sour milk seemed the most prevalent. Flies buzzed over some dishes on the cupboard.

Two men were sitting at a table, their card game interrupted by Ruth's arrival. They stared at Ruth. A third man took a step toward her and peered at her carefully. "Ya lookin' for somebody?" he finally asked. He was not the man who had shouted at the dog.

"I'm here to see Amos Armstrong," she answered. "Is he here?"

"Ole Amos, he ain't goin' nowhere," the man assured her. "Git in here closer.... it's easier for you to come see him. He ain't goin' to come over here and shake your hand. Right, Amos?"

Ruth walked further into the room. She could now see that one of the men at the table was obviously Amos Armstrong. One leg was stretched out alongside the table in an enormous cast from his ankle to the top of his leg. A leg of his pants had been cut away to accommodate it. A second smaller cast covered the other lower leg and foot. The bottom of his second pant leg was slit to the knee. The dog she had met on the steps now sat at his side and growled at Ruth.

Ruth tried to ignore the dog as she walked up to Amos and stretched out her hand. She recoiled at the thought of touching him. When he didn't return the handshake, she gratefully let her hand fall to her side.

"Hello, I'm Ruth Gottlieb. You don't know me, but I'm here to apply for the job of taking care of your cattle. I know I can do it—I'm used to milking and doing chores. Several people in town said you needed help since your accident. I'm here for the job."

When no one responded, she continued. "I can help you in your situation. I'm good with animals." The dog's obvious animosity seemed to contradict her statement.

Ruth realized she was talking too loud and too fast. The three men stared at her open-mouthed. The one who had met her at the door grabbed a chair and sat down on it backwards, never taking his eyes off her. There was an awkward silence, and then he burst out laughing.

"Hey, Amos, your problems is solved. This here little woman will take care of your cows, and me and Pa can go home without listening to your belly achin' about your chores. Heck, she's probably goin' fix your fences, plow your fields, and move in your haystacks right next to the barn. She must weigh at least 100 pounds—should be no problem for her."

"Naw, I bet she weighs closer to 120 pounds," the older man at the table responded, looking her up and down closely. "Probably solid muscle, too." He laughed loudly as he nudged Amos.

"Hey, we're forgettin' our manners," he finally said. "There's a lady here to visit Amos, and we plumb forgot to offer her a chair. Sit down in my place, Miss. Let me warm up some coffee and find something to eat. Nobody around here knows nothin' about manners."

Ruth sat on the edge of the chair facing Amos Armstrong. So far, he had not said a word since he had yelled at the dog. He was a big man in his mid-thirties. His full cheeks sagged, giving him a look of perpetual sadness. Straggling hair, long and unkempt, covered his ears and the back of his neck. It obviously had not seen a comb for a long time. His dark eyes squinted at her, giving him a menacing look. Several days' growth of beard, streaked with gray, covered the large features of his face. Perspiration, spilled food, and coffee stained the front of his work shirt.

Ruth spoke again, "Mr. Armstrong, I know you need help, and I know I can do the job. Will you consider hiring me?"

Amos finally spoke. "Who told you about my accident?" His voice was loud and jarring.

"Just some people in town. I was supposed to have another job, and that fell through. So, I'm looking for work." Ruth didn't tell him she was supposed to be the teacher. Somehow, she knew his companions would find that an object of hilarity. "I've done a lot of milking."

Amos looked at the other two men rummaging around in the cupboards. They were lean; their bib overalls hung loosely over their tall frames. Both wore shirts like Amos's and were in the same state of cleanliness. The younger man was about Amos' age; the older man was certainly his father. They had the same thin cheeks and sandy hair.

Amos finally broke the awkward silence. "Them's Neil and his pa George. They're s'posed to be helping me since I got hurt. Takes two of them to do my chores—a couple lazy louts. Neil's my cousin from over the Minnesota side of the border. They have to go home the day after tomorrow to thresh their oats. I need a man to help with things here. You ain't a man."

Neil slapped his thigh and laughed loudly. "Amos, you is the most observant guy ever borned. We're glad to know this here lady ain't a man. Take notes, Pa—Amos is teaching us great things we'd never know without his wisdom." They both continued to chuckle.

Ruth spoke up quickly. "What choice do you have? It seems like you either hire me or sell your cows. And sell them within the next two days. Let me work with your relatives this afternoon while they do chores. You'll see that I can handle the job." Ruth had never spoken to strangers with such determination. She surprised herself.

Amos hesitated. Finally, he said, "I ain't selling any of my cows. What do you know about taking care of things in a barn?"

"Aw, come on, Amos—selling your cows is easier than us teaching her what to do," Neil, the younger man, said.

"Shut up, Neil. I ain't selling nothin'."

George finally entered the conversation. "Well, we're leaving in two days. We don't much care what you do when we skedaddle. We'll show her the barn after we eat."

The opportunity Ruth wanted brought a whole new batch of fears. True, she could milk the big, gentle cows that belonged to Ben and Karl, and she knew how to do summer chores. But she had never been in charge—she had followed Ben around and did things as he did.

Neil plunked thick slices of unevenly cut dry bread on the table and a plate of cheese. George had poured very black thick coffee into stained and chipped cups. Ruth had had a sandwich and two cookies on the train—the lunch Hattie had packed her—and nothing since, but she was afraid she would gag on the food set before her. She nibbled the bread and washed it down with the bitter coffee. The men shooed away flies and ate with enthusiasm.

While they ate, Ruth found out more about the job. Amos had eight milk cows, eight young calves still living in the barn, ("But they're ready to get out with the rest of the cattle," Amos complained. "I've told these guys fifty times to let the calves out and they're still in the barn.") and five yearling steers in the pasture. There was a team of horses ("They'll be as wild as a cyclone if they don't get worked,"

Neil warned her) and about thirty chickens. The big dog, Brute, and six barn cats completed the list of livestock. Amos had broken his left leg in several places and smashed his right foot and ankle when he fell from a grain wagon.

"How can a feller fall off a wagon?" Neil wondered in mock bewilderment.

Amos looked at him impatiently. "You know very well how it happened—Brute chased a rabbit right under the horses' feet and spooked them. The wagon almost tipped."

"It don't take much to spook that team," George remarked. Ruth was making mental notes to stay away from those horses.

"How long will you have to wear the casts?" she asked Amos.

"The doc said he'd see me again in maybe six months. He'll decide then how much longer."

"It'll be much longer," Neil put in. "It's going to be spring before you see the inside of that barn of yours—maybe you'll never get those legs to work again. This here house is as far as you're going for this winter. You should sell your cattle now while they're milking good and in good shape."

"My legs'll work again," Amos retorted sharply. "You could do a little more to encourage a fella. Paint as black a picture as you can; that's what you do."

Ruth looked at the casts. One stuck out at an odd angle. Going through doorways would have to be sideways; going down steps, especially Amos's steps and with the other foot also in a cast, would be impossible. A stool with some wheels haphazardly nailed to the bottom sat beside him. A set of crutches also lay against the table. These contraptions must be how he moved about the house.

The three men were getting on each other's nerves. The heat in the kitchen was overwhelming. Flies buzzed on the screen door, and many easily found their way through the tears in the screen. The cheese seemed especially attractive to them. The men continued to talk, becoming louder and more disagreeable as time went on. They seemed to forget that Ruth was sitting there with them. Her apprehensions, the heat, the flies, the bread sitting heavily in her stomach all made her feel nauseous. The whole scene was like a bad dream.

It was a relief when Neil said he'd get the cows into the barn for the afternoon milking. "I'll come with you," Ruth said quickly. She needed to see how the procedure was done and was only too glad to leave the hot kitchen and the accompanying conversation.

Neil became a little more pleasant out of the house. "I don't envy you, working for Amos," he told her as they walked through the pasture looking for the cattle. "Everybody knows he should sell those cows. He'll probably never be able to farm again. He's too stubborn to talk sense to. And you're crazy to take the job. I ain't got no idea how you plan to do what needs to git done. You should be cooking and cleaning inside a house instead of doing a man's job. If you do work here, stay away from those wild horses."

Ruth was not feeling up to conversation. She nodded and watched Neil open the barn door for the cattle.

"Here, boss, here bossy cows," he called to the milk cows.

Despite the situation, Ruth had to smile. Those were the exact words Ben had used, calling the gentle milk cows into the barn back home.

She felt better as the cows walked placidly into the cool barn and immediately went to their own stanchions. She stood back until the stanchions were securely closed.

"Each cow gets a pint of ground feed," Neil said. "Amos said not a tablespoon more or less—one pint. You take care of the feeding; I'll be back."

Ruth began measuring out the feed and taking it to each cow. They snorted in fear of her at first, but she talked quietly to them, and they soon forgot her in their enjoyment of the feed.

Neil came back into the barn with three milk pails, followed by George. Ruth was soon feeling the enjoyment of pressing her forehead against the cow's flank and hearing the splashing of the milk in the pail. She relaxed, and she felt the cow she was milking relax also. For the first time, she thought this might work.

Ruth milked two cows while George and Neil each did three. *Not bad*, she thought. The cows were put out to pasture. She made mental notes as she watched the men put the milk through the cream separator. They cooled the cream by putting the can in the water cooler and fed the skim milk to the calves. After taking care of the chickens and pumping water to fill the tank for the outside livestock, they returned to the house. Ruth noted it took about an hour for them to complete everything.

As they climbed the rickety steps to the house, Amos called through the screen door, "Did ya feed the cats?"

"Aw, Amos," George replied, "Cats are supposed to catch mice for a living. Anyway, we didn't see no cats."

"I told you to put some milk in their pan for them. I tell ya that every time you do the dang chores."

"I'll take something out for them if you have some table scraps here in the house." Ruth offered quickly.

At Amos's directions, she cut some of the dry bread and soaked it in sour-smelling milk from the pantry. She hurried back to the barn and put the food in a pan in the milk room. She didn't see any cats but figured they'd come when she left.

George and Neil had started the cook stove and were frying chunks of meat when she returned to the house. The stove made the kitchen hotter than ever, even though it had begun to cool off outside. She declined to have supper with them; she knew she would have to start back to town soon.

"Mr. Armstrong, I'm confident I can handle your chores. Will you let me have the job?"

The other men looked at Amos as he sat by the table chewing on his lower lip. "We got to leave whether you find somebody or not, Amos," Neil said. "My missus ain't happy with me being gone so long leaving her with all the work, and that oats is sure to be ready to cut."

"I know, I know," Amos growled. "You told me that hundreds of times. Okay, miss," he turned to Ruth, "You got the job, but if stuff gets left undone, you're fired right off."

George snorted. "First off, Amos, how will you know if stuff gets left undone? You ain't goin' be checking on her work. Second off, who would you get if you fire her? Use some sense, man. Tell her you're glad she's here and stop all the stupid threats. Now, what are you goin' to pay her?"

Amos looked at Ruth for a long moment. "I'll pay you $15 a month if things is done right."

Both George and Neil began talking at once. "Fifteen dollars a month is fine for now when chores is easy. But it'll be a full-time job when cold weather comes," Neil pointed out.

"All right, all right, $20 a month when the cows start staying in the barn," Amos conceded.

"The $20 starts October one whether the cows are in the barn or not," George said. "She'll be feeding hay by that time."

"And, where's she goin' stay?" Neil asked. "Will she eat here with you? Makes a difference in what you pay her. Think she's going to want to stay here with you? It won't hurt you to start using some of that there money you got stashed away."

Ruth listened to them argue back and forth. Her opinions were not asked for, and they weren't arguing to benefit her, she realized, but just to be disagreeable. They definitely were getting on each other's nerves.

"She can probably stay at the Edmonds' place," Amos said. "They was goin' to house a teacher for the Section 9 School, but that school never opened. Not enough kids. The Edmonds live less than two miles away. She can check there when she goes back to town."

Amos finally looked at Ruth and directed the conversation to her. "I'll tell you where they live, but I doubt they'll want you to eat dinner with them. You'll have some time on your hands now when the weather is nice. You can eat your dinners here if you make them. The Edmonds woman don't know how to cook anyways from what I hear. I cook good, but these casts slow me down too much."

Both George and Neil erupted with loud laughter. "He cooks good, he says?" George said. "Little lady, he'll lie about other stuff, too. But at least you can have some food here during the day."

Ruth was only too glad to leave the house. The sun was almost setting, and she still had to stop at the Edmonds' place to ask about staying with them. She would need to hurry to get back to town before dark.

George walked outside with her. He kept clearing his throat, and Ruth realized he wanted to tell her something. She couldn't wait much longer; she needed to get back to town. She would have to make arrangements at the hotel.

"Yes?" she asked almost impatiently.

George hung his head sheepishly. "Ah, you see, Amos can't really do much on his own at all," he started. "Me and Neil's been takin' care of personal stuff for him. So, when you come into his house during the day to make dinner, ah, could you empty his commode?"

"Empty his what?"

"His commode, you know—a pot. He's got one of them pots by the back door. Remember, he can't get out of the house to take a dump."

"To take a...But how...where would I empty it?"

"See, there's that little ditch running back into the trees behind the house, there. Dump it out there. I'll leave a spade out there where there's some sand. After you empty it, you can shovel a little sand into it. Kind of settles the stink, ya know."

George looked vastly relieved as he entered the house, his message given. He didn't know that the first time Ruth followed his directions for emptying the commode, she hurried deeper into the trees and threw up.

Chapter 10

It had been a week since Ruth had gotten the job milking Amos's cows. She had made the arrangements to stay at the Edmonds' and had gotten her trunk there with the reluctant help of Matt Edmond. The late summer days fell into a pattern. She woke early, before the sun rose, to walk from Edmonds' farm to Amos's barn. The walk was pleasant now; Ruth shuddered to think about what it would be like when it was dark with snow flying. She had heard stories about people getting lost in blizzards and not found until spring. She tried to laugh at her fears of the unknown future—the present problems were more than enough. Blizzards could stay hovering in the future for now.

Staying with the Edmonds seemed unreal to Ruth. She saw very little of the family; and maybe it was her imagination, but they seemed to delight in being antagonistic toward her. Why would that be, she wondered; they hardly knew her. She agreed to pay the $10.00 they asked for to board her. Anyway, she had very little contact with them, so she would try to put them out of her mind. Right now, she must focus on doing the best job she could with the chores.

The chores themselves were going well. Ruth had become friends with the big gentle brown milk cows. They now walked confidently into the barn at milking time, always went to their own stalls without hesitation, and waited for Ruth to close their stanchions before they got their feed. They trusted her; there was no fear in their eyes as they calmly watched her get ready for milking. Resting her head against the cow's warm flank as she milked was soothing to Ruth and the cow she was milking.

The chickens accepted her presence without flying into a panic. She liked to stand in their coop and listen to them sing. She was learning to tell each one apart, and she could even tell which ones laid certain eggs with distinctive markings and sizes.

The horses, though, continued to be a problem. They kept their distance, even when she tried to offer them a few kernels of oats in her outstretched palm. They were large and skittish. They tossed their heads and put back their ears. They were afraid of her but not nearly as much as she was of them. They were nothing like friendly, docile Dolly and Nelly at the Gottlieb farm.

Hcr grcatcst joy was thc barn cats. Aftcr thc first two days, thcy overcame their shyness and waited at their pan to be fed. It was not long before they wound around her legs or stood up with paws on her knees, hoping for some cuddling. Soft, friendly meows greeted her each morning when she opened the barn door. *It's good to be loved*, she thought. At present, the cats and maybe a few of the other animals seemed to be the only friends she had.

At first, Ruth tried to be friendly with Amos. At least, she thought she tried. Conversations with him were difficult at best. He scowled when she talked about the animals. He gave no reply to her comments but peppered her with his own questions.

"How much milk are you gettin'? Do you give the ground feed to the cows before you milk? Are you getting' the cream cold right after you do the separating? Put the egg basket here in the kitchen, so I can count how many eggs you're gettin'. Do you check for eggs a couple times during the day? Are you sure the hens ain't laying their eggs outside somewhere?"

Ruth started the second week with more confidence. The days had settled into a routine. After this morning's chores, she had time on her hands—time that she didn't want to spend in the house. The cows were in the pasture after the morning milking; the can of cream was cooling in the cold water. She made sure things were tidy in the chicken coop and checked for early morning eggs. She talked to the hens. The cats were always ready to play. Finally, she could put it off no longer. It was time to go in to find food for dinner. She braced herself as she entered the kitchen.

As usual, Amos was sitting at the kitchen table, playing solitaire. The cards he used had probably been a full deck at one time. Now many corners had worn off, and the faces and numbers were faded almost beyond recognition. A few cards had been completely replaced with pieces of heavy paper approximately the same size.

For the first week, there was food from thoughtful neighbors' provisions. Several farmers had come to finish up Amos's harvesting of crops. Their wives had left items of food for Amos and Ruth. That food was used up yesterday, and no one had stopped in this morning.

Ruth hesitated. Where did she start? Was she in charge of this meal, or did she ask for his help or at least his advice?

"What would you like for dinner?" she asked tentatively.

"I got a bigger question.... what do you know how to make? I can handle makin' the coffee by pushing this stool around. You figure out what eats go with the coffee. I hear you were supposed to be a schoolmarm. Do schoolmarms know what a kitchen is fer? How much milk did you get this morning? Did you cool it first thing?"

"Yes, I put it through the separator and put the cream can in the cooler. I did everything just like George and Neil did."

"Well, ain't you the one then? You watch somebody do the chores once or twice and now you're the big expert. Those guys didn't know what they were doing in the first place. Did you give the milk cows their pint of oats?"

"Yes." She was going to add, "Not a tablespoon more or less just like George said," but decided against it.

"How many eggs did you get?"

"Well, I didn't count them. The pail was almost half full. But it was early when I picked them; maybe there are more by now. I put the egg basket by the door."

"You've been done with them chores for a couple hours.... I saw you dawdling out there with the cats. You could have checked for more eggs. I'm paying you big money. If I'd a knowed you was a schoolteacher, I'd never have hired you. What do schoolteachers know about taking care of cows? From now on, keep track of the eggs you get...they might be laying outside some place. Pay attention to what needs to git done, not sitting in the barn doorway and dawdling with the cats. How many cats are you seeing out there? George and Neil probably scared the young ones off."

Before Ruth could answer, Amos continued, "What are you making for dinner?"

Ruth had no idea what she was making. She found stale bread in the breadbox and some soft potatoes, including a rotten one, in the pantry. "What should I make?"

"Well, ain't you the one? I pay you big money, and you ask me what to do. Never thought I'd miss George and Neil.... maybe I was wrong."

Ruth blushed. "I think I need to throw out that rotten potato first thing. It smells really bad. Maybe I should throw away the bread, too."

Amos grunted angrily. "You're too uppity to know what's rotten and what's edible. Think I'm made of money? I'm paying you big money to figure out how to make dinner. Cut off some of the outside of the bread. Brute's not too high class to eat some crusts. The inside's good enough for us to eat yet."

Ruth remembered the eggs she had brought in with her. She peeled a few of the better potatoes and sliced them to fry. Then she fried some of the eggs and cut some slices of bread from the inside of the loaf. It was not a spectacular meal, but it was food, and she got it done. She would need to see what kind of food Amos had in the house and where utensils were. She better think of a plan for tomorrow's dinner.

While she was washing the dishes, a visitor stopped by. He got off the wagon carrying two large bags and banged at the door.

"Hey, Amos, you home? Good joke, huh? You're always home. The missus said I should bring you some stuff. She's tired of making sauerkraut, so I got a couple heads of cabbage in the sack and a bunch of potatoes. I think she threw a squash in there, too. Then, in this sack, she put in a loaf of bread and some cookies. She probably feels sorry for you. I can't understand why."

He put the sacks on the table and turned to Ruth. "And here's the little milk maid I heard about. How do you do, Ma'am? Actually, I think my missus wanted me to come so I could see what you looked like. Not everybody would want to milk Amos's cows…or step foot in his house, for that matter. Are you sure you're big enough for barn chores?"

"How do I know she's doing any chores?" Amos interjected. "From what I can see from the window, she out there dawdling with the cats."

The visitor laughed loudly. "Amos, you spent too much time playing with those cats yourself. Let this little lady figure out what needs to be done and talk nice to her. Don't expect us neighbors to come do your chores if she gets huffy and leaves."

While Ruth hated being in the filthy, smelly house, and she hated to try to make meals, her stomach growled for food. She was very grateful for the supplies the neighbor had brought. There would at least be bread and vegetables for tomorrow's dinner—and some cookies if Amos didn't eat them all before tomorrow.

As the days passed, Ruth saw that neighbors rarely drove by without stopping. She didn't know what she would have done without their garden produce, the home-canned items, and baked goods. Several of the men stopped by weekly. It seemed an odd relationship—Amos never expressed any appreciation for the items brought, but the men took for granted that there would be coffee and a tasty baked treat that they had brought themselves. What they seemed to want more than anything was the visit. Enough people stopped in so that Amos knew all the neighborhood news, and he was quick to share it. He always added his own commentary.

He told one story after another to the listening neighbors. Don Reynolds had to put down his best cow when the cow slipped on manure in the alleyway in the barn and broke her hip. Reynolds could keep his barn cleaner and things like that wouldn't happen. Pigs almost ate one of the Erikson kids when the kid fell in the pig pen. What could Old Man Erikson expect? Those pigs had never got decent feed in their lives. The Mattson kids are sick all the time, coughing all their germs on each other and spreading around their sickness. The missus is so tired of it all, she's ready to up and go back to her ma and pa in South Dakota—whether she'll take that pack of kids with her is anybody's guess.

The stories and the coffee seemed to run out at about the same time as the baked items.

At first, Ruth stayed in the barn when Amos had company unless she was fixing dinner. The condition of the house was an embarrassment, and she tired of Amos's gossip. But she hungered for human contact, and besides, the visitors usually brought food. She started making a point to go to the house when someone came if she wasn't in the middle of some barn chore. Amos ignored her, and the visitor would greet her quickly, maybe offer some of the food he brought, and get on with the visiting. She was never invited to sit at the table with them, so she used this time to wash dishes or wash the eggs. Sometimes, she worked on the impossible job of cleaning something in the kitchen. At least she could listen and hear something of the outside world.

Ruth was surprised at how helpful the neighbors were. Besides the food they brought to Amos, they took cans of cream and any extra eggs to the General Dry Goods Store for credit on Amos's account. On their return from town, they delivered grocery items and occasional letters or newspapers. And sometimes a tidbit of gossip. Amos would remember this to share the next time he had company.

However, when the wives accompanied their husbands, the men made only quick stops. There was no coffee or visiting. The women stayed seated on the wagons while the men made any transactions that needed to be made. Ruth felt curious eyes looking for her. Why did they seem to be unfriendly? Maybe it was only shyness on Ruth's part, but she never felt comfortable going to the wagon to greet them. They looked about the place with scorn. Perhaps they wondered what kind of person could be working for Amos and doing barn work at that. It became easier to stay out of sight when she saw the men were not alone.

Even with food items from neighbors to supplement the dinners, Ruth still felt her cooking skills woefully inadequate. She knew that extra eggs could be taken to The General Dry Goods Store, but the hens were laying well, and eggs were quick and easy to prepare. Ruth almost always made fried or scrambled or boiled eggs for the dinners. She sometimes added fried potatoes or other vegetables. And usually, there was bread from the neighbors. Despite the filth in the house, Ruth was ravenously hungry and surprised herself by often consuming four eggs beside the four she made for Amos. It made quite a dent in the number of eggs to be sent to the store.

Amos had told Ruth that there were garden vegetables stored down in his cellar. Neighbors had harvested some of his garden when they did his fields. She knew she should be using those things, but Ruth hated to go down into the dark, chilly storage area under the house. Dusty shelves and frightening shadows lined the walls. Mice droppings littered the shelves, and the vegetables that she quickly snatched up had tiny teeth marks on them—the result of mice taking their fill first.

"I'm paying you big money," Amos reminded her often enough. "Seems like you could find a little variety in what you cook."

Ruth had tried to get used to the cellar. Scattering mice and tiny beady eyes watching her from the shelves made her decide to rely on eggs or what the neighbors brought.

Ruth never asked Amos what he made for his own breakfasts and suppers. He probably didn't find much to eat with his limited mobility. But the coffee pot was always hot and the black liquid ready to be poured whenever anyone stopped in.

While the barn chores were going okay, Ruth never did make friends with the unpredictable horses. They were fine on their own in the pasture, but what would Ruth do when they would have to be in the barn during the winter? She dreaded to even think of it. However, this concern was taken care of when Paul Thompson, one of the neighbors who lived several miles to the south, stopped by.

"Amos, what are you going to do with that wild team of yours come winter?" he asked as soon as his coffee cup was filled.

"You're sure not up to doing anything with them," he continued. "They're going to be as wild as polecats with too much sassy energy if they're cooped up in the barn all day eating your hay. I don't think your chore girl hired on to handle horses—at least not your horses."

"She's got her hands full trying to get some victuals on the table, let alone take care of my horses," Amos quickly interrupted. "And they ain't wild—they need careful handling."

"Yeah, and look where their careful handling got you—stuck with busted legs. Let me finish my offer. I'll take them off your hands for the winter. I'm going to do some logging on my riverfront acres, and I'll need a strong team to haul them logs. My team of mares are both going to have foals in April. I don't want to work them too hard hauling timber. Let me use your team. The work will do them good, and they'll be ready to settle down for field work in the spring—if you even want them back. Who knows if you'll ever be able to use them again."

"Hah, 'course I'll need them in the spring. How would I get my field work done without horses? What kind of hay you got?"

"You know I've got the best horse hay in the country. I ain't going to beg—you want to swap your horses for the winter or not?"

"And how do I know you'll treat them right? They're used to the best—warm barn and good feed and rub downs after working."

Ruth held her breath as she listened to the men haggling over the deal. *Oh, please take the horses*, she silently implored Paul Thompson. Chores would be so much simpler without dealing with the large unruly animals.

Much to Ruth's relief, Amos finally agreed to the deal. Arrangements were made that Paul would tie the horses behind his wagon and take them home that very day.

With all his seeming reservations and arguments about the details, Ruth was surprised at Amos's reaction after the neighbor left.

"Hah, I bested him on that deal," he told Ruth gleefully. "He feeds his stock well. I can save my hay, and he can keep them horses in good condition for me, free of charge. Takes a lot to put one over on ole Amos. I got the best deal in the county."

Ruth felt like she had gotten the best deal in the county.

The barn work during those late summer days was pleasant.

Working with the animals was Ruth's favorite time. While her hours in the house during the mid-day were an ordeal, she dreaded the evenings even more.

I'm not giving the Edmonds a fair chance, she told herself for the hundredth time. *I'm in an unusual situation, doing an unusual job for a woman. They're just not used to it yet. It could be so much worse.* Ruth had a room to herself—one that had been meant for the schoolteacher for the country school that never opened—in the upstairs of the big farmhouse. The room was comfortable; the house was clean. The family consisted of Matt, his wife Dora, and their two daughters, Agnes and Agatha.

Ruth's boarding arrangement was that she would have breakfast and supper with the Edmonds, and the noon meal would be with Amos. She seldom saw the family in the morning. She left before sunup, long before they were up. That was fine with her. She fixed herself a piece of jam-covered bread and a cup of milk for her breakfast.

Suppers seemed strange for Ruth. When she returned in the evening, the family had already eaten. Perhaps it was her imagination, but she had the feeling they hurried through the meal and quickly left the kitchen when they saw her walk up the driveway. When she gave a quick greeting to the family seated in the living room, the girls swallowed giggles, Dora was threading her quilting needle, and Matt was finding his place in the newspaper. The dirty dishes were on the table as the family left them, with the chairs still arranged around the table. A small amount of food remaining in the pans for Ruth was pushed to the back of the stove. The food was dry and hardened onto the pans, making it difficult to get out. Long shadows filled the kitchen as the sun set before Ruth finished her meager meal. She washed the family's dishes and cleaned up the table. Pangs of loneliness settled over her as she scrubbed the dry pans.

During the first days of her stay, Ruth went immediately to her room after finishing the tasks in the kitchen. She was exhausted and needed the sleep. As she became more accustomed to her schedule, she thought she should try to be more friendly. Perhaps she had been rude to not join them. Besides, her loneliness pushed her into the living room.

Dora was sitting on the worn couch with the children on either side of her. She did not look up from the quilt she was working on, but ten-year-old Agnes and eight-year-old Agatha leaned on their mother's shoulders and openly stared at her. The family did not acknowledge her presence; Ruth awkwardly sat down on a straight-backed chair with some mending she brought down from her room. Silence. The girls continued to watch her. When they were certain their mother was engrossed in a stitch, one or the other would stick out her tongue or cross her eyes while smirking at Ruth. Ruth had never spent much time with children, but she thought these two were the most horrid girls she had ever met.

She pretended not to notice the mocking girls. "The pleasant weather is continuing," Ruth ventured softly as she prepared her needle and thread. Dora scowled as she continued to sew.

"If we don't get cooler weather and rain soon, we can forget about grass in the spring. It's too late in the fall for such hot weather." She spat the words out and clamped her jaws shut. Agnes and Agatha giggled into their mother's shoulders.

Matt seemed engrossed in his newspaper and remained silent.

Ruth tried to concentrate on her mending, but she felt the tension in the room building.

"Why do you wear overalls like my pa?" Agatha finally asked. "Ladies don't wear clothes like that." Agnes did not try to suppress her giggles.

"I wear these clothes because I do chores in a barn," Ruth explained. "My work is easier in overalls than in a dress."

Agatha wasn't done. "Mama said you're working in a barn because you don't have other stuff to do. Why don't you stay in your own house?"

"Well, I don't have a house of my own."

"Why don't you get your own house? Ladies are supposed to work in a house, not a barn. If you had your own house, then you wouldn't have to stay with us."

The girls' smirks changed to sullenness. Agatha continued, "If you didn't stay with us, I could have my room back. I don't like sharing a room with Agnes. She's messy. Mama says I have to be with her because you're in my room."

"You've said enough, Agatha," Matt finally interjected. "If you girls can't be pleasant, you might as well go to bed."

"I can stay up later than Agatha," Agnes whined loudly. "I'm two years older than she is. She can go to bed, and I'll wind the yarn into a ball for Mama."

"We have to go to bed at the same time," Agatha fumed. "Otherwise, she'll wake me up when she comes into the room. Ma, make her go to bed if I have to." She leaned across her mother's lap and scowled at her sister. "If you were in your own room…."

"I can't be in my own room. That barn lady is in my room."

Matt finally threw down his newspaper. "I'm going outside," he mumbled.

"And, I guess I'll say good night," Ruth quickly added. "Morning comes early."

She got no response from the family, but as she went up the stairway, she could hear Dora talking to Matt as he put on his cap to go outside. "You don't have to be short with the girls. They're right. Sure, we can use the ten dollars a month, but I can't say things have improved around here. You get the $10, the girls lose a room, and I get the extra work."

"What extra work?" Matt retorted. "She eats leftovers, and you get the dishes washed."

Ruth sighed as she closed the door to her room. Her thoughts drifted back to Daddy and her happy childhood. Daddy was always smiling, always approving of what Ruth did, and always loving her. Then Ben's face replaced Daddy's, and the tears came.

Chapter 11

As the weeks dragged by, Ruth purposely began sleeping a little later in the mornings and loitering a little with her bread and jam in the Edmonds' kitchen. She didn't set out for Amos's barn until she noticed a faint light in the east. *This is crazy*, she thought. *It's hardly October—I have months of winter ahead of me. I must get used to walking in the dark.* She had never liked the dark. She remembered walking to church meetings in the evenings with her family. She would hold Anna's arm even after she reached her teen years. Now that she was an adult, she scolded herself for her fears. *How silly to be frightened; there is nothing that will hurt me. I know every step of the two-mile walk.* Yet, familiar shrubs and rocks took on menacing forms. Soon it would be pitch dark both in the morning and evening. She shivered.

The darkness would have to be dealt with soon enough. For now, the walks were pleasant. Ruth was glad when she could get to Amos's farm each morning. She looked forward to getting to the barn, not the house. The sight of Amos's driveway and sturdy barn was comforting. She opened the heavy door of the barn and smelled the sweet aroma of hay and animals. How good to be here among her friends—and no people to deal with. The cats ran to welcome her with soft meows, and the chickens began their happy early morning clucking. By now, the eastern sky was turned red, and the songbirds were shouting out their songs as they prepared for their long migration south.

Dora Edmond had complained about the hot fall and dry weather, and so it was. But as October began, the weather took a nasty turn, and Ruth's walks were no longer pleasant. Winds howled, and cold rain drenched the fields and roads. The walks back and forth from Amos's farm to the Edmonds' home were pure misery. The roads were soft and muddy; at times, mud went over her shoes and squished down between her toes. The pain of cold feet caused her to limp as she walked the two miles each way. She wrapped a wool shawl over her heavy coat, but she was still chilled to the bone when she arrived at her destination. She didn't even pretend to be social in the evenings anymore. She immediately went to her room after eating a lonely supper and doing a cleanup of the Edmonds' kitchen.

In such weather, the barn was especially inviting. The cows still stayed outside, but as soon as they saw Ruth, they quickly stood, stretched, and made their way to the barn. They walked quietly to their own stanchions after giving a friendly nod to Ruth. The ritual of chores began. Ruth loved the routine of it. She lit the lantern and then quickly measured out the feed. While the cows ate, she opened the door of the chicken portion of the barn and spread their grain into the troughs. She no longer fed them outside. This weather was causing the chores to change quickly. Before long, the winter chore schedule would include a frozen water tank and cows needing care while being in the barn most of the time. That would not be so pleasant, but the dark walks would be the worst.

By the time she was ready to milk, the barn was light enough to put out the lantern. Milking was Ruth's favorite chore. She prepared the ten-gallon milk can topped with the strainer. She set the milking stool by the first cow and began the milking. She loved these large animals, so quiet and dignified. She loved their warm bodies as she pressed close to them. The plink-plink of the first milk in the pail turned to a frothy squish-squish as the pail filled. When the first cow was finished, she filled the cats' pan so they wouldn't be underfoot and in danger of being stepped on by the cows. Then she poured the rest of the milk from her pail into the strainer on the can and continued with the next cow.

Ruth felt her shoulders relax as she absorbed the contentment of the cows after their feeding and being relieved of their milk. She released them from the barn and separated the milk. She divided the skim milk between the chickens and the young calves still living in the barn. The cats were full of whole milk; they had no interest in drinking skim.

The cream can was put in the water cooler. The cooler was a wooden tank in a small building next to the windmill. Cold water was piped to the cooler from the windmill, and then another pipe went to the outside tank in the cow yard. Ruth pumped water to quickly cool the milk and filled the tank with drinking water for the cows. Neighbors would be sure to see that the cans of cream were taken to the General Dry Goods Store for credit on Amos's account.

Now all that remained for Ruth to do was clean the cow stalls, rinse out the cat pans, and gather some early morning eggs. She sighed as she looked at the house. Entering it would mean another round of hostile conversation, another day of making the quickest noon meal she could, another round of Amos's questioning of her methods with the chores. She knew Amos would be looking out the window and checking her progress as much as he could from the house. She could not put off the inevitable any longer.

Ruth slowly climbed the wobbly steps with the broken railing still lying where it fell months ago. Before she even got inside, the smells assaulted her—spoiled food, body odor, and human waste—reminding her that emptying the commode would be the first item of business.

Amos was sitting at the kitchen table playing solitaire as usual. Ruth felt nauseous as she looked at him in the filthy undershirt he wore every day. The left leg of his bib overalls, cut to the upper thigh to make room for the cast, was now covered with food stains and dirt. The smaller cast around his right foot was soiled brown, giving no indication that it had ever been white. This cast was Brute's favorite place to lay his head, and the dog often licked it as if to make it heal faster. Ruth had occasionally tried to coax Brute outside with her, but he never left Amos's side except to go out to relieve himself. He even walked with Amos as the man maneuvered his crutches or his little stool between the table, the stove, and his bedroom.

"What is spoiled in here?" Ruth asked brusquely, holding her nose. Her voice was unpleasant even in her own ears.

"And good mornin' to you, too," Amos answered sarcastically. "How should I know what stinks or not? Using food before it spoils is your job, not mine. You don't know the first thing about cooking. I'd have starved a long time ago if people didn't drop off stuff to eat.

"What time you getting here now?" he continued. "Those cows need to be milked at 6:30 in the morning and 5:30 at night. You're getting 'em off schedule. They needs to be milked same time every day. Ain't you the one thinkin' you can laze in bed half the day. Don't think I don't see you gettin' to the barn in the mornings later every day. You think I'm made of money, paying you big bucks and you milk whenever you feel like. Who knows what's goin' on in that barn? When I get these blasted casts off, I can see for myself what's not getting done."

"And, when you get those casts off, you can do your own chores, because I'll be leaving."

Ruth had hoped that Amos hadn't noticed she was milking later in the mornings and earlier in the evenings. She was not about to tell him she was afraid to walk in the dark. She could hear his derisive laughter. She quickly defended herself.

"What difference does a half-hour make? I don't hear any complaints in the barn. It's only in this stinky house that complaining goes on."

"Well, ain't you the one, all uppity. I could tell everybody who stops here what a lousy cook you are."

"And they already know what a lousy housekeeper you are by the looks and smells of this house."

Ruth couldn't ever recall talking to another person the way she talked to Amos. *Well,* she thought defiantly, *I've had a good teacher. Nobody has talked to me the way he does.*

Amos continued to ask questions about the chores and animals.

"Are the cats staying around the barn in this wet weather? Do you understand about 'drying up' the milk cows? The blue roan is going to calve in mid-winter. When she's down to giving a fourth of a pail of milk, start milking her just once a day. I'm paying you big money to keep track of everything out there."

Ruth knew about "drying up" cows from her short months of work with Ben. The cows needed to have a dry time before having another calf when they would begin another lactation cycle. She knew this, and she had noticed that the blue roan was not giving much milk, but she hadn't realized the reason. She hated to ask Amos questions; she felt vulnerable enough as it was.

Some of Amos's questions were the same every day: "How many eggs did you get this morning? Is there enough grass in the pasture yet?" (She didn't know). Are you sure you're giving the cows a pint of grain every day? There's not much nutrition in the dead grass now—they need the grain."

Ruth didn't pay much attention to his questions. She wondered what to make for dinner. The chickens were laying fewer eggs now with the shorter days, but cooking eggs was so much easier than other things. She hated to go down to the dark cellar for vegetables. The scampering mice were so much bolder now as they took refuge in the cellar from the nasty weather. Ruth was afraid of coming across spiders when she quickly sorted through the shriveled vegetables. Today there were no supplies from neighbors except a few biscuits. Eggs, it would be.

Ruth retreated to the barn as soon as she washed the dinner dishes. The cloudy morning had given way to a cold rain. She stood inside the barn looking out at the wet brown grass. What would she do when really nasty weather came, and it was no longer comfortable in the barn? At least here, she had a place of solace. It was her only one.

The cold, rainy weather continued over the next several days. Clouds hung low and heavy, making the days even shorter and Ruth more despondent.

She was walking back to the Edmonds one evening when she noticed the first snowflakes in the air. She tried not to panic. Snowstorms would be much more serious than darkness. That would be a real danger in the months ahead. In her agitation, she imagined hearing noises in the early evening darkness. She stopped to listen—was it the creaking of a wagon? Perhaps horses walking? She stared at the road ahead of her. She seldom saw anyone in her traveling back and forth, especially now when she walked in the near dark. She definitely could hear a wagon and horses now. It soon materialized just yards in front of her. The driver looked startled to see her and called "Whoa" to his horses.

"Are you the woman who works for Amos Armstrong?" he finally called out after a few minutes of silence. He stared at her through the darkness.

"Yes, I am."

"Are you on your way to the Edmonds?" he asked.

Ruth sighed. She knew very few people around here, talked to just about no one, but everyone knew her and her business. "Yes, I am." She repeated.

"Do you want a ride?"

"Who are you?"

"I'm Richard Hunter. I have a farm about four miles west of Amos. I got late in town. One too many games of cards. I go right by the Edmonds if you want a ride."

Ruth accepted. She grabbed hold of the side of the wagon seat and boosted herself up. Not very lady-like; she had a fleeting vision of her mother's horrified face. But wearing overalls made things like climbing into a wagon easier.

Richard proved friendly enough. He asked about Amos, how much milk she was getting from the cows, when they were going to calve, and if Amos had enough hay for the winter. As they talked, Ruth remembered she had met him before. He was one of the many farmers who had come to help Amos with the harvesting and plowing. That was when neighbors had spent two days at the farm finishing all that be to be done for fall work. Women had left food for meals and had harvested produce from Amos's garden. This had happened just as she had begun her work for Amos and at the time Neil and George were leaving. She hardly was aware of it—it was one of the many things that blurred in her mind as she adjusted to her job.

The walk to the Edmonds that had seemed endless on these wet, cold nights now just took a few minutes in the wagon behind the clopping feet of the horses. Richard stopped the horses at the end of Edmonds' driveway.

"Thank you so much for the ride," Ruth said quickly, jumping down from the wagon seat. She could feel her overalls were wet from sitting on the damp seat, but she had been glad for the ride. She had walked halfway up the driveway before she wondered if she was supposed to wait to see if he was going to help her down.

That's silly, she thought. *I can easily get off a wagon myself. He knows I do barn chores. Why would I suddenly act like a helpless female?* Still, the thought that she hadn't even considered acting more feminine concerned her. *What kind of a person am I turning into? I can't have a civil conversation with Amos, I can be as insulting as he is, and I have no idea how to act like a lady.* Again, Mother's face appeared in Ruth's imagination. Ruth had written a few letters to her mother, but she was careful to leave out many details—like the condition of Amos's house, his surliness, the hostility of the Edmonds, the emptying of the commode.... Her trail of thoughts ended with the growling of her stomach. As she approached Edmonds' house, she wondered what morsels of food would be waiting for her.

After finishing the chores the next evening, Ruth quickly left the warmth of the barn and hurriedly started her walk. *I can tell it's darker tonight than last night,* she thought, *even though there is no rain. It's colder, too. I must go through my trunk tonight to try to find a warmer wrap for my head. I know every step of this walk. Seeing strange objects in the field is just my imagination. There is nothing to fear.*

She approached the intersection in the road and made the turn to the south to Edmonds' farm. She noticed the outline of a team and wagon not far ahead of her. *Strange,* Ruth thought, *I didn't hear the horses or the wagon until I turned onto this road. It was almost as if they were just standing there and then started going as I arrived.* The wagon was going so slowly she easily gained on it, and then it stopped in front of her. Ruth saw that it was Richard Hunter's wagon.

"Hello, again," he said to her. "Can I give you a ride tonight?"

"Another late card game in town?" she asked.

"No, I'm just taking care of business. Climb in."

Ruth thought the whole scene seemed surreal. *Why would he be out on the same road the second night in a row when they had never encountered each other before last night?* She reluctantly grabbed the side of the wagon seat and climbed in.

Richard slapped the horses' rumps with the reins, and the wagon started with a jolt.

Without any preliminary small talk, Richard said. "There's a dance in town Saturday night."

A dance? On Saturday? She searched her mind. Was she supposed to know that? Did she have some responsibility regarding the dance? Did the neighbors supply food or music? She remembered socials in Rolling Valley as she was growing up—sometimes different areas of the town would provide the lunch for the evening. All the houses south of the church would....

Ruth realized she hadn't answered his comment when he continued, "Well, I'm asking you to go with me. I could pick you up with my wagon either at the Edmonds or Amos's place. Maybe you don't have any of your duds at his house, but that would be the shortest way to get to town for me...."

"Oh, but I couldn't possibly go to the dance," Ruth found her voice and interrupted when she realized what he was asking. She felt short of breath; she hadn't seen this coming. "You see, my husband..."

"Your husband! Did you get married to that skunk Amos? I thought it was funny you was willing to milk cows for him and work in his barn. But who would ever marry him?"

"No, no. I mean I did have a husband, so I couldn't possibly go with someone else. I mean it wouldn't work for me to go with you. I mean—I can't...I don't want to..." Ruth was aware she wasn't making any sense. Courting again had never entered her mind. This invitation had been so unexpected she wasn't able to think rationally.

"Okay, okay, I get the hint," Richard said sourly. "You're really strange; one for the books. If you have a husband, why are you here working for a guy like Amos? Why ain't your husband taking care of you? I'm not getting mixed up in this mess. I'll just let you off here." He jerked the horses to a stop. "Goodnight."

Ruth climbed down from the wagon and watched it rumble down the rough road before her mind cleared somewhat. What had she told him? He must think she was still married. It would have been simple to tell him her husband was dead, and that it was too soon to be with someone else. Why hadn't she thought of that? *I could have said my husband is dead, my husband is dead.* Ruth realized she had never said those words except in the telegram to her mother after the accident. "He's dead, and I might as well be, too. I cannot take another day of this unending work, the walks in the dark. No one cares, and my husband is dead."

Chapter 12

Ruth's despondency continued to hang over her as November's short days brought more gloom. To add to her woes, the weather was not only wet and cold—it began to feel like winter. Every night brought new snow and freezing temperatures, sometimes already getting down to zero degrees.

"This early cold doesn't bode well for the coming winter," neighbors agreed when they visited Amos. "Too dry, too hot all fall, and now too cold with all this snow. What's coming next?"

Ruth's work began even before she entered the barn each morning. It was necessary to shovel snow to get the door open. She kept the shovel leaning against the barn next to the door; it was needed almost daily. When the door could be opened, it was a relief to enter the warmth of the sturdy building. The cows now spent not only the nights but most of the daytime hours inside keeping the building comfortably warm even in the frigid temperatures. She knew her entrance into the barn would be met by friendly sounds from the animals. The cows mooed softly for their grain; the cats waited just inside the door. They began to purr with Ruth's arrival. Only the chickens remained silent—it was too dark in the barn for them to wake up.

Ruth was trying to learn how to change the chore routine with the change in the weather. Amos had been the one who had insisted the cows needed to be inside most of the time. Of course, he was not the one to do the barn cleaning either. Now, after the morning milking, Ruth would pump water into the barnyard tank until it was full. She would need to fill it once more during the day to satisfy the cows' thirst, but she knew that any remaining water would quickly freeze and must be chopped out with the ax. It was a fine line between giving them enough water and not having to chop any ice remaining in the tank the next morning.

The cows were eager to be released from their stanchions and get outside even with the cold weather. Standing confined to their stanchions had to be tiresome. And the prospect of fresh water urged them to the tank. While they pushed and shoved to get at the water, Ruth hauled forkfuls of hay from the outside haystack into the barnyard. Once the cattle were fed and watered, she returned to the barn and took care of the chickens. It was necessary to carry the water from the well into the barn for them. Finally, all the animals' needs were met, and Ruth took a few moments to relax and watch the animals eat. The young stock stuffed their mouths full and observed her as they chewed the hay. They began to get playful as they no longer felt hunger. They butted at each other and danced away from head butts from others. The cats had finished their morning milk and began washing their faces and paws. Mouse hunting would come later. The chickens sang their clucking song as they relaxed in squares of sunshine shining through the windows. They cleaned their feathers by throwing dust and straw over themselves. They began to check out nest boxes for laying eggs. Ruth sighed. It was hard to pull herself back from enjoying the animals to the work at hand. The companionship she felt from the animals was her only break in the monotony of work and loneliness and sadness. She pulled on her mittens and went out to check the water tank again. After pumping a little more water, she began the barn cleaning. She placed the wheelbarrow between the gutters of the barn and slowly filled it with forkfuls of manure. It was surprising that the forkfuls no longer seemed heavy to her. The full wheelbarrow was easily pushed to the manure pile behind the barn and dumped there.

The last thing Ruth did before going to the house was to pick the eggs. She had an idea of how many eggs she would find from the number of triumphant cackles she heard from the chickens. With the cold weather and short days, the chickens were laying fewer and fewer eggs. Ruth now usually took less than a dozen to the house.

Ruth took both the eggs and the cream into the house so they wouldn't freeze. The cream would be added to what was already in the ten-gallon cream can stored in the unheated back room of the house. Neighbors were faithful about picking it up and taking it to town. Amos would get groceries in exchange for the cream and the few eggs that were taken in.

The chores inside the house were also different with the cold weather. The first thing Ruth did was fill the kitchen wood box with split wood from the outside wood pile. The wood pile beside the house was huge—Amos must have spent many days cutting and splitting wood before his accident. Despite filling the wood box as full as she could twice each day, the box was empty and the house chilly when Ruth entered after finishing the chores.

The busy days of winter chores repeated themselves with unending monotony.

Ruth had trouble dressing warm enough for her walks between the Edmonds and Amos's barn. She crawled out of bed one morning, remembering her frigid and wet walk the evening before. She had gone through her trunk before retiring and taken out every piece of warm clothing she owned. She would be warm enough today, she told herself determinedly. She put on two pairs of long woolen socks and a pair of Ben's pants. Then she added one of his warm flannel shirts over her blouse before putting on the bib overalls. As she slipped on her coat, she was thankful she had lined it with heavy flannel. Before going out the door, she wound a veil over her face and around her fitted knit cap. She stepped out on the Edmonds' porch and was immediately surprised. The weather was not as cold as last night; it was extremely mild.

The eastern sky showed definite signs of light.

I must not take time to change my clothing, Ruth thought. *Amos would be looking out the kitchen window before long, looking for the lantern light in the barn. Maybe it will feel cooler as I get away from the buildings.* But that was not the case. Sweat was dripping down her back before she was halfway out of the Edmonds' driveway. Even though she unwound the veil as she walked, it already stuck to the back of her neck.

Exhausted from being so warm, she was relieved to enter the barn and hear the friendly welcome from the barn animals. She took off some of her outer clothes and wiped sweat. She tried to dry her damp hair.

I don't even know how to dress properly, she thought. *I don't know how to have a meaningful conversation with anyone. Amos and I can't have a civil word between us. My life is meaningless.*

"Except for taking care of you animals," she said as she began the chores. "Thank goodness I have you to talk to. No one else cares about me.

"Cats, you deserve a little extra milk this morning for being so friendly. And, cows, you can expect just a little more ground feed in your rations—not a tablespoon extra, but a little. When the weather turns cold again, you're going to need more hay, too"

She spent time talking to the animals as she fed them, did the milking, and strained the milk. She turned out the cows and tidied the stalls.

Ruth suddenly realized she had been dawdling. It must almost be time for the noon meal. She grabbed the egg pail and left the barn just as a wagon carrying a man and woman came up the driveway.

Her first inclination upon seeing a woman in the wagon was to duck back into the barn and wait until they left. But, when they both waved enthusiastically to her and motioned that they would meet her at the house, she reluctantly joined them.

"We're Art and Frieda Weiler," the woman said warmly, giving Ruth an unexpected hug. "You probably don't even remember us. We were here with the other neighbors in late August to help Amos finish up field work. You had only begun your work here; I'm sure there were too many people for you to recall everyone. I told you that day that I would be back for a visit, and here it is almost two months later."

Ruth did vaguely remember Frieda. She was so pretty and talkative. She had a large, sturdy frame and looked like she could take on any job with strength, determination, and good humor. Her rich brown hair was pulled back in a bun, but loose ringlets hung around her forehead and full, rosy cheeks. Her most remarkable feature, though, was her soft brown eyes. They glowed with happiness and warm friendliness. Ruth had not thought of her or her promise to come and visit since that day they met. She did remember that Art had stopped occasionally to visit Amos.

"I was going to visit you to see how I could help you adjust to our community," Frieda went on. "But then it was time to take care of my garden produce. I had a bumper garden despite the hot, dry summer. Then, Art and I added a room to our house. We wanted it done before the snow flies. I'm not much of a carpenter, but Art seemed to think I could help him."

"She's better at building stuff than I am," laughed her husband good-naturedly. "She can drive in a nail in two blows from the hammer. Besides that, she knows how to assemble shelves and make dressers and all the fancy stuff that women need in a room. It's mighty pretty now that we've got it done," he said proudly.

"He's a little prejudiced," Frieda said, smiling at her husband. Then she turned to Ruth, "You'll have to come see it someday."

They had been talking outside of the house. Ruth was hesitant to invite them inside even if they had been there before. Maybe they thought she'd have it cleaned up by now.

"Are you goin' stand out there jawin' all day?" Amos demanded from the doorway. "Get in here and let's see if you brought something that a hungry feller can eat. I got hot coffee ready for drinkin'. I sure hope you brought something besides eggs. I don't know what my chore girl does out in my barn, but I ain't too impressed with what she does in my kitchen."

"Hey, Amos, you don't look like you're starving," Art said genially. "I'm also sure your animals are well cared for. I'd say you're pretty lucky to have such good help."

Before Amos could reply, Frieda bustled about the kitchen taking pans out of her bags and filling the table with containers of wonderfully smelling contents.

"Here is a pan of mashed potatoes. There are meatballs and gravy in this kettle and some cooked squash with butter in here. They were hot when we left home, but I'm going to heat them just a little on the stove. Amos, I'm glad you have a fire going, even with this unexpected warm weather. You'll find some baked goods in the container on the cupboard."

While she spoke, Frieda quickly moved Amos's cards and old newspapers onto a chair and washed off the table. She set it with Amos's cracked plates and put the warmed food on the table in a matter of a few minutes.

Art said, "We had planned to visit with you longer, but this weather has me a little worried—too warm for mid-November. I keep thinking it might take a quick change for the worse, and I don't want the two of us to be too far from home when that happens. We got some errands to do in town, and I'll be relieved to get home."

"But we'll stop again on our way back," Frieda assured Ruth, "We'll pick up our containers then. Ruth, do you need anything from the store?"

"I think we could use some sugar and, of course, coffee. We do use a lot of coffee."

"That's easy for her to order groceries like they're free. I pay her big money; I can't afford everything in the store. There's brown sugar in the cupboard. We just need coffee."

Art laughed. "Amos, you have to spend your money somehow. We'll bring coffee and a little bit of white sugar."

He said it so amiably that Amos had no objection.

As they were going out the door, Art continued, "Say, Amos, do you have a steer that you want butchered? We've got a pig that's going to be ham and pork chops pretty soon. I thought maybe we could swap a little meat, and we'd both get some beef and pork."

Frieda explained to Ruth. "Once the weather turns cold to stay, it'll be easier to make meals. We'll do our butchering soon. You can keep meat frozen in Amos's back room or buried in lard. It will give you a few more options for cooking."

"Options, you say?" Amos snorted. "Hah! This lady don't know nothing about options unless it includes eggs."

Art and Frieda went on their way to town with Amos's cream and eggs to sell at the General Dry Goods Store. They promised to bring back some sugar and coffee and any mail there might be.

Amos sat down at the table before Art and Frieda were out of the driveway. Ruth watched him fill his plate with mashed potatoes. He poured the gravy over the potatoes and laid five big meatballs on top. Then he covered everything with a layer of cooked squash. He began to eat ravenously, forkful after forkful. Ruth became fearful that she wouldn't get her own share of the food. She also grabbed a plate and quickly filled it. Her hand gripped her fork like it was a shovel. The taste of the delicious food was hardly noticed. She was determined that Amos would not get more than she did, which meant she must gulp it down. She had almost finished the food on her plate when a vision of Mother's face appeared from nowhere. "Remember, a lady always puts down her fork and chews quietly between bites," Mother lectured. Ruth fled from the table and busied herself at the stove so Amos couldn't see her face. Not that he took any notice of her with his preoccupation with the food. Tears pricked her eyes. What was happening to her? Was she turning into a barbarian who fought for her share of the food? Would her mother even recognize her? She was no better than Amos. Ruth steadied herself and took a deep breath.

She sat back down at the table and refilled her plate with a mountain of food.

"Hah," Amos said as he cleaned up his plate with a piece of bread. He wiped his mouth with the back of his hand. "This is the way women are supposed to cook. And I'll take them up on the meat swap, too, that Art's been talking about. One of his pigs for a half of one of my steers. I'll get the best part of that there deal. They'll have to get the ham cured for me. I'm goin' make sure they throw in some bacon, too. That'll make those eggs go down easier."

Ruth was hardly listening. She felt sick from all she had eaten. Frieda had probably thought she was sending enough to make two or three meals. They had devoured it within a matter of minutes.

She felt shame when she realized the friendly couple would be back soon. How could they even want to step foot in this filthy house? Ruth so wanted to be friends with someone like Frieda. Ruth remembered that Frieda had said Ruth should visit them and see their new room. How nice that would be. Maybe they could visit back and forth during the winter.

Ruth looked at the house as others must see it. She had to make at least a few changes before the couple returned. She washed off the cupboard and then grabbed a bucket, found a mop in the back entry, and rid the floor of some of its dirt before Art and Frieda returned from town.

"Here's your coffee and sugar, Amos," Frieda said as the couple entered the house. "You'll find some stick candy in the package, too. That won't be on your bill. It's a treat from us."

"Looks like you've got a couple farm publications in the mail," Art told Amos, handing him some magazines. "Something new to read in the evenings."

"Did I get mail?" Ruth asked hopefully.

Art glanced at Frieda. "Not today, Ruth," Frieda answered. "But everyone is busy at this time of year. I'm sure there will be something next time."

Ruth felt the quick sting of tears. Her mother couldn't be so busy that she didn't have time to write to a lonely daughter. Ruth had written two letters since she had heard from her mother. She had described her job as delicately as she could without being untruthful. She knew Mother would cringe when she read that her daughter was doing barn chores and milking cows. But even if Mother was not happy with the situation, she could surely still write something.

"We have to go," Art said quickly. "I don't like this weather. Too warm for November."

Chapter 13

Art was right in his concern about the weather. It became sharply colder the day after their visit. Heavy dark clouds were building all day. Amos seemed especially sullen when Ruth came into the house to make dinner. She had been looking forward to the leftovers from Frieda's food and was dismayed to see that Amos had eaten them all for his supper the night before. She fumed as she looked at the meager provisions in the cupboard. There was still bread and cooked squash and part of an apple pie from what Frieda had brought. That would have to do. They had sent all the eggs to town with Art and Frieda. Ruth didn't feel like making any anyway with Amos always complaining about them.

After they finished their meal in silence, Amos began stomping back and forth on his crutches. "What's takin' you so long to do them blame dishes? This weather don't look good. Get out there and put all the young stock in the barn. After you milk, let the cows out to drink. But be sure you get them locked in the barn before you leave. And brace the barn door shut; this wind could whip it open. Put out a little extra milk for the cats so they don't go out hunting."

Fat flakes were falling by the time Ruth had her wraps on. How would she see the road to Edmonds? The ground and any tracks would be concealed by the snow before she even started out. She wrung her hands as she hurried to the barn. The wind had come up, hurling snow into her face and blurring her vision. The yard looked unfamiliar with the woodpile covered with snow and tree stumps standing dark against the white background. Her breath was whipped away by the gusts of wind. She would do the chores as quickly as she could, no matter what Amos thought about the milking time. He was so concerned about his animals but didn't give a thought to her being out in this weather.

The last of the afternoon light was still lingering when she finished in the barn and started for the Edmonds. She wasn't proud of the way she had done the chores. The milk cows had only a taste of water at the tank before she chased them back into the barn. She put all the milk into the cooler; she could separate it tomorrow morning.

If I'm alive to be back here tomorrow morning, she thought grimly. But she realized again how needed she was for the animals if not for anyone else. Who would relieve the cows of their milk if she couldn't get back? Who would sing back to the chickens when they did their clucking songs over their morning feed? Who would pet the cats as they lapped up their warm milk? But, of course, the chickens wouldn't have any feed, and the cats wouldn't have any milk. Who would provide for their needs? She remembered Ben talking about the relationship and inter-dependence of farm animals and their caretakers. For the first time, she felt her job was important.

Ruth could only guess where the road was as she trudged through the snow. *This is what I dreaded since I started this job in late August,* she thought. *Making this walk in the dark and now in the blowing snow. I could freeze to death, and no one would find my body for days. Who knows if I'm even on the road anymore?* Panic was rising in her throat. Her thoughts were in a jumble. *I might have wandered onto the fields. I won't be found until spring.* She strained her eyes to see if she was in the field. Just then, she bumped into a fence post. The fence! She had not thought of that. She could follow the fence all the way. There was only a short distance without a fence, and there the road was dotted with trees. She would be able to find her way. Tears of relief filled her eyes. She walked along the fence line with confidence, sometimes even running her mittens along the top wire. It became her companion; it was her savior in the storm. She thought of the walk ahead of her. She knew the fence would continue right to the Edmonds' driveway. When the fence stopped, she would be at their place. It worked out just as she planned. When the fence stopped, she followed the driveway up to the house without difficulty. Dora and the girls did not come out of the living room when Ruth fell into the kitchen, exhausted. "I see you made it," Matt said. Maybe he sounded concerned for her. "I told Dora to fix a little extra for your supper. It takes energy to be out walking in this weather."

I shouldn't be out walking in this weather at all, Ruth thought. She mumbled her thanks and reheated what was left on the stove. She fell into bed as soon as she had washed the dishes.

Light was coming into the room's only window when Ruth awakened. She lay still, trying to rid her mind of the nightmares that had plagued her sleep—nightmares of being lost in a storm. As reality settled in, she knew she had badly overslept. Even with the frost covering her window, she realized it was fully light. The wind was still blowing, although not as forcefully as during the night.

Ruth dressed quickly. The Edmonds were already at the breakfast table when she came down.

"We thought you were never getting up," Agnes announced.

"You should have awakened me. What's the weather like?"

"We've had six, seven inches of snow overnight, but it looks like it's going to clear off," Matt answered. "The wind is starting to calm down some. I don't think you would have been able to get to Amos's before now anyway. You need daylight. Amos's cows aren't going to die if they don't get milked or fed at exactly the right time for once. Although he thinks they will, of course. I'm just going out to do my chores now. Have some breakfast before you start out. There's hot cereal left, isn't there, Dora?"

Dora frowned slightly. "There might be some left in the kettle. Help yourself."

A few minutes later, Ruth was trudging through the snow. The gusts of wind still took her breath away. She was glad she hadn't started out before now, but she imagined Amos staring out the window, wondering what had become of her. In places where the snow had drifted, she floundered with the snow well over her knees; in other places, she was walking on smooth ground. I must remember that I can always hang onto the barbed wire fence when I walk in the dark, she consoled herself.

The snow had completely stopped, and there was even a hint of morning sunshine when Ruth arrived at the barn. She was greeted with impatient sounds from the animals as she fell into the barn door. She sighed with relief as the warmth enveloped her.

"Yes, yes, I know everyone is hungry. You'll all get your food as fast as I can get it to you. Be thankful I'm here at all," she admonished the hungry stock. "We did have a bad storm last night, you know." She added to herself, "I need to practice that same speech for Amos."

Ruth was finishing the chores and preparing herself to meet Amos's complaints about being late when she heard a team and wagon go by the barn and on up to the house. The wagon was on runners that glided smoothly over the new snow.

I'm surprised anyone is out and about so soon after the storm, she thought to herself. Most errands could wait until the weather settled a little. Curiously, she quickly gathered the few eggs in her egg basket, picked up the cream can, and headed for the house. She didn't recognize the team or wagon.

From inside the house, she heard Brute bark several times. It was not a regular visitor.

When she entered the kitchen, she saw the visitor was the talkative man she had met at the dry goods store when she first arrived last summer. His name didn't come to her, but she did remember that he did odd jobs around town. He was sitting at the table with Amos drinking a cup of hot, black coffee.

They looked up at Ruth when she entered. She started taking off her wraps. Amos was scowling. Ruth steeled herself for the reprimands she expected from Amos for doing chores late.

"I'm right glad you got here to Amos's safe and sound this morning, Ma'am," the visitor told her. "Don't know if you remember me—I'm Stanley Cooper. That was a bad storm last night—not fittin' for nobody to be out in. I'm stoppin' at some of the neighbor folk this morning with bad news. Clyde at the livery told me I could use his team and wagon. Wanted some of the folks around to know. Just told Amos here."

Ruth realized that Amos's scowl was not meant for her. He stood up to pour more coffee for the two men and then stood looking out the window.

Stanley began his story to Ruth, one he had probably already shared several times that morning. "Don't know if you ever met Stubbs Johnson, Ma'am. He worked for the Clanceys for years—good stock man. Got his nickname when he lost a couple fingers—got them caught in a threshing machine belt. Didn't stop him from being a good hired man, though. He usually stayed with the Clanceys, but oft times he'd go into town to play checkers at the store. Was a good checkers player. I didn't like to play with him, though—took him too long to figure out his moves. But he was good. I think only Nels Arnson could beat him regular. Sometimes he'd just sleep right there in the back of the store. Arnson sure didn't care if he stayed there—even gave him grub to eat in the morning. Why he didn't stay last night, we can't figure. Had to get back to the Clanceys, he told the guys. When they said it was too bad a storm to go out, ole Stubbs says he'd just hold on to the barbed wire—hand over hand on the wire, he says—and get back to Clanceys just fine. Said he'd done it a hundred times before and in worse weather. The Clanceys don't live but two miles from the outside of town, over on the north side."

Ruth was having trouble breathing. She waited wordlessly for Stanley to finish the details of his story.

"Well, it would have worked for ole Stubbs last night, too. Except that for some reason Clancey closed the barbed wire gate at the end of his driveway. Stubbs didn't even know he was going hand over hand on the gate and just kept going following the fence on the other side of the driveway, farther and farther out into the country. He must have gotten all tuckered out and stopped to rest. Anyway, me and a couple of the guys from the store found him this morning, froze solid. His hands froze right to the fence. Kneeling down there by the fence, you'd have thought he just stopped to catch his breath. We went up to him, and there he knelt—froze. Face as white as the snow. I never seen the beat. Ain't never seen no one froze to death before. Hopes I never see another. Too bad. Stubbs was a good guy. A good stock man. The Clanceys are really going to miss him. They'll miss him at the store, too. Was a real good checkers player. I ain't goin' to be able to play a game of checkers from now on without thinking of ole Stubbs.

"Thanks for the coffee, Amos. I'm going to stop at another couple places before I head back to town. Worst thing I seen in my life—I'll dream about it tonight, I tell you. Just was kneeling right there by the fence.

"Glad you made it here this morning safe and sound, Ma'am. Sure ain't safe in these storms. We're going to miss ole Stubbs."

Stanley went out the door, letting in a rush of cold air. Ruth shivered and sat down on a kitchen chair. Her stomach quivered; she thought she was going to be sick. She pressed her hands against her mouth. Horror washed over her. Hand over hand on the fence, Stanley had said. Her plan of survival for walking in the dark. It hadn't worked for Stubbs Johnson.

Amos was still staring out the window. She talked to his back. "I'm moving into your upstairs today," she said quietly. It was not a question. "I'm leaving now for the Edmonds' to get a few things that I'll need. Maybe Matt can bring my trunk sometime when they go to town."

Amos spoke for the first time. "What about my dinner?"

"I can't think about making food. I want to go now in the middle of the day before it gets any colder. I'll make something when I get back."

Amos didn't answer. She put on her many wraps that she had just taken off. Ruth made record time in getting to Edmonds. She felt propelled to get there immediately, take care of business, and get back. She wanted to walk only in bright sunshine.

The Edmonds were sitting at the dinner table, just as she left them at breakfast some hours before. They looked at her in surprise when she entered the house.

They had not heard about Stubbs Johnson. Quickly she told them the story and explained she would be moving out. That brought an immediate reaction.

"What about your payment? November isn't over yet; I don't think we ever promised a refund if a month wasn't finished," Dora huffed. "Money doesn't grow on trees, you know. That payment gets used up for essentials right away. There's nothing left to give back."

Matt put in quickly, "What did you have in mind, Ruth? Were you hoping for money back?"

Before Ruth could answer, Dora added, "And how will that look, you living with a single man? This is a God-fearing community. Neighbors are not going to like that living arrangement under their very noses. Think about your reputation."

Even Agnes had a comment. "I think people already talk about you because you don't wear dresses like you're supposed to."

Ruth pressed her lips together to keep from answering in anger. Her voice was rigid, and she spoke slowly trying to control her emotions. "Thank you for your concern. Right now, I'm more interested in staying alive than what people think of me. I hadn't even thought about getting money back on my rent, so you don't need to worry about that."

She turned to go up to her room but couldn't resist looking back and adding, "Thank you so much for your hospitality and all the good food during the months I stayed here." She hoped they realized she was being sarcastic. *I've become proficient at sarcasm with all my practice with Amos*, she mused.

Ruth took only what she would need immediately—some undergarments, her extra pair of coveralls, combs for her hair. She stuffed them into one of the pillowcases she had made years before. What if Amos didn't have any extra bedding? She took the other pillowcase and pushed in her sheets. On impulse, she grabbed the muslin delaine. Every other thing that she possessed in the world was in the trunk. Carrying both pillowcases, she descended the stairs and explained to Matt and Dora that the trunk would have to sit there until arrangements could be made to move it.

"I should take you and your stuff over to Amos's, but I hate taking the horses out on such a cold day," Matt apologized. "I tell you what, though. I'll bring your trunk over to you myself, soon as this cold breaks. You'll have them in three-four days."

Ruth quickly pulled on her outer garments. She couldn't get out of the house fast enough. She hoped there would never be a reason to go back.

It had not gotten any colder, and the sun was still shining brightly. Despite carrying the pillowcases filled with her things, she made record time getting back to Amos's house.

Ruth wasn't sure why, but she was angry. Angry at the weather that so capriciously took a life, at Amos for letting her go back and forth from the Edmonds' place to his when the danger was great, angry at the Edmonds for not helping her with her trunk today, angry at herself for being in such a miserable situation—a situation that had been life-threatening. *Not anymore*, she told herself. *I really don't care what people think. I'm staying in that horrible house with Amos until the snow thaws. I'm going to tell him all the things I should have told him months ago—that he should be grateful that I'm taking good care of his precious cows, that his house stinks, and I'm only staying there because it's too dangerous not to, that we must renegotiate what he pays me. I don't get paid nearly enough.*

Ruth had almost run the distance between the two farms. Despite the cold, her clothing was sticky with sweat. She burst into the house ready with her angry speech. Amos was sitting at the table wearing a red plaid wool coat and a wool cap with earlaps pulled far down on his head. He had gloves on and was unsuccessfully trying to hold the worn cards. Ruth had not seen him in a coat before and was about to ask in surprise where he was going. Then she realized the house was icy cold. A glance at the empty wood box reminded her that she had not thought about bringing in wood before going to the Edmonds.

Brute was lying by the cold stove, his body in a tight circle, his nose covered with his tail.

"I'm sorry I forgot about the wood." Her words surprised her. She had not planned to begin her tirade with an apology. She had never said the words "I'm sorry" to him.

Amos shrugged his shoulders. "I've been cold before. Though it ain't easy to shuffle cards with gloves on." His words didn't sound angry—it almost seemed like he was trying to show a bit of humor.

"I'll bring in some wood and find something for dinner. Then maybe we can talk over this new situation. I brought a few of my things, and I'd like to stay in your upstairs."

"I'd like to stay in your upstairs"?? Where were these words coming from? She had demanded to stay there just hours before. She realized she was exhausted; maybe she was too tired to be making demands.

"It's not pretty up there. I ain't been up there since mid-summer. I think there's an old mattress up there that George and Neil slept on when they were here helping me in August. I wouldn't be surprised if there'd be mice up there by now."

Ruth gritted her teeth and shuddered. Anything but mice! However, it took only a moment to realize that, while mice were not pleasant, they were better than walking in the dark or snowstorms. They were most definitely better than hanging onto a fence frozen to death.

When she returned to the house with an armful of wood, she was astonished to see that Amos had set the table. He had never done that before. She was about to ask what had taken possession of him but instead mumbled a thank you. He was probably so cold he needed some exercise.

After they had eaten and washed down the last of the bread and jam with scalding coffee heated on the now red-hot stove, Ruth asked how the new situation would affect her pay. "I'll need to be paying for my room and board now, but I'll be here more of the time to do more housework. I can try to do a better job of cleaning for you. Maybe"—she stumbled on the words, "Maybe I can try to make some better meals."

"Hah, I could use some better grub—and something besides eggs. You must be able to cook something else even if you was going to be a schoolmarm."

Eggs had been her go-to meal. Unless neighbors had brought something else to eat, she made them almost every day. She knew Amos was tired of them, but she hadn't given much thought to the fact that it gave him less credit at the dry goods store.

"I'm not proud of my cooking," she confessed. "I've just tried to get by with as little preparation as possible. If I'm here all the time, I'll try to plan ahead and do a better job. At least, I've mastered all ways to prepare eggs."

"I hired you to take good care of my cows. The grub ain't that important if there's enough of it. Take care of the stuff in the barn—that's what I'm paying you big money for."

"And I do take good care of your cows and the other animals. You have to give me credit for knowing what I'm doing out there."

"Do you know what you're doing? How long have you been taking care of milk cows? I've growed up with livestock, and most of them cows were raised right here on this farm. I've known them since they were born. There ain't no way I can check up on you, so you better do what's right. And do you even keep track about how much hay we got, what we're going to need to last to spring? Even with the horses gone, ya gotta keep track of things. You just play around out there."

Ruth flushed angrily. "Well, I've been milking cows and taking care of them since…." Ruth couldn't finish. How long had she been milking? Before coming to Ben's home, she had never even been in a barn. She had been his student absorbing dairy information like a sponge during their short marriage, but could she honestly say she knew a lot about taking care of cattle?

Suddenly, for the first time, she realized how miserable this time must be for Amos. It was evident she really didn't know much about her job. Was she doing the best job possible in the barn? Amos was truly concerned about his stock.

"I'll try to let you know more about what's going on in the barn.

We can make decisions regarding the cattle together. I am doing my best."

Amos did not comment. After some minutes of silence, he said, "I'll increase your pay from $20 to $35 a month."

"Increase? But now I have to pay you room and board."

"Naw, now I'm paying you to be a housekeeper, too. But git it in your head that from now on I expect to eat other grub besides eggs. You better look upstairs before it starts to get dark. It ain't going to be a picnic up there."

Ruth picked up her pillowcases and climbed the ladder to the upstairs. A closed trap door at the top needed to be pushed up. A hook held it open. "Leave the trap door open so it can get warm up there," Amos called after her. "Unless you're scared I'll come crawling up the ladder. In that case, you can close the trap door and hook it shut. Either be cold and safe or warm and scared. Ha, Ha!"

The upstairs was one room, and it was terribly cold. Frost lined the roof line, tall in the middle of the room and slanted down to just a couple feet high on the sides. Small windows, about a foot square, were set in the front and back walls. The west window showed the sun low on the horizon. Ruth saw the old mattress lying in the middle of the room. So far, she didn't see any mice, but she was definitely glad she brought her own sheets. The mattress was filthy. Various items of clothing hung from hooks along one of the low walls. There were three battered trunks along the other wall.

"Do you have any blankets up here?" Ruth called down to Amos.

"I don't even know what's in those trunks," he replied up the stairs. "Stuff from my ma and pa, I suppose. An' maybe some of my brothers and sister's stuff. I got some extra blankets down here you can use on the mattress. S'pose there's not much warmth in sharing the mattress with the mice. You can use some of the hooks for your stuff—throw my clothes on the floor."

Ruth did enough rearranging to find room for her few things. She brushed off the mattress and put her sheets on. It was beginning to feel a little warmer, but the dwindling daylight cast weird shadows on the walls. She shivered. She was glad she wouldn't be walking back to the Edmonds, but right now, she didn't want to spend more time than necessary in the darkened upstairs.

Climbing down the ladder, she realized with a jolt that she was very late in starting the afternoon chores. In fact, the cows had not been let out to drink since right after the morning chores. Amos had not said anything.

"Did you realize I wasn't keeping up with the chores today?" she asked sheepishly. "I had told you I knew what I was doing out there."

"Well, ain't you the one—actually admitting you ain't perfect. I figger today was your moving day," Amos answered dryly. "I'll get back to nagging you tomorrow. Ya gotta work for that big money I'm paying you, ya know."

The chores took longer because she was doing everything in the dark, and things had been neglected the last two days. She was exhausted when she returned to the house but relieved beyond words that she didn't have to walk to the Edmonds.

It was only after she took off her warm outer clothes that it dawned on her that she would now be expected to make supper. It was hard enough to come up with a meal once a day.

"What do you usually make for supper?" she asked Amos.

"I ain't choosey. Sometimes there's stuff left from what neighbors bring. Sometimes I throw some potatoes in the stove to bake, but it's too late to do that for tonight. Sometimes I make milk toast."

"Milk toast? I know how to make that. My mother-in-law made it for Sunday night suppers. That won't take long."

I should have thought of that meal months ago. I need to write down menu ideas and what supplies I would need to make them, Ruth thought as she quickly cleaned up after supper.

It was such a treat to climb the ladder to her own room, even though it was dirty and dark. The only light came through the trap door from downstairs. It was warm now after having the trap door open all afternoon and evening. She made up the mattress, tucking the sheets in tightly just in case some mice did live inside.

Exhaustion was Ruth's prevalent thought as she laid her head on her pillow and covered herself with several blankets and quilts. She was comfortably warm, warmer than she had been in her room at the Edmonds. Before sleep claimed her, she wondered if Amos worried that heating the upstairs would diminish the woodpile before spring. Strange, today was the first time she had anything close to a normal conversation with Amos, and he had only once said, "Well, ain't you the one!" Ruth's last conscious thought was of Stubbs Johnson. *Did he have any family? Was anyone grieving for him?* Except for the horror of his death, she had not thought of him before now.

Chapter 14

The weather warmed somewhat during the next few days. Most of the snow melted, and the late fall storm became an unpleasant memory. But to Ruth, pushed into moving to Amos's house, the storm had brought relief from the constant fear of her morning and evening walks. Amos was not pleasant company, but she preferred sparring with him than enduring the surliness of the Edmonds.

She found she had more energy and a greater awareness of her surroundings. The house smelled bad. Not just because Amos smelled bad. It was dirty. Ruth was surprised at her sudden burst of energy and enthusiasm. With the extra time spent in Amos's house, she realized a great need to CLEAN.

Where to start? The table was probably most in need. Getting it cleared of old papers and mail, worn-out magazines, and dirty coffee cups was the first challenge. For the past three months, she had merely been pushing the things around enough to provide room to set two tin plates and two tin cups for the noon meal for her and Amos. Dirty dishes from other meals sat on the table when Ruth would get to the house after chores in mid-morning. There was never any food left on the table. Ruth suspected that Brute cleaned up any leftovers from breakfasts, suppers, and snacks with neighbors. The table would be the place to start.

"What you doin' with my stuff?" Amos asked when she started removing the piles.

"I need to scrub the table," Ruth replied. "Where do you want your stuff?"

"On the table where it's been."

"I need to move it while I scrub the table."

"You can scrub the part where we put our plates."

"Amos, look at the mess. There are coffee stains and food smudges on all the papers. Who knows what the table looks like underneath all that junk? If you don't tell me where to put it, I'll pile it on the floor. But today, I'm scrubbing that table."

"Well, ain't you the one," Amos grumbled, but a few minutes later, he emerged from his bedroom. His arms struggled with his crutches while at the same time balancing a large empty wooden box.

"Put the stuff in here. I'll put it in my bedroom. And don't you even think about cleaning stuff in my bedroom."

Ruth scrubbed the table with a brush, soap, and water. It took several rinses before the water didn't turn a dirty brown. From there, she went to the cupboard and the stove. While working, she made mental notes about menus that she knew how to make.

Pancakes, she thought. That was quick, and she knew how to make them. The ingredients were always on hand. Now that she was in the house more, she could make potatoes and salt pork or other meat that was kept frozen in the cold box for the meal at noon. Oatmeal and bread would work for breakfasts, and pancakes or milk toast or noon leftovers would work for suppers. She did hope that others would continue to bring bread. Bread baking was a daunting chore; she would have to make herself practice that more often. She couldn't rely on the generosity of neighbors all the time, especially now that she was officially the housekeeper.

The job she was dreading most she put off until the next day. She did empty the commode each day, but it needed a scouring job with a strong bleach solution. The house would definitely smell better with that job done. *Tomorrow*, she thought. *Right now, the kitchen is cleaner than at any time since I've come here.*

She was exhausted but satisfied with her accomplishments when she put on her outer garments in mid-afternoon to start the chores.

The warmer weather brought a visitor who wasn't one of the regular coffee-drinking neighbors.

Matt Edmonds came with Ruth's trunk. He set it in the middle of the kitchen and didn't ask if there was a better place to put it. Ruth knew she should invite him to stay for coffee, but the words wouldn't come out of her mouth, and Amos didn't say anything.

Somehow just having Matt in the house was frustrating. However, it was good to have her trunk with her belongings close to her. She wouldn't ask Matt to move it—she'd wait until a neighbor stopped by and ask him to carry it up the attic ladder.

"Guess you're glad you don't have that walk anymore," Matt said before leaving. "You're lucky you got moved before winter gets set in. But I know Dora misses that ten dollars a month. She was hoping to buy an organ for the young 'uns for Christmas. I s'pose money don't mean so much to you when you ain't got family. Now Dora, she's always thinking of others, especially our young 'uns. Stop in and visit us sometime."

Ruth couldn't even sputter a goodbye. Was she supposed to feel guilty that she wasn't providing the funds for an organ? Dora had told her the money was used for essentials. And why should she visit them? They never talked to her while she lived there. And had he forgotten the terrible storm she had walked through "before the winter set in"?

For once, she was in complete agreement with Amos when he said, "Hah, how could that woman of his think of others? She ain't got a brain in her head."

Chapter 15

The warm weather didn't last long before winter settled in again. Everything was hard with the cold. Ruth's hands cracked and bled from chopping the ice from the cow tank and pumping fresh water. Try as she might, her mittens always became wet in the process.

Ruth was dragging forkfuls of hay to the impatient cows in the barnyard. They had drunk their fill and now complained that the hay wasn't coming fast enough. Usually, Ruth had a friendly conversation with the cows and fondly chided them for their impatience, but this morning she was rethinking her latest conversation with Amos.

Complaints about her cooking never stopped. She hated to admit, even to herself, that her cooking skills were non-existent. During her growing-up years, Mother loved making fancy things in the kitchen. Anna was an eager student and quickly picked up her mother's skills. They studied new recipes and combinations of foods. Ruth never seemed to have success with things in the kitchen. Mother often said things went quicker and easier when she and Anna did them; Ruth could help by staying out of the way.

It was different with Hattie. She never made anything fancy—just good, wholesome plain food. Ruth knew she should have learned more from Hattie; certainly, the older woman would have been willing to teach her, but the timing was not right—it was far more pleasant to be with Ben. There would always be "later." Later, when she and Ben had their own home, when they had children, when she had learned more about the outside farm work, when.... And now, the time would never be right.

When Amos wasn't complaining about Ruth's cooking, he drilled her about the outside chores. "How much milk are ya getting? Are you sure it isn't freezing? You're goin' have to bring it in right after milking and keep it in the back entry until neighbors take it to town. Are you sure you're finding all the eggs? The chickens should be laying better than that. How much are you feeding them?"

Most of Amos's questions were repetitions from the preceding days. She often would spit out a sarcastic reply or not answer him at all. Today, however, she realized she needed to get his advice on a matter in the barn, much as she hated to admit it. Before she went out that morning, she pushed her concerns out of her mouth.

"I think there's something wrong with some of the hens. They sit on the nests all day but don't lay anything. When I check under them for eggs, they feel like they're extra warm. Last week there was one like that, and today there are two more. And now I've noticed that they are losing some feathers and their combs and wattles are not a good color. I'm afraid they're sick. Maybe they'll spread some disease to the others."

Amos stared at her and then laughed in derision. "You don't know nothin' about nothin'. Those chickens aren't sick. Ain't you ever heard of broody hens? They want to hatch eggs, and they quit laying. Get them out of the coop, so they can't get to the nests. Put them in the main barn with the cows. Splashing some cold water on them will speed up the process. In a week, they'll be back to normal." Amos snorted in disgust. "This is what I get when a schoolmarm tries to do chores."

Ruth shook her head at the remembered conversation and reminded herself that she needed to get the barn cleaned before going in to cook some dinner. She had just picked up the manure fork when she heard horses and a sleigh crunch by the barn and go up to the house. Looking out the door, she saw it was Art and Frieda's sleigh. Maybe they brought something for dinner or at least would offer friendly conversation. She put down the fork, took off her barn coveralls, and headed for the house.

Amos was pouring the always-ready hot coffee for the two men by the time Ruth entered the house. Art had thrown off his coat and was sitting at the table. He had a box of delicious-looking cookies in front of him.

"Now, don't spoil your appetite for dinner with these cookies," Art said. "They're meant for your dessert."

Amos had a quick retort. "Ha, I need something to spoil my appetite."

"Couldn't Frieda come with you?" Ruth couldn't keep the disappointment out of her voice.

Art grinned. "You know that woman is busier than a cat in a barn full of mice. Right now, she's on a baking binge and can't leave the house. 'Course I'm not complaining about all that stuff to eat, but by spring, I'm going to be fat as a pig at this rate. She hardly has time to talk to me, so I have to get some company by visiting Amos here. But, as a matter of fact, she sent me. She said we needed more people to eat what she makes. So, I'm inviting both of you to our house for Thanksgiving next Thursday."

Ruth had not thought about Thanksgiving. She had not realized the event was only days away. Her days blurred together with chores, cooking, and working with the impossible job of trying to keep the house clean. Time had no meaning for her. *Thanksgiving.* So many memories of the activities of that holiday.... the wonderful aromas in the immaculate house, Mother rushing about, planning her guest list and menu for the big dinner, Anna busy at the sewing machine sewing another dress. "Ruth, for goodness' sake, don't you smell the cookies burning? Get them out of the oven for me, and then please stay out of my way." Mother's voice was exasperated. "I don't know how you can ruin a dessert merely by stepping into the kitchen."

Ruth usually retreated to Daddy's store when Mother was on a cooking binge. Ruth loved to listen to Daddy talking with his customers. He was pleasant to everyone, and they left, not only with their purchases but chuckling over some clever thing he had shared with them. Sometimes, Ruth heard them confide in Daddy about some problem in their lives, and they listened carefully to his advice. She had mentioned to Daddy once that she wished she had a way with words like he did. "Be a good listener, Ruth. Everybody likes to talk," he advised.

And then, there was Ben. There was no problem in finding things to talk about with Ben. They would talk far into the night, planning, laughing, never at a loss for words. Could it be that it was just a year ago that Ben had visited her and her family? He had declared his love for her and their desire to be married. A year ago? That was a different lifetime; she was a different person.

Ruth's recollections were interrupted by Art's cheerful voice. "Well, am I going to get any takers for Thanksgiving dinner?" he was asking. "Amos, Frieda and I are both pretty strong. Between her and me, we can get you down those steps and into the sleigh. It'd do you good to get out. And, Ruth, if you don't mind my saying so, I think a good meal would do you good, too. You could use a little meat on your bones. Frieda would be only too happy to oblige."

Ruth held her breath. Oh, to sit down to a delicious meal with friends! Could that actually happen?

"Shoot and tarnation," Amos replied. "You think I'd take a chance getting' down them narrow steps with my crutches? And then trying to get through all that dang snow and ice? I ain't goin' nowhere until these casts get off. I don't care if you have six people tryin' to lug me around. I'm stayin' right here."

"Oh, but I would love to go," Ruth quickly interjected. Would the invitation still be offered if Amos wouldn't go?

Art answered quickly, "I understand your caution, Amos, but I think you can get along without Ruth for a few hours. What about if I pick up Ruth and we'll bring some food back for you? If you change your mind, we'll haul you out of here one way or another."

Amos started to object. "I'm paying her big money, but what do I know if she doin' any work out there anyways. She might as well go and bring back something to eat as long as it ain't eggs."

Art laughed. "I have a feeling Frieda will send back a whole basket of food and probably not one egg. It'll give Ruth a little break from cooking besides doing all those chores."

Amos snorted. "Cookin' you say? I can tell you never been here to eat one of her meals."

Art smiled at Ruth. "I'll be here about 11 o'clock on Thursday morning then to pick you up."

He carried the hot coffee pot to the table and refilled cups for Amos and himself. "Lots of cookies left," he said, offering the plate again to both. "They should last for a few days."

She grabbed a couple to eat on her way outside. Most likely, they would be eaten by the time she returned to the house. She hurried back to the barn to finish the cleaning. She counted the days until she could have a real meal and pleasant conversation with pleasant people. Tonight, she would look at her dresses and decide what to wear.

***

After supper that evening, Ruth took the lamp from the kitchen table, carried it up to the attic, and set it on the wooden box she used for a nightstand. Amos groused about having to get his lamp from his bedroom for his light on the table, but Ruth argued that it was necessary that she had some light in the attic for this evening.

She kneeled in front of her trunk and hesitated. She had not opened it since moving into Amos's house. On top were her two cotton house dresses, dresses that she never wore now that she wore Ben's overalls for her barn work. Digging down, she pulled out her dark blue taffeta dress covered with tiny light blue flowers. It was made by a dressmaker, a luxury Mother had insisted upon for the party for Ruth's high school graduation and Anna's engagement announcement. This had been her Sunday dress when she attended church with Ben after their marriage. Its shiny material rustled as she laid it on the bed. Attending church with Ben…another world, another life. She remembered him helping her from the wagon in the churchyard, his hands on her waist. Sitting next to him during the church service always gave her a feeling of euphoria even after months of marriage. He was so handsome in his black suit, white shirt, and black string tie. His dark blonde hair was slicked back instead of falling onto his forehead as it did when he was working outside. Ruth hoped it was not a matter of gossip when she sat so close to Ben that their shoulders sometimes touched. Ben didn't seem to mind. He occasionally gave her a secret smile as their eyes met. Ruth was aware of the envious looks of the young unmarried girls in the congregation. She noticed they poked each other and stifled giggles when he walked by their pew and greeted them as he joined Ruth and Hattie and Karl after taking care of the horses. She was so glad to have him sit down beside her and have him adjust her cape across her shoulders.

Ruth shook her head and reluctantly pulled herself back to the present. She pulled out another dress from the trunk. This was her gray muslin delaine, the dress that Mother had made for her after her engagement announcement. "This will be your second best dress, the dress you wear when you call on your neighbors or shop in town." Ruth had never called on neighbors and had only rarely worn it to town when she accompanied Hattie on shopping errands. Hattie always wore a housedress with a clean apron when she went to town. Ruth didn't want to look like she was trying to out-dress her mother-in-law.

Ruth laid the muslin delaine on the bed next to the taffeta. One more dress lay in the trunk at the very bottom. Ruth had not looked this far down into the trunk for several months, and for the moment, she had forgotten it was there. Tears filled her eyes as she looked at her wedding dress. The beautiful white lace collar lay delicately on the dark green material. Covered buttons went from the high neck to the fitted waistline accented by a light green sash. She didn't dare touch it. Her hands were so rough and chapped that she might snag the silk material.

The trunk was quickly closed. That life was closed, too, Ruth told herself. I can sit here and cry for what will never return, or I can decide what to wear for Thanksgiving next week. She had purposely avoided thinking about her situation, didn't want to think of the future beyond the present day. Each day was too busy, and most nights, she fell exhausted into bed. Her life was her work—one foot ahead of the other with no vision of what would come next. There were no solutions in the future. Best not think of it. There was nothing else ahead, nowhere else to go, not even anyone's shoulders to cry on.

Ruth forced herself to turn from the trunk to the bed. *It'll be the muslin delaine for Thanksgiving*, she decided. She stepped out of her overalls and tried on the dress. *Something must be wrong*, Ruth thought. *It's not fitting me at all.* The hem came close to her ankles, and the waistline sagged down unto her hips. It took Ruth a moment to realize that the dress was several inches too big. She had no mirror to look at upstairs, and wearing overalls seven days a week kept her from noticing her size. Now, as she removed the dress, she saw how her ribs protruded from her backbone, and her stomach was flat and hard. *I work like a man, and now I'm built like one*, she thought ruefully. *But now I guess my problem is how to make this dress somewhat presentable.*

She tried it on once more, this time pinning the seams to fit her smaller size. She would need to redo all the seams of the bodice before next Thursday. She worked on it each evening at the table after the supper dishes were done.

***

Thanksgiving morning was clear and cold. Ruth had hung her dress on a hanger in the attic, hoping the wrinkles would smooth out. She also hoped it wouldn't absorb odors from the house.

She hurried through the morning chores and gave the cows a little extra hay. *I might be late feeding them this afternoon*, she thought, *and Amos will never know.*

But it was as if he had read her thoughts when she returned to the house. He was sitting at the table drinking coffee and was in a foul mood.

"How long will the hay in the upstairs hay barn last?" he demanded before she even closed the door behind her.

When she shrugged her shoulders, he exploded, "Shoot and tarnation, don't you pay attention to nothin' out there in the barn? All you can think about is traipsing around to eat somebody else's food and wearing them fancy dresses and acting all high and mighty. I'm paying you big money to take care of my cows. I got to get the haystacks in from the hayfield before we get more snow. I should have kept the horses so you could bring in the haystacks yourself. Hah, you don't even know how to harness a horse. And I know you were afraid of that team. I had to give them away for the winter to make it easier for you. Start earning your pay. I'm giving you big bucks to take care of everything out there."

Ruth felt anger surge through her. "Fire me if I'm not worth my pay," she retorted hotly. "I don't see too many people lining up out there begging for my job. You better be glad I do what I do."

"Ain't you the hoity-toity one? So, I should be giving thanks to you on this Thanksgiving Day, eh? I seem to remember you wanted this job. People weren't begging you to be the schoolteacher, either, as I recall," Amos added sarcastically. "And it's only because of my generosity that you're going off partying today when there's work to be done."

The ticking of the clock in the angry silence that followed kept Ruth from prolonging the argument. She would have just enough time to do a quick washing up and change into her dress. She'd plan a suitable answer for Amos later.

Ruth filled a bucket with cold water, took the soap from the kitchen sink, and found a towel of questionable cleanliness. She awkwardly carried it all up to her attic room and let the trap door slam shut. Getting clean and putting on a dress soothed Ruth somewhat, but not as much as the anticipation of a holiday meal and pleasant visiting with people who talked without sarcasm or anger.

The bodice of the dress seemed to fit nicely now after Ruth's revisions, but she still had not seen herself in a mirror. She wound her thick brown hair into a bun at the back of her neck from memory. She hardly remembered what her hair looked like. She came down the attic steps just as Brute barked once.

Brute had done his duty in announcing company and then slunk beside Amos's chair and laid his head on Amos's cast.

Ruth hurried to open the door for Art. "Anybody hungry here?" his loud voice boomed out. "Hey, who's this good-looking, high-society woman? I don't know if my farm wagon will be a fitting carriage for you. You clean up good!"

Ruth felt her cheeks redden at his teasing. "I'll just get my shawl and bonnet," she said quickly. She couldn't get out of the house fast enough.

"We'll bring you some leftovers," Art called over his shoulder to Amos. "I have a feeling you won't go hungry. I'll have your girl home before chore time. We don't want her to turn back to Cinderella."

"A Cinderella, she ain't," Amos murmured. "Cinderella must have known how to cook."

Ruth was in the wagon before Art closed the kitchen door. The four-mile ride in the brisk air was soothing and invigorating at the same time. Art's cheerful and loud conversation kept her entertained and even made her laugh. She felt herself relax.

Frieda was in the doorway waving a welcome as the horses trotted up the Weilers' driveway. The house wasn't visible from the road, so this was the first time Ruth had seen their home. It was a solid two-story white house with an open porch that extended across the entire front side. There was also a large barn and several outbuildings. Everything was in good repair. The entire place was neat and inviting.

"Oh, Ruth, it's so good to see you," Frieda called out. "Come in, come in. My, you look wonderful. What a lovely dress! We had hoped that some of Art's cousins could be with us today, but they couldn't come. It'll just be the three of us. Having you here will make the day special. Happy Thanksgiving."

What a knack she has to make a person feel good, Ruth thought. *She seems genuinely glad I'm here.*

The meal was delicious. Pork chops and dressing, mashed potatoes and gravy, squash, green beans, buns, and cucumber and beet pickles. Large wedges of pumpkin pie completed the meal. The table was set with attractive china, and a bowl of gourds made a colorful centerpiece.

Ruth marveled at the variety of colors and flavors of the meal. Frieda was not only a gracious hostess, but she was a wonderful cook.

Ruth found herself enjoying every part of her visit—the meal, Art's jovial conversation, Frieda's gentle voice.

"Bring your coffee into the sitting room, Ruth," Frieda said when they could eat no more, and Art went out to check the animals. "The dishes can sit for a while. I want us to finally have some girl talk without menfolk around. Please tell me honestly how things are going for you. Is your situation very hard? Amos is not easy to work for, is he? And please tell me about yourself. All I know is that you planned on the teaching job that fell through."

Ruth reflected for a minute. How could she describe to Frieda what her life was like?

"I was disappointed about not getting the teaching job, but truth be told, I'm not sure I would know how to teach. I do know how to take care of cows. It's just that Amos is so…."

"Difficult is probably a good description for Amos. I'm sure he's more that way now when he's so disabled. Can you imagine what it must be like for him? Those cows are pretty much his whole life, and now he can't even get out to see them, much less take care of them. How does he spend his time? He was always such a busy man before his accident. I really feel sorry for him. I pray for him every day."

Ruth was startled at Frieda's words. She was not expecting to hear sympathy for Amos. In the months that Ruth had worked for Amos, she had felt frustration, anger, even disgust for him, but never compassion. And, she had never heard anyone say they would pray for another person. She had learned a couple memorized prayers as a child, but now she was far too tired when she fell into bed to even think of saying a prayer.

"I just don't have any future in my life. Sometimes I don't even seem to have a past. I was very close to my dad and was devastated when he died. Then when my husband was killed…."

"I didn't know you had a husband, Ruth," Frieda said softly. "Please tell me what happened."

Ruth started slowly, almost reluctantly, measuring her words. "We were married just four months when the accident happened. The bull…" The scene was suddenly as vivid as the day it happened. Tears filled Ruth's eyes. How long since she had felt enjoyment with her life, how long since she had felt anything except a growing hardness and bitterness that was consuming her? Her words came faster. She told about the accident, then about making the decision to come to Four Corners, then backed up to tell about her childhood home, her father's death, and her mother moving in with her sister. The more Ruth talked, the faster the words came until they tripped over one another. She paused only to wipe tears from her cheeks and blow her nose. She felt exhausted when she finally stopped.

Frieda looked at her for a long moment, then hurried to Ruth's chair and wrapped her arms around her. "Oh, my poor dear," she said, rocking Ruth like a little child. "My poor dear. May Jesus help you. I often pray for you, but my prayers will be much more fervent now."

For the second time, Ruth heard Frieda say she prayed for someone; this time the someone was her. It gave her a strange sensation to think about Frieda asking God to watch her or help her or however Frieda prayed. Ruth didn't think she felt comfortable about having God see her. She wondered if she could ask Frieda not to pray.

But Frieda changed the subject. "Ruth, I'm glad you moved from the Edmonds to Amos's house. I remember being in his upstairs onetime last year when we stored some meat up there for him. It's not pretty by any means, but I don't remember it being drafty. I bet you could make it cozy—at least it's your own space, a place for your own things."

"What do you think people are saying about me, living with Amos?"

Ruth was thinking of her mother. She could see her mother pursing her lips and raising her eyebrows. She heard her mother's voice saying primly, "Really, Ruth, that just would not be proper."

Freda laughed. "I think if people say anything about the situation, they'll wonder how anyone can live with Amos. But it's really not anyone else's business, is it? And think of Amos. He was never much of a housekeeper, but he must be bothered by his disabilities. There's so much he can't do. It must be very hard, even depressing, for him. Maybe having you in the house more would boost his spirits. It's a challenge for you, but you've gone through many challenges in these last months."

Their conversation ended with Art coming into the house. "I hate to break up all this lady chatter, but I suppose we have to think about getting Ruth back for afternoon chores."

The time had gone so quickly, Ruth could hardly believe it would soon be chore time. She was terribly disappointed. She wanted to continue to talk to Frieda. How badly she had needed someone to talk to!

Frieda jumped up. "Oh, I want to send some food home with Ruth. She can heat it up for herself and Amos the next couple of days. Ruth, I'll fill a basket with things, and we can pick up the basket sometime on our way to town."

On the way home, Art asked what needed to be done for Amos beyond the daily routine. Ruth said more haystacks needed to be brought in from the hayfield.

"Of course. I should have thought of that myself," Art exclaimed. "I'll talk to a couple neighbors about bringing some in and getting it up in the hay loft next week. It was good you noticed that more hay was needed."

Ruth didn't tell him that Amos had questioned her about it. She hadn't even noticed the dwindling supply in the hayloft on her own.

***

So, the special day was over. Ruth thought about her conversation with Frieda repeatedly as she pressed her forehead into the cows' warm flanks during milking time that evening. It was good to have something pleasant to recall.

Chapter 16

December arrived. Thanksgiving Day became only a memory; the days blurred together with sameness and monotony. Ruth was putting on her outer barn clothes one forenoon to pump more water for the cows before she needed to decide what to make for dinner when Brute announced company with one short bark.

Amos looked up from his solitaire game, and Ruth saw with surprise that the rig stopped at the door belonged to Matt Edmond.

He entered the house rather sheepishly and pulled some mail from his pocket.

"I was to town awhile back. The postmaster said you both got mail. Guess he didn't know you wasn't at my place no more, but I said I'd get it to you eventually."

Matt gave Amos some letters and periodicals and immediately left. Ruth caught her breath when she saw there were two letters for her—from her mother and Hattie. She hadn't heard from her mother for many weeks, and Hattie had written only a couple brief notes.

Amos was looking through his mail. Ruth turned her back to him and quickly tore open the letter from her mother.

Dear Ruth,

With winter here it surely is a worry having you working outside doing all those barn things. I hope you have had a chance to inquire about getting a school to teach. That would be so much more fitting with your interests and skills. I would surely think there would be a changeover of teachers now during the coming holiday season, so do investigate the matter of finding a school.

This is such a busy time to be living at the parsonage. There are Christmas gatherings several times a week. Of course, we have most of the get-togethers here, so Anna and I are baking goodies every day. It is hard to keep up with the demand.

The twins are already nine months old. They are crawling everywhere. Little Andy is a climber. We hardly turn our backs, and he is on the table. Of course, Alice tries to follow his lead. Anna must constantly watch both of them. What a busy girl she is with being a parson's wife, a mother to such active youngsters, and all this entertaining. She does it all so graciously.

I'm sure Anna plans to tell you herself, but she is too busy to write. She and Kenneth are expecting another baby early next summer. She has been sick several mornings. I am so glad I can be here to help her. Everyone says how good it is that I am here.

What are your plans for Christmas? It would be nice to have you visit here, but this is such a busy time, and we never know about the weather. We will have about ten guests for Christmas Day. Maybe the spring would work out better for a visit.

Anna and Kenneth send their regards for a merry Christmas.

Love,

Mother

P.S. Be sure to inquire around for a school.

Ruth quickly climbed the ladder to her room and sat down on her mattress before the tears came. Nothing has changed since an hour ago, she told herself. Why does it feel like I've been punched in the stomach? It's not Mother's fault that she doesn't understand my situation. It's her first Christmas without Daddy, the first time she's not in her own home. She's glad to be needed. Besides, I'm not free to come and go. I wouldn't be able to visit her even if I was invited. But I'm not invited, and that's what hurts. Ruth had never felt more alone. She lay down and sobbed.

She realized as her sobs subsided that she was very cold. She had closed the trap door to the ladder when entering the upstairs. Her breath made misty clouds. She would have no option but to go back downstairs. She needed to make something for dinner. She rubbed her checks vigorously and hoped Amos would not notice her red, swollen face.

Amos was engrossed with his mail when she entered the kitchen.

"About time for some grub," was all he muttered as he continued reading a letter.

Ruth quickly put more firewood in the cook stove, glad for its heat. She held her hands out to the warm stove and kept her back to Amos.

"I gotta letter here from Neil—you remember my cousin who was here last summer when you started workin' for me?"

"I remember."

"Well, he's pretty much caught up with his work—ain't that much to do at his place right now, and ol' George is pretty much takin' care of things. I wrote to him a while back about spending a little time here during Christmas. He might like to get away from that wife of his. Anyways, he's comin' December 23 and staying until New Year's Day. So, you can have a little vacation—go stay with your family or somethin'."

Ruth whirled from the stove to look at Amos. "You arranged to give me a vacation?" She was amazed. There had never been any talk about days off; she had never even thought ahead to Christmas until she received her mail. Only then did she remember her mother's letter and realized that she had no family to go to. With Neil coming, she really had no place to be.

The tears were threatening again. She would not let Amos see her cry.

"You forgot your other letter here on the table."

Ruth had forgotten the letter from Hattie. She snatched it up, hoping Amos wouldn't notice her tear-stained face or the threat of fresh tears. With her back to him, she tore the letter open and read the short note.

Dear Ruth,

Karl and I would like you to spend Christmas with us. Do you think you could arrange some time off? We hope you can come for several days during the holidays. Let us know. We will meet you at the train depot in Twin Oaks if you can come. Hoping to see you soon.

Love,

Hattie

Chapter 17

The next days were bittersweet for Ruth. She had people who wanted her to spend the holidays with them, with an actual invitation. To top it off, she had the freedom to say yes, thanks to Amos arranging for Neil to come to do chores. She still couldn't wrap her mind around Amos doing that. Was he doing it to be kind? Or did he want someone to check up on the job she was doing? She didn't know. Looking forward to a vacation was truly an unexpected anticipation.

But the trip back to Karl and Hattie's home would be returning to the memories of Ben—their few short months together, their hopes and dreams smashed with the bull's attack, their love gone forever. How would it feel to enter that house again?

There were preparations to make before leaving. She wrote a quick reply to Hattie's note, saying when she would be arriving in Twin Oaks. What clothes would she take? Dresses would need to be altered.

Frieda and Art stopped in one morning while Ruth was still working in the barn. Frieda ducked her head inside the barn door. "Yoo-hoo, Ruth! Are you soon done with chores? Art and I are on our way to town. I think you should go with us. You might want to do a little Christmas shopping. It'd be easier for you to do that for yourself than have me try to find things for you. Finish up here as quick as you can. I brought some baked goods that I'll take up to the house for Amos. Art and I will have a cup of coffee with him while you get ready."

Ruth hardly had a chance to say a word before Frieda was on her way up to the house. A trip to town! Christmas shopping? Ruth had not even considered getting gifts for anyone. Just being around Frieda would lift her spirits, but it had been so long since she had socialized with anyone else that she felt fearful of going to town.

"I am so glad you can get some time off for Christmas," Frieda told Ruth as they rode together in the sleigh on their way to town. "It will do you good to have a change of scenery for a few days."

"I'm not sure I'm ready to face all those memories," Ruth confessed.

"I'm going to be praying for you the whole time you're gone, Ruth. It's going to be hard, but Jesus will make it work out. I bet He's got some good plans for you. Now tell us about Ben's family."

As Ruth described Karl and Hattie to Frieda and Art, she suddenly missed their gentle and kindly ways. She had never felt close to them—her own fault, she supposed. She had hardly thought of them in the months since she had left their home. Now she looked forward to seeing them. Maybe Karl would have helpful advice about the livestock, and Ruth certainly needed some basic cooking and household hints from Hattie.

As the sleigh skimmed over the frozen ruts, Ruth tried to concentrate on gifts she would buy. Amos paid her regularly on the first of each month; she had taken enough with her in her handbag to cover what she thought she would need.

Ruth contemplated her shopping plans to Frieda. "I'll need to buy something for Karl and Hattie, Mother, Anna, Kenneth, and their little ones. What do nine-month-old children want for Christmas?"

Frieda laughed. "From what I've seen of little ones that age, I'd say an empty box would be the best gift."

"That may not impress the parents, though," Ruth replied.

"I have dozens of empty wooden thread spools. Why not tie some of those together for them to clunk or rattle or whatever they want to do with it. I'll send the spools along with Art the next time he goes to town."

Frieda continued, "What are you getting for Amos?"

"Amos? I hadn't thought about getting him anything. Of course, he wouldn't be getting anything for me."

Immediately, Ruth felt childish. She wasn't giving gifts because she hoped for something in return. It was just that Amos would probably just have something derogatory to say about whatever she would get him. He certainly wouldn't appreciate it.

As town came into sight, Ruth felt butterflies in her stomach. She had not been in town since last summer when she first arrived. Her only contact with people besides Amos and the Edmonds were Frieda and Art and the various neighbors who occasionally stopped in to visit Amos, and then, of course, Richard Hunter, who had asked her to the dance weeks before. Her encounters were usually one-on-one. Facing a group of people in the store made her very nervous. When she expressed her fear to Frieda, Art entered the conversation. "Don't worry, Ruth," he reassured her. "At this time of year, women are going to be thinking about supplies they need for the holiday meals, and men will be worried about how to pay for it all. People may not even notice you at the store, but that's probably not what a lady wants to hear."

"To give Ruth a little extra time shopping, I'm going to finally go through our account with Mr. Harlowe," Frieda said. "I need to compare his figures with ours for our transactions with cream and eggs and then the groceries we get in exchange. I'm never very confident of his bookkeeping skills."

When Ruth, Frieda, and Art entered the store in the late forenoon, it was busy with customers. As Art predicted, women were buying supplies for extra baking and fabric for new outfits for themselves and family members. Frieda immediately sat down with Mr. Harlowe to check the store ledger, figuring in the eggs she brought in that day to her account.

Ruth tried to smile and greet some of the women, but they seemed preoccupied with shopping. She started putting gift items in her basket—some lightweight flannel for Anna for sewing baby outfits, a lacy handkerchief for her mother, a pipe for Kenneth.

As Ruth roamed the aisles, trying to think of something practical for Karl and Hattie, she noticed that the men gathered around the stove at the back of the store just as they used to do in her father's store. Some looked absently at farm tools hanging on the walls, but they mostly wanted news of the community. The death of Stubbs was still uppermost on many minds. Conversation got around to the challenges of farming. The early winter weather would already make seed prices and supplies more expensive in the spring. "Do you think Harlowe is going to have enough seed wheat for us come April?" one asked. "I think hay is going to be scarce by the time spring gets here," another commented. Ruth used to hear similar conversations when she worked at her father's store.

Ruth used to tell her father that she wished they would buy more and talk less. Father always responded, "They are good men, Ruth, concerned about providing for their families and their livestock. I'm glad we can provide a place for them to get things off their chests and exchange ideas. It's good for them. Besides, they'll eventually buy what they need."

Remembering her father's words gave her a feeling of goodwill towards these men. They were hard-working people trying to make a living just as she was. She felt some of her apprehensions of being with a group melt away as she wandered through the store.

Thinking of the customers in her father's store gave her the confidence to smile and exchange a word of greeting when she found herself standing next to others. However, the other shoppers hardly returned her greeting. *Maybe they don't know who I am*, Ruth thought, *so why should they pay any attention to me?* She did notice, though, that two women in the next aisle whispered together, and their eyes often strayed to Ruth. *What can they be saying about me? If it's said in such hush-hush conversation, it can't be something good.* She felt her newfound confidence slipping away from her.

Richard Hunter, the man who had asked Ruth to the dance, was one of the men gathered around the stove in the back. As she was picking out a large red handkerchief for Karl, he called out loudly to her, "Hey, Miss Gottlieb or Mrs. Gottlieb or whatever you go by, how's that man of yours? Which man, I don't know. I never did figure out if you're married, going to get married, or what. Leave it to ol' Amos to get mixed up with a woman who doesn't make any sense."

Ruth froze as all conversation stopped and eyes turned to her. She felt a deep flush creep up her neck to her cheeks. Were people so hesitant to talk to her because she was living in Amos's house? What were they saying behind her back?

Before she could think of any words to say, Art looked up from the tools in front of him on the counter. "Well, Richard, Amos Armstrong is doing well. His legs are healing pretty good, I think. Ruth is taking good care of his livestock and running a smooth household. I know Amos is indebted to her hard work. He wouldn't be able to keep his cows if it weren't for Ruth. We can all thank her for the fine service she is doing for our community in helping out someone in need."

Ruth appreciated Art coming quickly to her rescue, but she felt the blush stay on her cheeks. The familiar hardness and bitterness returned to her heart, and most of all, the loneliness. These people were just busybodies and gossipers. She must hurry to get her grocery items and finish the Christmas gifts.

She heard Richard grumble to the group of men sitting by him. "Sure, we should all appreciate the fine lady," he said sarcastically. "I tried to help her out once, gave her a ride to the Edmonds when I happened to be driving by. She never did make any sense. I couldn't figure out what she was saying…something about being married or used to be married or wanting to get married. I'm keeping a safe distance from her, you can bet. She's crazy as a hoot owl."

Tears stung her eyes. What had happened to her since she happily shopped for Christmas gifts just a year ago? She and her mother and Anna had debated for hours on just the right gifts for one another. And, of course, she bought several things for Ben. She always found just one more thing that would be perfect for him. A pair of leather gloves, warm socks, a book on birds of North America. Her favorite gift to him was a Parcheesi game; she pictured long winter evenings of games by the fire, teasing each other in friendly competition about who would win the most games. Now just a year later, she was alone. No one looked after her; no one really cared if she gave them a gift or not.

She willed herself to look at the merchandise on the counters. She must finish the job at hand before Frieda and Art were ready to leave. She added the large red handkerchief for Karl to her basket. For Hattie, she bought a package of dates for baking. Hattie probably wouldn't indulge in something that costly for herself. As she was going up to the front counter to pay for her items, she suddenly thought of Amos and at the same time saw the perfect gift for him—a deck of cards. The cards he continually used for playing solitaire were so faded she wondered how he could see the patterns on them, and he must surely have memorized which cards were now pieces of cardboard. The new deck had pictures of a train going around a grove of trees. Funny—buying something for Amos gave her the most satisfaction.

The ride home was quiet. As Art turned the horses into Amos's driveway, Frieda took Ruth's hands in hers. "All will turn out well, Ruth. You'll see."

Was Ruth just imagining things, or did Frieda's words sound hollow and unconvincing? Maybe even optimistic Frieda couldn't see how things would turn out well.

Chapter 18

Christmas Eve morning was cold and clear. Ruth began her walk to town to catch the train to Twin Oaks just as the sun rose above the horizon. She marveled at how easy it was to carry her suitcase the four miles to town. What a change from when she could barely handle her heavy luggage when she arrived in Four Corners in August.

Ruth fidgeted as she sat on the hard bench inside the depot. It was a relief to hear the whistle in the distance. Few passengers got on the train. Most people were already at their Christmas destination by this time.

Ruth was glad she had a seat to herself. She realized she was rigid with tension. She forced her shoulders to relax and tried to concentrate on the flat, snowy landscape rushing by her window. So much had happened in the past week or two. She would need these quiet hours on the train to sort out her thoughts.

Neil had come to do the chores the evening before as he promised. Ruth almost smiled to herself as she realized the situation was just reversed since last August. At that time, Neil showed Ruth the barn and the routine of chores. Now, it was Ruth who showed Neil how things were in the barn. Of course, the winter chores were much different than they had been in August.

"How are things out there?" Amos had asked when the two of them had returned to the house.

"Well, the barn ain't fallen down yet if that's what you're wondering. Looks like the schoolmarm did an okay job. Cows look purty fit. Cats are fat. You going to have enough hay to last till spring?"

Ruth had hoped for a little higher praise but realized now that coming from Neil, it probably was the most she could expect. At least Amos seemed satisfied and didn't demand more information. Everybody worried about having enough hay to last until spring, Ruth knew. But she probably had been overly generous with feeding. She would have to be more careful in January.

Thinking about giving her gift to Amos did bring a smile to Ruth's lips. "What's this?" Amos had asked when she pushed the small box to his place at supper the night after her shopping excursion.

"It's your Christmas present. Open it."

"What'd you give me something for? I ain't giving no presents."

The gift lay unopened on the table for a time. Curiosity finally got the better of Amos, and he ripped off the old newspaper that Ruth had wrapped it in.

His eyes lit up with surprise and then pleasure when he saw the new deck of cards.

"I think they'll be easier to shuffle when each card has four corners, and you don't have any cardboard substitutes. You might even win a little oftener when you can read the faces of the cards."

Silence followed for a few moments. Amos finally found his voice.

"Well, ain't you the one!" For the first time, the expression didn't sound sarcastic.

***

How glad Ruth was that Frieda had suggested a gift for Amos. It was embarrassing that Ruth had not thought of it herself. That evening she watched Amos admiring the picture of the train coming around a grove of trees on the backs of the cards. He laid the cards out on the table and studied each of the faces of the jacks, queens, and kings. He practiced shuffling them, but Ruth didn't think he even played a game that first evening.

"I ain't never had a new deck before," he murmured at one point.

I hope the others like their gifts as much, Ruth thought to herself as she swayed in her train seat. The package for her mother, Anna, and Kenneth had been sent off. It included a dozen empty spools tied together with yarn for the twins.

Ruth reminded herself again to relax her shoulders. She would have a dreadful headache if she kept her muscles so tense.

Ruth feared going back to Twin Oaks. That was why she was so tense. It had been easy—or necessary—to freeze her emotions during the months she had worked for Amos. Long hours and hard work had kept her from thinking too much.... thinking about Ben, about her life, about her future. Everything had been frozen in time, and now it was moving again. She would face all over again that Ben was gone, and she needed to take control of her life. It would not work for others to make decisions for her, as had always been the case before. She was alone. She also knew that she would have to start concentrating on something else, or the tears would start.

She thought of Karl and Hattie. What would the Christmas holidays be like in their home? Would they be so filled with memories of Ben's death that they would be unable to celebrate? She remembered her first meeting with Ben's parents, his brother Daniel and Daniel's family. She had been so enthralled with spending the time with Ben, so excited about her approaching marriage, that the other family members hardly registered during those days.

She did remember Karl as being quiet and almost a little embarrassed to have her around. “He’s shy around women,” Ben had explained to her, “especially beautiful women.” Ruth had laughed at him, but she felt warmed by his words. “Maybe it’s because I don’t know how to talk farming with him,” she ventured. At the time, it really did not matter if Karl talked to her or not.

Even with Ruth’s absorption with being with Ben, it was evident that Hattie excelled in homemaking. Simple but abundant and delicious meals appeared on the table three times a day. Doughnuts, fruitcakes, and all kinds of cookies appeared on the platters after each meal and for forenoon and afternoon coffee. Not the fancy little delicacies that Ruth’s mother and Anna labored over, Ruth noticed, but always satisfying. Neighbors had stopped over several times with holiday greetings during the three days Ruth was at the Gottlieb home. Ruth couldn’t help wondering if they knew she would be there and were coming to find out what “Ben’s girlfriend” was like. The guests automatically sat down at the large kitchen table, knowing coffee and goodies would be part of the visit.

While Karl was quiet around Ruth, he was talkative with the other guests. He was a gracious host, as was Ben. She realized both were knowledgeable in all aspects of farming—things she knew nothing about like crop rotation, milk production, and marketing crops. *Ben will be just like his dad*, Ruth thought proudly at the time, *a pillar of the community*. While the men talked farming, the ladies visited about recipes, holiday meals, sick people in the community, and their latest sewing or knitting projects. They tried to include Ruth in their conversations, but recipes and sewing projects were not subjects she could easily talk about.

While the home was spotless as Ruth’s had been during her

growing-up years, there was always a comfortable, hospitable atmosphere. *Peaceful would be the word*, Ruth decided. Karl and Hattie neither doted on her nor ignored her—Ruth hoped that meant they would accept her as a future member of the family. Surely, they would have no objections when Ben told them about the approaching wedding in the spring.

As the train swayed and clattered, Ruth's memory of that visit sharpened into focus. Every hour of that visit almost a year ago returned in startling detail. She could hear Ben explaining to his parents that he had not had an opportunity to ask permission of Ruth's father to court her, but he had made his intentions known to her mother, older sister, and brother-in-law. Ruth and Ben were planning a wedding in the spring, and Ben asked his parents for their blessing.

The scene was so vivid Ruth could see the details of the room, the small Christmas tree in the corner, and family pictures on the organ. She could even smell the pleasant aroma of the home—cinnamon and other spices and coffee. They were sitting in the living room, Ben and Ruth together on the couch. Hattie sat erect on a straight-back chair close to Ben's end of the couch. Karl sat across the room in the large homemade rocker, the newspaper draped across his knees. Ben had spoken quietly of his love for Ruth and their desire to be married. When he finished, the silence that followed seemed louder than his words. For several minutes there was no sound except the ticking of the mantel clock. Karl and Hattie exchanged quick glances. *They've been expecting this*, Ruth realized. And now they're ready with something. Do they have objections to her?

Hattie finally spoke. "Ruth, we know Ben loves you. Goodness, he talks of you all the time. But we do have a few questions we'd like to ask you."

Ben looked surprised. Ruth's breath caught in her throat. What was this inquisition? What could they possibly ask her that would change anything? Would they ask something that would make Ben think less of her? But that was impossible. She was confident of his love and loyalty. "Of course, please ask anything you like," Ruth replied, but she couldn't keep her voice from trembling.

Hattie took charge of the conversation. In fact, Karl seemed detached and glanced down at the newspaper from time to time. "You know, Ruth, that Karl and I are hoping that Ben will take over the farm. We aren't getting any younger. Ben's brother—or maybe his wife—has no interest in our land. Karl's arthritis is already making the chores difficult for him. Our farm has been in our family for three generations. We welcome Ben as a partner here; we need younger ideas and strong help.

"You've always lived in town. Would you be able to support Ben's decision—and it would be his decision to make—to be a farmer and someday take over this place? Would you be happy making the adjustment to farm life and making it your lifetime commitment?"

Ruth was relieved. This would be easier than she thought. "Oh, yes! I love the farm and all the animals. I'd love to live here and help Ben with the chores. Watching Ben milk the cows is fascinating. I've always preferred to do things outside rather than housework. Living in the country would be wonderful! Yes, it could and would be my commitment."

Karl cleared his throat and spoke for the first time. "Ach, we don't like for our womenfolk to have to do too much in the barn. There are times, of course, like during harvesting and such when the men need help with the chores. Usually, though, the women have plenty to do running the household. They don't need to be milking."

Ruth felt like a little child being reprimanded, and her cheeks began to burn. But the questioning was not over.

Hattie continued, "Ben says that you and he are planning to be married in March. If the spring cooperates at all, the field work will begin in April. That will leave no time for building a house of your own until after harvesting and plowing in the late fall. It certainly doesn't work to build in the wintertime. Can you be content living here in this house with us for a time?"

It surely won't be for long, Ruth thought. *Ben will find time even during the busy summer to build our house. It doesn't have to be big.* They could add on some rooms later.... when there were babies....

Ruth realized she was slow in answering when Ben entered the conversation. "It's probably not the best situation for newlyweds to live with the parents," he said quietly. "We could wait to be married until we have our own house built. But Ruth's life is in transition right now with her home being sold and her mother going to live with her sister. It just seems like this is the right time for us to be married. Besides, you two are wonderful parents. I know we'll all get along very well."

Ruth nodded. She hoped she looked agreeable.

Ben reached over and covered her hands with his. "As I said, you two are wonderful parents. And you are getting a wonderful daughter-in-law. The best. I'm a lucky man. Ruth and I haven't spent much time together, but we know this is right and God-pleasing. We are good for each other. And we'll all be good friends as well as family, living here together, helping each other."

.... *Until we have our own home,* Ruth thought.

Karl told Ruth that Ben would receive the adjacent forty acres for payment for working on the farm. He would buy the remaining acres when Karl and Hattie wanted to retire. Ruth knew of the agreement; Ben had described to her just where he wanted to build their house. "There are large oak trees on the corner of the forty," he had told her in one of his letters. "It's a perfect place for the house. It's within easy walking distance, so I can still help Pa with the chores and use any of the outbuildings that I have need of. I'm thinking that maybe someday, Ma and Pa might want to exchange places. They can have the little house that I build, and we can fill this big house with kids. How does that sound?"

"That sounds perfect," Ruth answered in her following letter. She didn't ask if the location of their house would be in view of his parents' house. After meeting his parents, she hoped that it wasn't. Why did she feel so intimidated by these good people?

"I have another question," Hattie said firmly, bringing Ruth back to the present conversation. "I do apologize for asking these questions and sounding so nosy. But we don't know you or your family or your background. By not choosing someone from this community for his wife, we want to make sure Ben has considered all the options and not just fallen in love with a pretty girl."

"Aw, Ma," Ben protested. "Give me credit for having been raised with more sense. Ruth and I are committed to each other for the rest of our lives. We will have a happy, good home. You just watch and see. You and Pa will be proud."

"We are very proud of you, Son, but this conversation is necessary," Hattie said determinedly. "After we talk tonight, I will forever hold my peace. Now, Ruth, the last question—are you and your family church-going people?"

Of course they were. Everyone in her town attended church. Thoughts of her early years came quickly to her mind: Mother, Daddy, Anna, and she walking the two blocks to the large community church; Mother making sure their dresses and Father's suit were the latest styles. "It's good for Father's business to look successful," she often reminded the family. People calling out greetings as they arrived at the church. It was not unusual for one of the farmers to quietly approach Daddy and whisper, "Mr. England, as long as I'm in town I was wondering if I could quickly buy something at your store after church." Daddy always obliged before going home, where Mother would be running back and forth putting the finishing touches on sumptuous meals for them and their frequent guests. It was all part of the routine. Ruth could not imagine a Sunday without attending church.

"Of course, we attended church," she replied to Hattie's question. "My whole family attended every Sunday."

"I'm glad to hear it," Hattie said. "Now again, I'm sorry to have all these questions for you. Karl and I agreed we would need to bring these things up before we could give our blessing to your marriage. We do know that Ben could have married you with or without our blessing."

"You're right, Ma…but it's much more pleasant to have your blessing. Thank you."

Ben bounded up from the couch to give his mother a bear hug and then shook hands with his father, who had stood up and joined them, the newspaper falling to the floor. For an instant, Ruth felt like an outsider watching the three of them, but Ben quickly motioned her to join them. Hattie kissed her cheek, and Karl shook her hand with an embarrassed laugh. Ben put his arms around her and pressed his cheek against hers. *We will be a happy family together*, Ruth thought. She remembered wishing again that Daddy could have met Ben's family. Daddy would be happy for her and approve of her choice.

The wedding was small and took place at Ruth's home in Rolling Valley. Only Mother, Anna, Kenneth, and two of Ruth's closest friends attended. Ben's parents hosted a dinner party at their home when Ruth and Ben arrived there two days after the wedding.

Ruth's thoughts wandered over those first months of marriage. While Ruth loved being Ben's wife, living with his parents was trying at times. They settled into a routine. Ruth did not spend much time in the house; she followed Ben outside like a shadow. He patiently explained the chores to her. She loved all the animals but was especially drawn to the large, gentle milk cows. They regarded her with curious, unafraid eyes and had no objection to her first awkward attempts at milking. If Karl thought she spent too much time in the barn, he never mentioned it.

After a few awkward attempts, Ruth took on no responsibilities in the house. Hattie had that covered. If Hattie could have used some help, Ruth never noticed.

Meeting new people was never easy for Ruth, and it did not become easier now as Ben's wife. One evening as Ruth and Ben prepared for bed, Ben remarked that Hattie was going to her monthly quilting get-together with several ladies at the church the next afternoon.

"I think you would enjoy that, Ruth," he said. "Why don't you go along with Ma? She'll show you how to get started. I would think making quilts would be very worthwhile."

Ruth couldn't conceal her disappointment. "But I thought we were going over to our forty and stake out our garden plot there tomorrow afternoon."

Ben hesitated a moment. "Sure, I guess we should do that. Although Ma's garden is big enough to feed an army. Maybe you could just work in hers for the first year or two."

Seeing Ruth's reluctance, he agreed to stake out their own garden plot. He'd work it up as he had time during the summer, and it would be ready to plant the next spring. That was the plan. The plot never got worked.

Memories were coming fast and furious to Ruth. They didn't do much to ease her tension. She seemed more immature with each episode that came to mind.

She remembered the evening that Ben showed his worn overalls to Hattie. "Ma, I tore the knee out of my pants today. Could you patch it?"

Hattie glanced quickly at Ruth. Looking back, Ruth knew what she should have said. She should have explained to Hattie that she didn't know how to patch; would Hattie show her? It was something

Ruth had never done. Daddy probably would not have even noticed if his pants were patched, but Mother would have been horrified to have Howard in patched clothing. Ruth said nothing. Hattie told Ben she would fix them the next day. *This will all be so different when we have our own house*, Ruth thought. *Ben won't ask his mother to do things for him.*

***

"Ten minutes to Twin Oaks!" the conductor boomed, walking through the swaying aisle. "Gather up your things if this is where you get off."

Last year slipped back into memories. She was here, facing the present, ready or not.

Chapter 19

Ruth looked through the train window anxiously. Suddenly she was seized with the fear that no one would be waiting for her. What if Karl and Hattie had second thoughts about her visit? Perhaps they wanted to put this tragic year behind them, and her presence would only bring back terrible memories. Would they want to go through that, especially at Christmas time? Christmas without Ben would be hard enough as it was.

Then she saw Karl standing on the platform. She looked twice, though, not sure at first if the tall, stooped man was indeed Karl. He had aged years in the less than five months since she had seen him.

Ruth quickly gathered her belongings and hurried down the train steps to the platform. She waved at Karl, who was studying the departing passengers. When he saw her, relief flooded his face, and he strode toward her. They stood awkwardly face-to-face for an instant. Should they embrace, shake hands, what? Karl quickly took her suitcase, ending the awkwardness.

"Good you could come," he said in his quiet, pleasant voice, so like

Ben's. "Hattie is waiting at home. She's glad to have you come."

"Thank you for the invitation, Karl. I'm glad to be here. I had no other place to go for Christmas."

Ruth was embarrassed. She meant it as a friendly statement, but it sounded like she accepted the invitation because of no other options.

They walked silently to the farm sleigh (the same farm wagon, now with runners on for the winter), where Dolly and Nelly waited patiently, warm under the blankets that covered them. Ruth touched their noses gently as she walked to the other side of the wagon to get in. They both blew into her mitten. *They remember me,* she thought gratefully.

"Been a cold winter," Karl was saying as he crawled up into the wagon after putting her suitcase in the back. "And, hardly getting started yet. Hattie sent a couple extra blankets to put over you. Some good hot coffee will taste good when we get to the house."

Ruth felt like she was in a dream.... the gentle horses that she was so fond of.... this familiar farm wagon.... hearing Karl's voice. Surely Ben would be in the house when she got there. He would look up from his newspaper when she entered the door and smile at her—a smile of love and welcome. But that wouldn't happen—he wasn't there—she knew he wasn't. How could she walk in, how could she sit at that table and drink coffee—sitting in her usual place with Ben's place empty? How could she go upstairs to their bedroom?

They talked little. The farm sleigh skimmed over the snow-covered road, and too soon, they arrived at the house. As the horses trotted up the driveway, the door of the house opened, and Hattie waved her apron in welcome.

"Here we are—we're home," Karl said. She had lived here for such a short time, but she did have the strong feeling that she was arriving home.

"It's so good to see you, Ruth!" Hattie hugged her tightly. Ruth was surprised at Hattie's show of affection. She was not a demonstrative woman. As they stepped back from their embrace, Ruth saw tears streaming down Hattie's cheeks. Ruth was bringing memories of Ben to the house. But with the memories came a bond. They shared their grief. Perhaps this would make it easier to bear.

"Come, come, let's get your outer clothes off," Hattie said warmly. "Karl will bring in your things after he takes care of the horses. Such a cold day. Oh, my, Ruth, there's nothing left of you! You're too thin, dear. Sit down at the table."

Someone to fuss over her. How Ruth had missed that. What a spineless child I am, sitting here soaking up the warmth of this kitchen, watching Hattie hurry back and forth from stove to table, noticing that the older woman looked her over carefully but lovingly. It was so good to have someone take charge, someone to care for her. She had no responsibility but to sit.

Hattie had also aged in the months since Ruth had left. Her hair was grayer, her tall thin frame was bent, her face sagged into wrinkles where there were none before, but she worked with the same efficiency and skill as she put food on the table.

A leaf had been removed from the table, making it smaller. There were just places for the three of them. Ben's place was not there.

When Karl came in, Hattie quickly served supper even though it was just four o'clock. "I knew you'd be hungry when you got here," Hattie explained, "so this is our evening meal now. We have Christmas Eve services at eight, so by the time Karl finishes up in the barn, it'll be time to start out. We'll have more coffee and some Christmas goodies when we get home from church. Then we want to hear all about how things are going for you."

Christmas Eve services? "Oh, but I couldn't attend church tonight," Ruth blurted quickly. "I'm sorry, but I'm really worn out. I'm sure I'll want to go another time, but not tonight."

Karl and Hattie looked surprised and then disappointed. "We

have a new minister—Rev. Schwartz. His sermons—they'll help you. They've helped us so much," Hattie said slowly. "I'm sure tonight will be extra special. It is Christmas Eve, you know."

Karl added, "We don't want to go off and leave you your first night here. You better come."

I must do this, Ruth thought. *They want me to go so badly. If I don't go, they may feel like they need to stay home with me.* She reluctantly agreed to attend. She had not been in a church since Ben's funeral. And, she had never once thought about going in the months since.

Both Karl and Hattie looked relieved at Ruth's change of mind. Hattie served the simple, delicious supper—chunks of roast beef, potatoes cooked with apples, and thick slices of warm bread. Ruth ate ravenously, remembering she had not eaten since her piece of toast for breakfast. Hattie encouraged her to refill her plate several times. Her coffee cup was filled repeatedly.

Ruth caught herself looking back and forth between Karl and Hattie. They looked like old people sitting there at the table, yet she saw a resoluteness that she had not noticed before. Perhaps their limited physical strength made them more determined to face life. Karl especially looked fragile. His thin stooped shoulders bent over his supper plate; his chin lowered as he ate. Ruth saw his hands showed the effects of arthritis. When he left the table to go out to do the evening chores, he slowly rose from his chair by pushing himself up from the table.

The meal was quick, with only brief, casual conversation. Hattie went to change her clothes for church. Ruth picked up her suitcase and climbed the stairs to the bedroom she had shared with Ben.

Chapter 20

The air was frosty, with the entire sky filled with glittering stars. The country churchyard was already filled with sleighs and buggies. Farmers were hurrying their horses into the makeshift shelter where they were blanketed. Oat bags were slipped over their heads, and the horses quickly began enjoying their Christmas Eve treats. Hattie and Ruth waited for Karl inside the church entry.

People entered the church and came to greet her. "Good to see you…" "Hattie said you were coming…" "We're glad you came…" "Hattie was so happy you were able to get away from your job…" (Did they know what her job was?) "You need to put a little meat on your bones…."

Good people, genuine friendliness. She was not the odd person who was the butt of gossip as she was at…

She would not think about Four Corners, about Amos, any of it. She would be here for another five days, among people who cared about her. But looking into the church proper, seeing the familiar front of the church, the large tapestry of Jesus praying in the garden, the pews—the pew where she had sat next to Ben—how could she do this? How could she sit through this service? She felt like she was drowning, and panic filled her. Why had she let Hattie and Karl talk her into coming?

Karl joined them, and the three of them went to their usual pew. She noticed that Karl and Hattie spent several moments in silent prayer before the service began. Had they always done that? She didn't remember. She tried to ease her mind and busy herself by looking up the hymns posted on the hymn board—Christmas carols. She would just listen, she decided; she would not engage herself in the service but just bide her time until it was over. Maybe she could even catch a few winks of a much-needed nap.

Her thoughts were interrupted by the entrance of Pastor Schwartz. He was probably nearing sixty, was rather short and heavy, and wore a black robe. After bowing towards the altar, he turned and faced the congregation. His coarse, iron-gray hair stood straight out from his head. His scruffy beard covered his chin and hid his neck. There certainly wasn't anything attractive about this man whom Hattie and Karl had spoken of so highly.

The pastor looked over his congregation in silence. His eyes seemed to linger on Ruth. They were a piercing blue, and Ruth felt his gaze penetrating her soul. *He must know about me,* she thought, *the poor young widow whose husband was so tragically killed.* But she felt no pity in his eyes as they rested on Ruth before he looked over the other worshippers.

"We begin in the name of the Father, Son, and Holy Spirit," he began, his voice gruff and guttural. *It's not even a pleasing voice. Ministers are supposed to speak winsomely. Didn't Kenneth always speak to please the people?*

Rev Schwartz's voice cut into her thoughts. "You've come tonight to worship the Christ child, and we will. Perhaps my message will not be what you expect, however. Let's begin with the first hymn…."

The congregation sang with fervor, enjoying the familiar carol. "Oh, come, all ye faithful, joyful and triumphant…" How long had it been since Ruth had sung anything? Certainly not since before the funeral. Indeed, was it even possible to sing anymore?

Ruth didn't try to join in. She knew she couldn't sing—her throat was much too full, her heart too sad with memories of past Christmases. After the carol was over, she mumbled through the responsive readings with the congregation, not thinking about the words she was reading from the hymnal.

Her thoughts came in waves. *I'm drowning in my tears; they are threatening to take over. If I cry now, I'll never stop. I'm so weary in grief and despair—I just keep sinking without anything solid to cling to.*

I should not have come to Karl and Hattie's home. Even their kindness and the kindness of these people sitting around me show what a failure my life has become. People in my real life have disdain for me; the man I live with can't say a civil word to me. But at least with Amos, there was routine, busyness, no time to think about the past, no time to wonder about the future. She could vent her sadness by trading sarcastic and unkind words with him. And there was no time to think about the tears that always threatened to swallow her up.

Finally, Pastor Schwartz entered the pulpit. Again, there was that pause, that looking around the congregation, the eye contact with Ruth.

"Save me, O God, for the waters have come up to my neck!" he began and then paused. Ruth sat up a little straighter. *Those words—how familiar they sounded—like my very own thoughts. What a strange way to start a Christmas sermon.* Pastor Schwartz's unpretentious face and his gruff voice penetrated the fog of Ruth's mind.

"My Christmas Eve sermon tonight is not Luke 2 as many of my Christmas sermons have been in past years," he continued. "My text is

Psalm 69, verses 1-3. 'Save me, O God! For the waters have come up to my neck. I sink in deep mire, where there is no standing; I have come into deep waters, where the floods overflow me. I am weary with my crying; my throat is dry; my eyes fail while I wait for my God.'

"Let's look at other selected verses in Psalm 69. 'Those who hate me without a cause are more than the hairs of my head. Deliver me out of the mire, and let me not sink. Let not the floodwater swallow me up. But I am poor and sorrowful.' These sound like desperate words, don't they? The person or people that God was talking about must have been at their wits' end. Have you been there? Are you there right now?

"Some of you may have come here tonight to hear about a little Baby being born in a cozy little barn to parents who love Him. Gentle Mary and strong Joseph settling down in the hay to rejoice over this cute little boy. Ahh, isn't that sweet? No! This Baby came not to be sweet—let King David tell us why this Baby came in Psalm 72, verses 12-14. 'For He shall deliver the needy when he crieth; the poor also, and him that hath no helper. He shall spare the poor and needy and shall save the souls of the needy. He shall redeem their soul from deceit and violence; and precious shall their blood be in his sight.'

"It was for those people with the water coming up to their necks that God sent a Savior. In their desperation, they cried for His salvation. Why does God let us face desperation but to turn us to Him?"

Ruth glanced around at Hattie and Karl and the others sitting near her. Did they realize he was reading her thoughts? How did he know that those were the very words Frieda had spoken on Thanksgiving Day? Ruth knew few words of Scripture; how could he have chosen those very words?

Rev. Schwartz continued, his voice becoming louder and more forceful. "Jesus told us that He came that we may have life and have it more abundantly. He came to relieve our pain, to bear our burdens for us by walking along beside us.

"Is this year's Christmas observance the same as last year's and all the years before that? The same traditions, the same people at your table, the same kind of food…"

Ruth felt tears stinging her eyes. *I don't even have a table. My Christmas traditions from childhood are dead. I don't have a place to live. I don't have anyone to help me; I don't have a future.*

"Or," Pastor Schwartz went on, "is this year completely different from past years?"

Ruth felt his eyes on her.

"Is there a place missing at your table—a loved one gone from your midst?"

Ruth felt the need to leave; this was becoming too personal. Could she walk out? But where would she go? It was too cold to stand outside.

"Is God trying to get your attention by shaking up your routine? Is He plowing on hard, stony ground, trying to make a harvest of faith? How is He doing that? Has He sent someone or something to soften the ground of your heart?"

Ruth thought of Frieda. She could certainly soften anyone's heart with her gentle words and loving actions. Ruth would rather think about Frieda than this loud, gruff speaker who talked about her personal life in his public sermon. Tears were stinging her eyes, yet she felt anger, too. What gave him the right to speak this way to her in front of the congregation?

"Does God have your attention yet? When change comes into your life, be assured that God is working. Changes sometimes come quietly without much notice. Sometimes changes come violently, so violently that your whole life is turned upside down." Pastor Schwartz's voice rose. "Does He have your attention yet?

"Why did Jesus come? He came to be our strong deliverer when we're reeling with the change that has hit us. He is our rescuer when we can't rescue ourselves. But the most important reason that Jesus came is to be our SAVIOR, a Savior from the devil, from the world that doesn't know Him, from OURSELVES. He saved us to be in heaven with Him for all eternity. That's why that Baby came. When the waters of grief and despair come up to our necks, we shout, 'Save me, O God!' That's why He came—to answer that call. His answer is not a figment of your imagination, but His answer is a real personal God giving you His hand. There was nothing imaginary about Jesus rescuing Peter when he tried to walk on the water. St. Matthew tells us that Jesus immediately stretched forth His hand and caught him. A powerful hand that would not let Peter fall or be drowned. My friends, that Baby came for YOU. Let Him be all for you that He wants to be—your best friend when you have no friends, your helper when you have no help, your foundation when you have no home, your Savior when you have no future."

***

The rest of the service was only vaguely remembered. Ruth knew Christmas carols were being sung, but she didn't know which ones, nor did she try to sing along. She had felt tired at the beginning of the service, but now she was so exhausted she felt like she couldn't move. The words of the sermon resounded in her head, but they made little sense, except for occasional phrases that suddenly clanged with great clarity. Hadn't she felt herself drowning in grief, actually using the term drowning? *Pastor Schwartz had said the waters have come up to my neck.* She had had no idea those words were in the Bible. "God will send someone to soften your heart," Pastor Schwartz had said. Didn't Ruth's heart feel uplifted and changed whenever she was with Frieda?

"And now I want to talk about that sweet Baby of Bethlehem," Pastor Schwartz concluded. "Why did God send His beloved Son into this miserable sin-filled place? And why did He choose the setting of a cold, dirty barn with its distinctive smell of manure? He sent His

Son because He LOVED US. He cared that the waters had come up to our necks, that we were sinking in mire, that our lives were filled with sorrow and violence. He sent His Son to deliver us from all our troubles. Can He really do that? He already has. He did that on the cross. He completed it on resurrection morning. Your problems won't automatically be solved in the morning, but He will go with you to meet them. Through the Holy Spirit, the Comforter, He will give you strength. Go now, and may the Baby of Bethlehem go with you. Amen."

Ruth sat stunned, dazed. Never had she considered that God was with her. She rarely, if ever, thought of God and certainly never considered that He loved her and could or would help her. As a child, she had mumbled prayers at bedtime and perhaps still did at times. But they were prayers of habit, not of conscious thought. Church attendance was a business opportunity for her father and a social occasion for her mother. Tonight, God had spoken to her. She felt it; she knew it. Perhaps she should be feeling elated or frightened, but she felt nothing. She would need time to sort it all out. She wanted to get her hands on a Bible and ponder on the things she heard tonight. But somehow, she knew that Pastor Schwartz's words were true.

Ruth was dimly aware that others were standing for the benediction. She rose slowly and absorbed the words: "The Lord bless thee and keep thee. The Lord make His face shine upon thee and be gracious unto thee. The Lord lift up His countenance upon thee and give thee peace." Peace: what a beautiful word—a word that had not been part of her vocabulary or her life.

The service was over. Again, kindly people came to greet her, to welcome her, to wish her a good Christmas. Everyone seemed careful not to say, "Merry Christmas." She had seen too much tragedy to be merry; but yes, perhaps she could have a "good" Christmas.

Chapter 21

Christmas Day. Ruth awakened early, not sure of her surroundings. The room was dark. In the moments that her mind tried to comprehend where she was and what day it was, she was conscious of a peace that seemed puzzling. It was an unfamiliar feeling, but it felt so good. She almost wished she wouldn't remember where she was; she didn't want to jeopardize losing this strange contentment. When her mind cleared, and she realized she was in her bedroom at Karl and Hattie's, she involuntarily reached out a hand to see if Ben was asleep beside her. His side of the bed was empty, but that didn't bring a sharp pain of sadness. In fact, the unusual and distinct feeling of peace did not leave her.

"The Lord lift up His countenance upon thee and give thee peace."

Where did those words come from? Perhaps it was just a relief that she didn't need to jump out of bed, don her work clothes and start in with the chores. Or perhaps because here with Karl and Hattie, she felt cared for. Those things were pleasant to think on, but.... and then she remembered. The Christmas Eve service from last night. She heard again in her mind Pastor Schwartz's words:

"Your problems won't automatically be solved in the morning, but He will go with you to meet them. Through the Holy Spirit, the Comforter, He will give you strength."

How did he know what she needed to hear? Of course, he would somewhat know of her situation. Even though he had been at this congregation less than three months, he surely would have heard about the circumstances of Ben's death. He perhaps had consoled Karl and Hattie when coming to pay them a get-acquainted visit. But no one, not even Karl and Hattie, knew the condition of Ruth's mind—her hopelessness, her increasing bitterness, her feeling of drowning in sorrow.

"I sink in deep mire, where there is no standing; I have come into deep waters, where the floods overflow me. I am weary with my crying; my throat is dry; my eyes fail."

Was it possible that God gave Pastor Schwartz the words to say in his sermon? It certainly wasn't a traditional Christmas sermon. She had never heard one like it. To be truthful, she couldn't remember any sermon she had ever heard.

Ruth knew there wasn't a Bible in this room. A large family Bible lay on the end table by the couch in the living room. Ruth didn't own a Bible—actually, she had never read the Bible on her own. She remembered being taught something about the arrangement of the books of the Bible as a child in a Sunday school class. Now she had a tremendous desire to find the verses read last night. Rev. Schwartz said the verses were in the Psalms. How did they happen to be written? Who wrote them? She needed to talk to someone about the sermon. Could she ask Hattie? Maybe Rev. Schwartz?

Ruth was suddenly very conscious of the clean smell of the sheets and the warm quilts around her.

"Peace" was the word to describe how she felt. She could think of this bedroom that she had shared with Ben for such a short while without being engulfed with grief as she had been yesterday. She dozed, waiting for sounds that would indicate that Karl and Hattie were up.

Ruth realized she was smelling coffee brewing. The first light of day was coming in the window. She heard Karl come in from the barn and wood being added to the kitchen stove. Soon other aromas drifted upstairs—rolls baking and sausage frying. Ruth was ravenous.

She dressed quickly and breathed in the warmth of the kitchen as she entered the room. Karl was setting the table, and Hattie was busy dishing the food at the stove. Fried eggs, browned sausage, fried potatoes with onions, and thick slices of toasted homemade bread were set on the table.

"You are right on time; I was just about to call you," Hattie exclaimed. "May you have a good Christmas!"

"Ja, a good Christmas!" Karl repeated. "We're glad to have you here."

They both smiled at her, and Ruth knew they meant their words.

"We expect Daniel and his family later this forenoon," Hattie said, "so I'll put the goose in to roast as soon as we finish our breakfast. But we don't need to rush. Let's enjoy this Christmas breakfast."

Enjoy it, they did. How could such simple food taste so heavenly?

"Hattie, I have many things to learn while I am here." Ruth was thinking mostly about asking questions about the sermon, but this didn't seem to be the time or place. Instead, she said, "I need recipes or directions on how to prepare foods and ideas about what foods I can prepare. My cooking is a disaster."

Hattie chuckled. "We'll work on it, but not today. Today is Christmas. We're going to concentrate on blessings today."

When Daniel and his wife Marie and their three little ones arrived by horse and sleigh some hours later, the house was smelling of goose and dressing roasting and pies baking. Daniel was a creamery operator in Ferndale, a town about seven miles away. They had visited a few times during the months that Ruth had lived here on the farm as Ben's wife. Daniel was a couple years older than Ben. He resembled Ben physically, but where Ben was open and friendly, Daniel was quiet and withdrawn. He seemed distant during much of the conversation. Marie was busy with her children, three little girls, the oldest being about six years old.

As the visiting went on around her, Ruth eyed the Bible lying on the table by the couch. A couple times, when the others seemed engrossed in conversation or the children, she opened it and paged through it. She located the Psalms but not the verses of last night's sermon. She was going to need some guidance in this.

Noontime came. The food was delicious and the gift exchange pleasant. Ruth enjoyed watching the three little girls squeal and laugh over their gifts. Hattie had knitted each one a sweater and matching cap. Karl had made wooden whistles that were put aside by the adults after a few loud blasts. Ruth had anticipated seeing them at Christmas time and had purchased three large lollipops when she had done her shopping before coming. She hadn't thought about the youngest one becoming a completely sticky mess. Hattie washed the child several times, pulled long hairs off the lollipop, and handed it back to the little girl.

Ruth listened to Karl talking to Daniel about the livestock. She wished she could sit down and be a part of the conversation, but it seemed to be for just the two of them. She wished she could ask Karl if the red roan cow was still so skittish. Did the little runt calf ever grow as it should have? All the questions she would have liked to ask about the cows that she had enjoyed so much when she lived here with Ben. But Karl may not appreciate her asking, especially when he seemed to be trying hard to make conversation with Daniel.

"Is the milk production at your creamery staying up during this cold weather?" Ruth heard Karl ask Daniel. "Is much of the milk frozen by the time it gets to the creamery?"

Daniel asked how many cows Karl was milking this winter and then surprised Ruth by his question: "Are you thinking of selling off the milk herd?"

There was a pause, and then Karl said softly, "Not yet."

Was it her imagination, or did Daniel seem like he wasn't really interested in what they were talking about? His questions were short, his answers often only a word or two.

Ruth attempted to talk to Marie, but she couldn't think of anything to say. Marie seemed to talk only to her children and ignored everyone else in the room.

Hattie was busy keeping coffee cups hot and the cookie tray filled.

By four o'clock, the children were tired and cranky, and Marie said they must be getting home. Daniel quickly agreed. "These days are short and cold, and we don't like to be driving about too long after dark. I'll harness up the horses."

"I'll go out with you," Karl said, grabbing his heavy chore coat.

Hattie was disappointed they were leaving so early. "I'll send some leftovers and an extra pie for you to eat when you're settled at home," she told Marie. "We don't see enough of these grandchildren. Please come back soon."

"We may wait for warmer weather," Marie answered shortly. "It's a worry taking them out in the cold."

They were gone in a flurry of activity. Karl went out to milk cows. Hattie and Ruth sat down for a cup of coffee.

"I wish they could visit more often," Hattie murmured. "The children are growing up, and I hardly know them. Daniel doesn't get a chance to find out what is going on with the farm, how Karl is feeling…or maybe he's past caring about what goes on here. We old folks probably aren't that interesting to them. He has a good job; we're thankful for that. We just wish we felt more a part of their lives."

Ruth was surprised to be included in Hattie's intimate thoughts.

"What did you mean, how Karl is feeling? Is he having health problems?"

"His arthritis is really bad in his hands—can't sleep lots of nights. I don't know how much longer he can keep farming and especially milking cows. It will become impossible before long."

When Karl came in from the barn, the three of them sat down to a good meal of warmed leftovers. For the first time, Ruth truly observed Karl's hands. *How could I have been so wrapped up in my own problems that I only noticed that his hands showed some effects of arthritis?* she thought. Now she saw that they were gnarled and deformed—the ends of some of the fingers turned up. How tragic if he could no longer farm. Farming was his life.

The evening was short; they sat at the table visiting. "Karl, there are many household things I want to talk to Hattie about this week," Ruth ventured, "but would it be okay if I spend some time out in the barn with you? I really enjoyed your cows and other livestock, and I'd like to see them all again." Karl looked a little startled. Ruth remembered his comment a year ago that women generally should keep busy in the house. But that was a lifetime ago. So many things had changed. He wouldn't feel she was intruding into his world, would he? Karl stole a quick glance at Hattie; Ruth felt rather than saw a slight nod of Hattie's head. "Ja," he said, "You can go out there whenever you want." With that, he covered a yawn and said he was going up to bed.

Here is my opportunity, Ruth thought as Hattie lingered at the table after Karl left the room. "Hattie," she began timidly, "Rev. Schwartz's sermon last night was very interesting, but there is so much I don't understand. I guess I haven't talked much about God stuff and haven't even thought about God too much. Could you help me?"

Hattie stared at Ruth for a long minute, so long that Ruth was afraid she had offended her. To Ruth's surprise, Hattie's eyes filled with tears. "Oh, Ruth," she said, half choking. "Oh, thank you, God."

Ruth was startled. Hattie continued, "Ruth, I have been praying that God would touch your lonely heart. I would consider it an honor to tell you about His love. But tonight, I am exhausted, and I want to pray about where to start and what to say before I begin. We will have a lot more than recipes and meals to talk about these next days. Thank you, God," she repeated.

Hattie slowly ascended the shadowy stairway leaving the lamp on the kitchen table. Ruth poured herself another cup of coffee and nibbled on yet another sugar cookie. She wasn't hungry, but the availability of good food made her continue eating.

She was surprised at Hattie's reaction to her asking for help understanding the Bible. It was almost as if Hattie was waiting for that question.

She brought the Bible in from the living room and paged through it until she again found the Psalms. She began reading.

As she reached for another cookie, she had a pang of guilt from a different source. She had gradually taken over the responsibility of preparing food for Amos, but her meals were sparse, uninteresting, and unappetizing. She needed to change that. While her mind was back at Amos's place, she wondered how he and his cousin were getting along. What was their Christmas supper like? She should have made something in advance for them to eat. There weren't many supplies in the house—she hadn't thought of purchasing anything extra for Christmas when she made out the grocery list for Amos. And were the chores getting done as they should be?

Those thoughts quickly evaporated as she became absorbed in the Psalms of King David. She was surprised when the old mantle clock struck twelve.

Christmas was over. *What next?*

Chapter 22

The following morning right after breakfast, Ruth asked if this would be a good time to go to the barn.

"Ja," Karl said, "but dress warm. We're not going to get up to zero today."

It was different going to the barn along the frozen, snowy path. Ruth remembered the spring and early summer days when the path was sun-splashed and green with new grass. But opening the barn door brought all the familiar and pleasant smells and memories of doing chores with Ben. A sudden rush of warm air greeted her as the animals kept the barn snug and comfortable. There stood the milk cows still in their same places. Their names were not names so much as physical distinctions—Bobtail, because she had lost part of her tail; Freckle Face, because of the small brown spots covering her head; Big Girl, because she stood several inches taller than the other cows, and so on. They turned their heads to look at Ruth as she hurried through the door and closed it quickly behind her. It seemed like they were greeting her; perhaps they wondered where both she and Ben had been. Ruth had spent so much time with them besides doing the milking—talking to them and petting them. After Ben was killed, she didn't remember if she had even entered the barn. She was in such a daze during those days that she couldn't be sure.

Karl soon entered the barn, too. "It's good you can come back out here."

Ruth was rather surprised at his words. She never felt like Karl nor Hattie approved of her spending so much time in the barn with the animals. At the time, she didn't care—it was an opportunity to be with Ben. And, during those months, she had decided she loved doing the chores.

Ruth spoke quietly to the cows. Their large eyes looked at her inquisitively. *I'm sure they remember me,* Ruth thought. The gentle horses nickered quietly to her. She checked the young stock pen. The newborn calves that had been so playful last summer were now mildly curious young stock mostly interested in their hay. Hearing people in the barn brought the friendly cats down from the haybarn. They purred and begged Ruth to pick them up.

Ruth turned to Karl while cradling a cat in her arms. "Do you feed grain to the cows before they have their calves? For how long? How far along in their pregnancy before you dry them up? Do the calves need ground feed if they have good quality hay? What's the best time of year for cows to have their calves?" Ruth threw question after question at Karl. All the things she and Amos had argued about, she now brought up with Karl. He answered her questions one by one, looking a little bemused by all the things she wanted to know. Ruth was chagrined to realize that most of the time Karl was unknowingly agreeing with Amos's point of view, not hers.

Ruth was beginning to realize that even though she loved the animals and had learned much in the few months she worked with Ben, she was not an expert in bovine care. Karl, Ben, and Amos had spent their lives learning the cattle business and how best to care for them. It was humbling to admit to herself that Amos probably knew more than she gave him credit for.

The days of Ruth's visit went by so quickly that when her final afternoon at the Gottliebs' home came, she felt like she couldn't remember any of the previous days—they all blurred together in her mind.

As she had promised, Hattie had written down recipes, meal suggestions complete with supplies needed, and some tips for cleaning areas of the house. They discussed schedules for baking—how long should bread rise—and how to control the oven heat with the wood-burning stoves.

However, though they discussed household tips for hours, the meaningful conversations were on spiritual matters. Hattie had decided to begin Ruth's Bible education with the Gospel of John. They read it together, and Ruth studied it on her own. "The Word became flesh and dwelt among us." The entire Christmas story was condensed in those few words, yet Ruth didn't remember hearing them before. She studied—*devoured* was a better word—not only John, but the other Gospels, the Psalms, and Romans. She read far into the night every night. During the week, she realized she wouldn't have access to a Bible when she returned to Amos's place. If he had one, she had never seen it.

As if reading Ruth's thoughts, Hattie herself asked if Ruth had her own Bible. It was embarrassing to admit that even though her family had attended church every Sunday, even though her brother-in-law was a minister, Ruth didn't own a Bible. Her family kept one in her parents' bedroom, but perhaps her mother had kept that one.

"I'm ashamed to say I don't have a Bible," Ruth told Hattie. "Would you have an extra one that I could borrow?"

Hattie smiled sadly. "Actually, there is one for you here. Ben had a

Bible. I know he used to read it often. I wish he would have shared it with you during your short time together. I have a trunk of his things upstairs. Anything in that trunk is yours to keep, including the Bible."

Ruth spent hours reading from Ben's Bible. He had underlined several passages and had written in the margins. Those notes made him seem close to her again.

She remembered him occasionally reading from it in the evenings as they prepared for bed. She was usually brushing her hair or laying out their clothes for the next day. She wondered why he had not spoken to her about his faith. As thoughts of those evenings came back to her, she remembered snatches of conversation that she had either forgotten or not given any thought at the time. Ben had said words like, "God is so good to us, Ruth. I'm so thankful for you. We owe all we have to our Lord. He'll provide for us as He's provided salvation."

As some of those words came back to her as she now read in that same bedroom, she was amazed that she hadn't questioned him about his faith or about God. His words seemed to her at the time like idle conversation—no more important than "I wonder if it will rain tomorrow."

How childish and immature she had been! She didn't know that person anymore.

***

During the last afternoon of Ruth's vacation, a visitor came to call.

Hattie and Ruth had just finished the dinner dishes, and Karl was dozing in his big chair in the dining room when they heard Rex barking outside. Karl went to the door.

"It's Rev. Schwartz," he called back to the women. "Put on some coffee, Hattie; I'll put up his horse."

Within minutes, the four of them were sitting at the table with hot coffee and kuchen. Rev. Schwartz looked even more fierce than he did at church on Christmas Eve. His cheeks were bright red from being in the cold, his stiff hair stuck out in all directions.

His steel-gray eyes had an unusual penetrating look. Ruth wasn't even sure he looked friendly. He was not a smiling man, but there was a magnetism about him that made Ruth want to hear him speak, yet she was a little taken aback by his appearance. His eyes often turned to Ruth as the four of them shared casual conversation. They talked about neighbors, illnesses in the congregation, the cold weather.

Rev. Schwartz then turned directly to Ruth and let his piercing eyes study her for some moments. "Tell me about your work, Ruth." Ruth realized that Amos had hardly been mentioned since she had arrived at the Gottliebs' home. She gave a highly condensed version of Amos and the work she did.

"How do you and Amos get along?"

No one had asked her that before. In fact, Karl and Hattie seldom mentioned her job or her relationship with Amos. If someone had asked a week ago what that relationship was, she would have readily volunteered that Amos was the most stubborn, sarcastic, dirty, hard-to-get-along-with person she had ever met. Now for some reason, all she could think of was Amos's surprised and pleased face when he had opened her Christmas present to him, his deck of cards.

"Oh, I suppose we have had differences of opinion quite often. But I'm sure he's very frustrated not being able to do his chores for himself. He wants to be sure they get done the way they should be done."

Where did that come from? Ruth realized that she spoke the truth—Amos's life must be very frustrating. His concern for his cows made him question the way she did everything. Anyone who had such affection for his animals couldn't be....

Rev. Schwartz interrupted her thoughts. "Remember every situation that God gives us is meant for our good. In our selfish way of thinking, it's impossible to see that all the time. Maybe years from now, as you look back on your life, you will see that is true."

For some time now, Ruth had tried very hard not to look at the future. The future had been a black shadow with no hope or plan. Was he saying that her misery in her job would someday work out for her good? That seemed to stretch the possibilities of reasonable thinking.

Ruth wanted to hear more about the sermon topic from Christmas Eve. That had been the only church service she had attended during her stay with the Gottliebs.

"I've read the verses from Psalm 69 many times since I heard your sermon," she ventured. "I'm not sure I understand all you said that night, but I had the strange feeling that you were giving that sermon directly to me, for my benefit."

For the first time, Rev. Schwartz smiled, and his eyes twinkled for just a moment. "I was."

Chapter 23

The train going back to Four Corners was almost completely empty. Ruth was glad. The quiet hours gave her a chance to go over in her mind all that had happened during the past week. Week? It seemed like it would be impossible for so many thoughts to bombard her mind in just a week. Even now, she tried to sort them into categories.

The day spent in the barn with Karl was so pleasant. How good it was to see the cows and cats again, to rub the horses' noses, to smell the good fragrance of the animals and the hay. It was also a revelation. Karl had been unusually talkative. Ruth realized that this was his domain; he probably felt more at home here than he did in the house. He shared many facts and opinions on livestock care. It was a revelation that Amos did know what he was talking about—many of the statements of the two men were similar.

Ruth had to smile when she opened her handbag and saw the many pages Hattie had written out for her—recipes, meal planning, and preparations. Ruth had added details in the margins as they had discussed the directions together. She was actually looking forward to putting some of the ideas into practice. It would be a challenge.

But the thing that dominated Ruth's thoughts was the sermon and her Bible reading. She held Ben's Bible in her hands the entire trip. She read, reread, and underlined passages and jotted down questions in the margins. She had learned so much about the love of God yet still had so much more to learn. How could she have sat in church for so many years and never been conscious of God's love, His help in daily situations, His compassion, and His salvation?

As the landscape rushed by her window, Ruth often closed her eyes with her finger in her place in the Bible. She had read all the New Testament and was now engrossed with the action stories of the early books of the Old Testament. Some were familiar to her. She had heard of David killing the giant, Noah building the Ark, Daniel in the lions' den, and some others. But they were nothing except adventures. God's providence in each of those stories had escaped her. Now she haltingly tried to pray. Praying to the almighty God who had created heaven and earth was intimidating, to say the least. What could she say to God when He already knew everything, even the thoughts in her head? But Hattie had told her that God wanted her to pray—to think of it as a conversation between God and herself. And each time she tried it, it became easier. In fact, it became a joy. She found she was praying even as she dozed in the comfortable train seat.

However, the act of talking to God made her do some self-evaluation. It wasn't pleasant. Tears came to her eyes when she thought about her preoccupation with herself. She had been pampered by her dad, and Ben continued that in their relationship. She was the perpetual child whom someone took care of. There was no need to be self-reliant or mature—someone else took care of that. How all of that changed with Ben's death! Suddenly she had no one, no one but herself. Now she realized that during these months, she had had God to turn to. Even though she had never asked for His help, He was standing by, ready to help. The help, though, wasn't that of a pampering, indulgent daddy or husband, but a God who sometimes led through the valley of the shadow of death.

"Oh, God, forgive me—forgive me for being so self-centered all my life. Help me now to make the best of my situation, to think of others, to be kind, to be helpful to Amos."

Amos. Showing compassion to Amos would be the challenge.

Chapter 24

As the train chugged into Four Corners, Ruth was glad the weather had moderated somewhat. She gathered her things together, prepared to walk the four miles to Amos's farm.

As she stepped out of the train car onto the platform, she was surprised to see Frieda and Art coming towards her.

"Ruth," Frieda called, "It's so good to see you. How was your trip? How are your in-laws?"

"What are you doing here?" Ruth questioned. "I wasn't expecting anyone to meet me."

"Amos said you were returning today. Since this is the only train that comes through Four Corners each day, it wasn't hard to arrange to be here. We had to get groceries anyway."

"Hey, Ruthie, I do believe your cheeks filled out a little in the week you were gone. Eating too many Christmas cookies, I suppose," Art teased her. "Anyway, it's good to see you. Is this all the things you have?" he asked as he took her suitcase from her hand.

Ruth was so glad to see her friends, probably her only friends in

Four Corners, she had to blink back tears. When Frieda hugged her, Ruth clung to her tightly.

"Let's get into the sleigh," Frieda said briskly. "It may be a little warmer than it has been, but we don't need to be standing here. We're done with our shopping, so we can visit on the way home."

"Here, you sit in the middle," Frieda directed as she tucked a horse blanket around both Ruth and herself. "We want to hear every detail."

Ruth suddenly felt shy. How could she explain the monumental things that had happened to her since she had left the week before?

"Well," she began slowly, trying to sort her thoughts, "Hattie and Karl are doing okay except for Karl's arthritis. We had a wonderful visit. But—oh, Frieda and Art—I don't know how to tell you, but I became acquainted with Jesus. I still don't feel like I know Him well, but I'm reading Ben's Bible every chance I get. It started with the Christmas Eve sermon...oh, and the pastor quoted something you told me."

"Whoa," Frieda laughed. "Ruth, this is wonderful news, but the pastor is supposed to be quoting the Bible, not the Gospel of Frieda. It sounds like you need to start at the beginning. By the way, Art and I have been praying that you would hear God's Word taught in its truth and purity, so I suppose we shouldn't be surprised."

The time it took for Art's work horses to cover the four miles to Amos's farm seemed but a few seconds as Ruth tried to tell of the impact of the past week.

"Here we are, time to dump you off," Art interrupted her good-naturedly. "I know Frieda wants to hear you tell all of this at least six more times, and I'd like to get in on the details, too, but I'm kind of worried about a cow who's going to have a calf soon. I want to get home before dark."

"We'll have you over soon," Frieda promised her. "Can Art help you with your things?"

Ruth quickly picked up her suitcase, assured them she could handle it easily, and watched them leave the yard. Frieda turned and waved gaily. Ruth had been so enthused, so eager to tell them all about her mountain-top experience. Now, as she stood at the bottom of the steps in the gathering dusk, she was filled with dread. Would she go back to the routine of chores and arguments, of bitterness and loneliness? Perhaps she had been kidding herself that everything would be different.

From inside the house, Brute suddenly started an ear-piercing howl. "Shut your mouth," Amos yelled almost as loudly as the dog.

"Lord, I don't know what to ask you. I'm here to do my job and live in this house, yet I don't know if I can. Would you help me? And would you help me please you? Amen."

She climbed the steps and hesitated. Should she knock? She hadn't knocked in all the time she stayed there, but perhaps this was different. Amos and Neil wouldn't be expecting her yet since she had gotten a ride. But they surely must have heard the sleigh, especially with Brute's outburst. The decision was made for her when the door burst open, and Neil shouted above Brute's barking. "Amos, would you get that dog to shut up? Your little woman is back again."

As Ruth entered the hot kitchen, the overwhelming smells of greasy food, dog, sweat, and a chamber pot that needed emptying hit her senses. Her stomach twisted, and for a moment, she thought she would be sick.

Brute finally decided he remembered Ruth and lay down at Amos's feet under the table.

Amos was sitting at his place at the table, the new playing cards dealt out. "Well, ain't you the one. Good thing you got back today—Neil's leaving tomorrow. I hope you learnt how to cook something besides eggs. Neil here is a top-notch cook—he burned something different for every meal!" Amos laughed loudly at his joke, while Neil glared at him without smiling.

"You may have had different food, but it smells like neither of you got around to doing any cleaning for the last week," Ruth said scornfully. She immediately clamped her mouth shut. It was going to be just as she feared; she would try to match every cutting remark with one of her own. How do you change a personality?

Neil sat down at the table and picked up his hand of cards. Ruth removed her coat; already, she felt too hot with the wood stove belching out heat. She wrestled her suitcase up the ladder to the attic. She stood for a moment, glad to be alone. She needed to cool off, both physically and mentally. Then she saw a pile of blankets in the corner and realized that Neil had been sleeping upstairs. Had he gone through her things, maybe even slept on her mattress? She shuddered.

She breathed deeply, trying to be calm. Tears of desperation slipped down her cheeks. I need help to deal with this. Then she heard those words, the words of Psalm 72 that she had read so many times. *"For he shall deliver the needy when he crieth; the poor also, and him that hath no helper."*

Ruth wiped her tears quickly, put down her suitcase, and descended the ladder. She forced herself to smile. The two men were engrossed with their hands of cards; they weren't paying any attention to her.

"Can I make you guys some coffee?" she asked brightly. "My mother-in-law sent some Christmas goodies that I can put out for you."

Amos turned to stare at her. "Well, ain't you the one. Neil, let's see if her coffee's improved any since she left. It sure was nothing to brag about before. Unless I made it, it was undrinkable."

They laughed loudly, threw in their hands of cards, and watched her while she made the coffee.

"How are things out in the barn? Did the old cat make it through that cold stretch of weather?" She turned to look at Neil.

"I didn't see but one or two cats," Neil finally admitted. "I don't take to cats, and they stay out of my way."

"What do you mean, you only saw one or two cats?" Amos shouted. "You said all the animals were fine."

"The animals are fine. I mean, the stock is fine. I don't think of cats as stock. They can take care of themselves. I put some milk out for them a couple times like you told me to. Cats are supposed to earn their own keep." Neil was becoming red in the face. "If you don't like how I do things, you sure ain't going to get me to help you again. I can walk to town tonight and sleep in the depot."

"Go ahead," Amos yelled back at him.

"Fellas, the coffee is just about done. Calm down so we can have some Christmas cookies. I don't know about you, but I'm starving."

Ruth quickly put out some of Hattie's tasty cookies. Within minutes, she poured steaming cups of coffee for each man.

The cards were dealt. The men contemplated their hands, bid loudly, and cursed when the desired card was not in the kitty. Without comment to Ruth, they pushed cookies into their mouths and gulped coffee.

"Is it pinochle you're playing?" Ruth asked while she ate cookies and wished she was back in Gottlieb's kitchen.

"I'm bidding until you pass, so you might as well pass right now," Neil threatened. Neither one answered her question.

Yes, sharing her faith with these men would be a challenge.

Chapter 25

Neil walked to town the next morning to catch the train home. He wasn't up when Ruth awakened, so she hurried out to do the chores. Despite the men's argument the night before, everything was in good shape. The barn was quite clean; the cows looked contented enough. The cats were glad to see her, and they didn't seem any worse off than when she left. They did appreciate the pan of warm milk, though.

Neil was gone when she returned to the house. Maybe things would be easier as they settled down to their regular routine.

"Amos," Ruth began as cheerfully as she could, "I got cooking pointers from my mother-in-law while I was there. I'm going to try hard to get a little more variety into what I cook."

"Well, ain't you the one," Amos automatically responded. "You and Neil need to both go to cooking school. Excepting he cooked oatmeal two, three times a day while you cook eggs. I ain't had eggs since you left, and the egg pail is running over. We better have eggs for breakfast."

"Well, as least I'm starting with something I know how to do. Fried or scrambled?"

When Ruth started a pan of scrambled eggs, she looked for bread in the breadbox. The only bread in there was badly moldy. "I'll cut out the mold and make French toast from the sections that are left. I'll make some syrup by boiling some brown sugar and water."

Amos had made a pot of coffee, and soon the kitchen smelled of cooking food and coffee that masked the more unpleasant odors.

"The barn looks good," Ruth offered as they sat down to eat. "Neil did a good job with the chores."

"I wouldna asked him to come iffen he weren't going to do the job right." Amos seemed to have forgotten their argument the night before about taking care of the cats.

"We really need bread, but I think I probably need to do some cleaning first thing. I'll make biscuits for our dinner and hope I can get to making bread tomorrow. I'll cut off some beef chunks from the hanging meat in the entry and cook that with some potatoes to go with the biscuits." Ruth thought her dinner menu was a great idea, but Amos's only comment was, "This here French toast still tastes moldy."

And so, the household chores began. Ruth emptied and scoured the chamber pot (holding her breath as much as possible as she did so) and scrubbed the kitchen floor.

When she peered into Amos's bedroom, he stopped her. "You ain't going into my bedroom," he said as he stood in the doorway with folded arms, his crutches leaning against him.

"I've already been in there to empty the pot, so there aren't surprises in there," she said, pushing past him with the scrub pail. "I think it's a matter of necessity to get some things cleaned up." She tried to talk in a friendly but firm way.

He mumbled something about "ain't you the one," but he sat down at the table and started a game of solitaire.

The day went quickly with cleaning, making meals, and going out to take care of the stock at noontime and then for the afternoon chores. When supper was on the table, she felt almost too tired to eat.

She forced herself to speak cheerfully. "I had a very good time at my in-laws' home over Christmas. I felt it was healing for me to go. Thank you for arranging for Neil to come to do the chores."

"Aw, Neil likes to come to get beat in pinochle. He always thinks he's good enough to wup me, but he never can. The chores is an excuse to come here." But Ruth noticed with surprise that Amos's face had turned several shades of red.

"Amos, do you ever go to church? I mean, before your accident, did you go?"

"Don't go tellin' me that you got religion while you was gone," Amos snorted. "I had enough religion stuffed down my throat by my ma and grandma. Pa and me made sure we didn't have to listen to all that woman sissy stuff from them. I don't want to hear it from you neither."

Ruth was about to say that going to heaven was not woman sissy stuff, but she clamped her mouth shut in time.

"I'll need to start a grocery list," she said, changing the subject. "Frieda said they would get things for us next week. Are there some things you would like me to make for you? Tomorrow I'm going to make a cake. We've got flour, sugar, plenty of eggs, and lard. I think I can do it from that. Cocoa would be a great addition, don't you think?

"You're talking stupid. Remember, I ain't made from money when you make that there list. All this talk about making fancy things sounds like money poured down the pothole to me. The big bucks I pay you will put me in the poor house without all this stuff you want to buy."

Ruth smiled sweetly at him. "I'll always check the list over with you first. You just wait and see what I can come up with from just a few ingredients. And now I think I'll go to bed. I'll wash the dishes in the morning."

Ruth was exhausted, but more than that, she was determined that

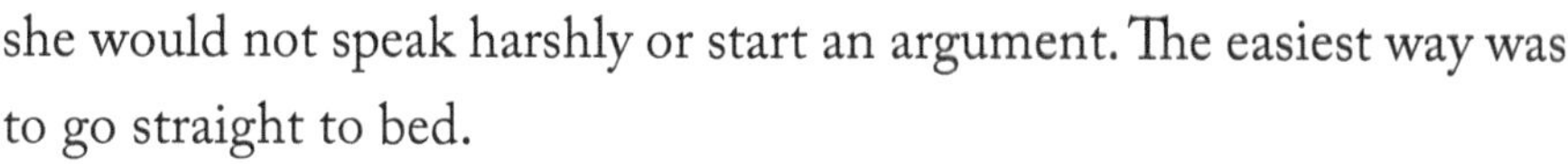

she would not speak harshly or start an argument. The easiest way was to go straight to bed.

Chapter 26

January brought a frigid grip that didn't let up. Cold weather made the chores so much harder. The ice had to be chopped from the tank before she could pump water for the cows to drink. Frost covered the walls of the barn, and the cold began to seep in from all sides. The cats slept long hours in cozy beds of straw, and even the chickens spent most of the short daylight hours huddled on the roosts.

Keeping the joy she had felt when returning from her in-laws' home seemed impossible. In the house, the wood box continually needed filling. The woodpile that Amos had piled high in healthier times was dwindling rapidly.

I can handle this, Ruth told herself over and over. She tried to keep the memories of her Christmas trip alive in her memory—rethinking Rev. Swartz's sermon, conversations with Hattie. They were becoming blurred in her mind. She tried her best to make use of Hattie's suggestions and recipes for making tasty and varied meals, but all of that took time. Besides, Amos never mentioned her efforts. Keeping the house clean seemed impossible when Amos seemed bent on making it dirty.

"Amos, please wipe up the stove when the coffee boils over. After it burns on, I can't get the stove clean," she said, trying not to spit out the words. This was at least the tenth time she had asked him.

"Well, ain't you the one," he replied loudly. "This here is my stove and my house. If I want burnt coffee stuck on the stove, what's it to you? You sure got uppity since you left for Christmas. I pay you big money to work here, not to be my hoity-toity boss."

Ruth had her retort all ready.... Words like living in a clean house during the Christmas visit were too pleasant to be satisfied to come back to this pigsty....She literally clamped her hand over her mouth to keep the words from coming out. It was impossible to be pleasant to Amos. It couldn't be expected of her.

When Ruth climbed the ladder to her attic bedroom that night, she arranged her things on a chair next to her mattress as she always did. In the evenings, the attic was comparatively warm; it would be icy cold in the morning. She wanted her clothes nearby so she could quickly jump into them. The attic trap door gave some light from the room below. Ben's Bible was lying on the chair; she had glanced at some verses since getting back from Gottlieb's home, but there was no opportunity to read it—the attic was too dark at night, the days were too busy. Her conscience pricked her soul; she was sliding back to the person she was before Christmas. She had no power to change as much as she wanted to. *Lord, help me*, she begged as she crawled onto her mattress. *I cannot be what you want me to be.* That thought brought a memory of a verse she had read in the Gospel of John: "Apart from Christ, we can do nothing."

The next day was a continuing struggle with the chores in the cold, with trying to keep the house warm, with putting meals on the table, with dealing with Amos.

When evening finally came and the dishes were washed, Ruth

was about to climb the ladder to the attic and fall exhausted onto the mattress, as was her custom. Amos was starting another game of solitaire. She turned silently to the ladder when she heard Amos grunt something.

"What did you say?"

Again, Amos was muttering something, his face looking down at the cards on the table.

"What did you say?" Ruth asked again, not trying too hard to keep the impatience out of her voice.

"I said it's kind of okay to play solitaire with a real deck of cards." He said it loudly this time, his eyes still on the cards. Ruth noticed even in the dim lamplight that his face was red. She couldn't think of anything to reply, so she climbed the ladder in silence.

In the shadows of the attic, she again saw the Bible on the chair beside her mattress—certainly too dark to do any reading.

On impulse, she grabbed the Bible, descended the ladder, and sat down at the table where the lamp gave out its light. Amos looked up from his cards in surprise and saw the Bible in her hands.

"Now, don't you be preachin' to me from that book," he said in his usual belligerent one. "I've had enough of that to last two lifetimes."

"But I can sit here and read it myself, can't I? It's too dark in the attic, and the days don't give me much time."

Amos gave his usual grunt that could mean anything and went back to his cards. Ruth read again from the pages of the Gospel of John. Slowly she felt her tense shoulders relax as she lost herself in the words. She was startled when the clock struck ten times. She closed the Bible and left it on the corner of the table on a stack of old newspapers. "Goodness, I didn't know it was so late. Good night, now."

Amos didn't reply.

The days settled into a routine. The cold eased a little as January crept to a close. Each evening Ruth read from the Bible at the table while Amos played solitaire or reread the old newspapers. She had read almost all the Bible, skipping a few of the books she felt would be too difficult without someone explaining them. She was rereading some of the books she had started with. During her busy days, she found herself looking forward to the evenings when she could fill her mind with the Scripture readings. Despite the weary work and drudgery of the days, she had a new feeling—a feeling she didn't remember ever knowing before Christmas. She noticed that the uncomfortable tightness she had carried in her chest for months was beginning to loosen its grip. Was it just the relaxing of muscles that caused her to feel differently about things? No, it finally came to her—she was feeling peace—the peace that had come to her with the Christmas Eve sermon. It felt good; it seemed to fill her up. Something else accompanied it—she began to feel gratitude. Gratitude not for her life that was still miserable, but for the love of Jesus, for His companionship when she was so lonely, for His help.

Without thinking one evening as Ruth was reading from Genesis, she blurted out, "The story of Noah and the flood is so amazing. What do you think it was like in the ark with all those animals?"

"Noah was probably worried about running out of hay," Amos responded.

Ruth felt a quick stab of anger. Did he always have to be so negative? But suddenly, she burst out laughing.

"Noah didn't know how long he would have to make it last," she agreed. "But he only had two cows to feed."

"Yeah, but he had horses and those other animals. I think elephants eat hay, too."

"Elephants would probably eat a lot more than cows," Ruth mused. "I guess Noah just had to trust God to make the hay last."

Amos shrugged his shoulders. "Hope He makes mine last till spring."

It was strange having this almost pleasant conversation with Amos. Interesting, too, that he must have some familiarity with the story of Noah and the flood.

After that evening, Ruth occasionally brought up a Bible story that she was reading, and then more often, a Bible verse that she found especially meaningful. She tried to be careful not to overdo it, but sometimes a verse or story was too fitting not to be mentioned.

"I don't put no stock in all that God stuff," Amos would say, but he never asked her to stop sharing the stories. In fact, they talked about what some things from the Bible meant. Ruth was surprised and a little embarrassed to find out that he knew more Bible stories than she did. But he ended every religious conversation with the usual, "I don't put no stock in all that God stuff. It don't mean nothing no how."

Ruth tried to become more proficient in her housekeeping skills, especially cooking and baking. Neighbors had been so good about dropping off loaves of bread, or cookies, or some meat during the fall. That stopped almost completely with these cold winter days. She never mastered bread making—her loaves were tough and often burned on the outside and doughy on the inside. But using Hattie's recipes and suggestions, her menus were more varied, and some things were quite good. She found she had all the ingredients she needed for soup if she used the potatoes, carrots, and onions other people had harvested from Amos's garden or shared from their own that were stored down in the cellar. Ruth still hated to go down to the cellar. It was half dark even in mid-day. Mice stared boldly at her, and spider webs clung to her hair. At this time of year, the vegetables were shriveled, and the potatoes were sprouting, but she cooked big kettles full to use them up before they went completely bad. With pieces of bacon or some other meat, and salt and pepper, Ruth thought it was quite tasty. Besides that, it was convenient to reheat leftovers for meals in the coming days.

"Do you like this soup?" Ruth ventured to ask Amos one day.

"The trouble with your cooking is you find something that's okay, and you make it over and over and over. Probably better than eggs every meal, though."

Ruth took that as a compliment.

She was about to reheat the last of a batch of soup when she realized the stove was again covered with spilled, burned-on coffee. Her frustration grew as she pried off the mess. She was about to say something about it being easier for her to make all the coffee instead of cleaning up after his coffee-making attempts, when she suddenly changed the words about to come out of her mouth.

"It's hard to catch the coffee between just boiling and boiling over, isn't it? I have the same trouble. Regulating the fire is always challenging for me."

Ruth surprised herself when her voice sounded almost pleasant—or at least not angry.

"I'm going to keep a rag right here just for wiping up boiled-over coffee. I'll probably need it often myself."

Amos stared at her for a moment before muttering something about sharing his kitchen with a fussy, bossy woman. But Ruth noticed that when the coffee boiled over after that, he used the rag to clean it up—after first casting furtive glances in her direction to make sure she wasn't watching.

It wasn't a complete or sudden change in the weeks after coming back from Gottlieb's home. Too many times, she matched his scornful words with her own harsh words, his complaining with complaints of her own. In fact, she sometimes was the one to initiate the bitter words. But little by little, even with the setbacks, she could speak with some pleasantness in her voice.

She tried to think of interesting things to share with him. She remembered that he had not seen the inside of the barn for almost six months—the barn and animals that he loved. She tried to fill him in on little details. "The chickens have a new nest right by the feeding trough…Yes, I know that probably means they need more straw in their nesting boxes," she added quickly before he could say it. "I'm also spreading a little straw on the floor, so it's not so cold on their feet. They are laying more eggs now, with the longer days. You should hear their loud talking. It's good company to hear them sing while I do the other chores. A couple of the cats have developed a habit of sitting on the cows' backs, probably to warm their feet. The cows don't seem to mind a bit. I'm so glad the straw is up in the haybarn, so I don't have it bring it in from outside during this cold weather."

She was rambling, she knew; but while he never made comments, he didn't stop her.

She started a chart for sun-up and sun-down times. "The days are getting so much longer; spring can't be too far away," she said cheerfully. Funny, she had never noticed lengthening days when she lived with her parents.

Ruth began talking to Amos about housekeeping details—when she planned to wash clothes or bake something. He never responded and probably was not particularly interested, but she realized that most days, he had no other communication, no new thoughts to occupy his mind. Visitors seldom came by in January.

Although Amos didn't answer her, at least he didn't have a sarcastic remark. The angry conversations between the two got fewer.

When the cold became less intense, Art and Frieda stopped by more regularly. When they asked for a grocery list, Ruth would occasionally ask them to bring back a magazine or newspaper for Amos. She would pay for these items with her own money. She always felt the need to save every penny of her earnings for the uncertain future, but Amos's surprise and grudging appreciation prompted her to keep on with the purchases.

"What are ya bringing that junk home for?" he asked the first time.

"I think it would do us good to have new things to talk about," she answered carefully. "In the evenings while I read the Bible, you can read your papers, and then we can share what we've read about."

"Well, ain't you the one," he answered. She wasn't sure what his tone sounded like.

"When do you see the doctor about getting your casts off?" Ruth finally asked one day. She knew it had to be continually on his mind.

"The doctor told me he didn't want to see me for six months. That'll be up in February. Sometime when Art stops in here, I'll tell him to send the doc out. Ain't no hurry…the casts don't itch no more—the cold weather musta kilt all the lice and such."

"It's February now, Amos. You don't seem very interested in getting those casts off," she observed.

"Why be anxious to hear that you'll be a no-good cripple all your life?"

Ruth realized he was afraid of what the doctor would tell him. And what would she do either way? What was her future? Amos would have to sell his cows if he could not work again. Whatever the doctor said, changes would be in her future, too.

Chapter 27

With some reservations, Ruth accepted an invitation to accompany Art and Frieda to town the next time they stopped by. She couldn't help but think of Richard Hunter's comments from her last visit to the store, but she did not want to be intimidated into staying home. This time when she went to the general store, she would know that Jesus went with her. That was not something she considered when shopping in December.

She felt better as she absorbed the late winter's sun as the sleigh went through the dirty snow. The rays were warmer than just a few weeks before. This was mid-February; surely, the coldest part of the winter must soon be over.

Frieda was talkative and bubbly as ever. She soon had Ruth laughing over the antics of their housecat. "Art and I said we would never have a cat in the house," Frieda explained. "But before Christmas, our favorite barn cat Spencer came down with distemper. We figured he wouldn't last more than a few days, and we wanted to make his end more comfortable. Well, I'm sure it was all an act on his part. Within two days, he was up and around, tangling my yarn and begging to sit on our laps whenever we sat down. Such a pest you would ever see, but now we would miss him if he wouldn't be in the house. He wakes me each morning by jumping up on the bed and chewing on my braids."

"Yeah, Frieda finally gets up before me," Art put in. "She's got to feed that cat before we have any peace in the house.

"Well, we agree he can say in the house until the weather is warm. It would be too much of a change to take him back to the barn now."

Art's voice became teasing. "And, Frieda, aren't you going to tell Ruth why we don't want a housecat next year? So far, you've written letters to your folks, my folks, your two sisters, and a whole cluster of cousins about the big news. She would only be the fortieth person to be told the big secret."

Frieda laughed. "It's not a secret, Art. I just don't want everyone staring at me wondering if I'm showing yet. You've guessed by now, Ruth, that Art and I are going to have a baby next summer—probably in August."

"Yeah, we picked the hottest part of the year so that Frieda could think about something else besides the heat."

Ruth felt genuine gladness for her friends, but it still brought a touch of melancholy to her heart. She wondered if she would ever have her own home and children—and another husband. Her life seemed so empty. *But not as empty as just a couple months ago,* she reminded herself. *Jesus walks with me; He directs my life. He has good plans for me.* Just the night before, she had discovered Jeremiah 29:11: "For I know the thoughts that I think toward you, said the Lord, thoughts of peace, and not of evil, to give you an expected end." So many comforting words in that short verse. *God thinks of me personally; His thoughts are for my peace; He will protect me from evil. My life seems so uncertain right now, but God has big plans, good plans.*

Thinking of the verse lightened her heart, and she gladly entered in the happy chatter of Art and Frieda. "Now, for sure, you must teach me how to knit," Ruth said. "I'm going to have to make some baby things for you before summer."

Art laughed. "Frieda can teach you to knit, but don't plan to make too many things for our baby. One drawer is full, and she's already after me to make shelves for baby stuff."

"Remember making the shelves comes after you make the cradle," Frieda reminded him. "Boxes will work fine to store baby things in for the time being."

"Cradles and boxes, I can handle," Art responded. "I'm trying to mentally prepare for the hints about needing more room, like a bigger house."

"That will only come with the third or fourth baby." Frieda smiled fondly at her husband, and he squeezed her hand right in plain view of Ruth.

It was so pleasant for Ruth to have friendly conversations with these warmhearted people. She began another topic that had been on her mind.

"Why do you think the neighbors are so willing to put up with Amos's negative attitude? He never thanks them for bringing food or taking his cream and eggs to the store or bringing his mail to him. Are they that eager for the local news that they continue to visit him and do things for him?"

"I think you hit it," Frieda replied. "Amos is like a walking newspaper. He knows everything that goes on in the neighborhood, and he's only too glad to share it. But there's something else, too. People who have lived in the area for more than a few years know the history of Amos's family. It's not pretty. I didn't live around here until after I married Art, but I've heard enough to understand Amos a little. Fill me in, Art, if I leave out something pertinent."

"Whatever I know, she knows," Art responded. "Marriage is that union thing, you know."

Frieda gave him a smile in agreement and continued. "From what I've heard, Amos's pa was a brutal tyrant to both the family members and the farm animals. Amos had two brothers and a sister who left home as soon as they could make it on their own. One of the brothers was killed when he fell from a train that he was hitching a ride on. I don't know what happened to the other brother or the sister. Amos's mother died when Amos was in his early teens. Apparently, she was a religious fanatic, but there was no joy in her religion. She was quick to tell everyone they were on the road to hell. The battles, verbal and physical, between those two parents would frighten the toughest of the tough. We heard she died of a heart attack. His pa continued to become meaner as the years went on. He took it all out on Amos."

"Why didn't Amos leave home, too?" Ruth asked.

"Well, somehow, it became Amos's responsibility to protect the animals from his pa. For all Amos's faults, he loves every animal on that place. He treats each one—even the chickens—with kindness. Maybe it's not nice to say, but I think it was a relief for people and animals when Amos's pa died."

"He probably died from drinking too much. I don't think I ever saw the man sober." Art added.

"Farmers round here respect someone who treats his animals right," Frieda said.

Art continued, "Not that Amos ever had any social graces. Gratitude isn't part of who he is. The way he was talked to as he grew up—that's the way he talks now."

"I think people are willing to overlook Amos's crude ways because they respect what he does. He was never treated well himself, but he rose above that and shows a kindness to his animals that he never received for himself. You have to give him credit for that.

"However," Art continued with a grin, "I don't think all that goodwill towards Amos extends to the neighborhood women. While they're compassionate enough to send along food items with their husbands, his personal hygiene and crudeness keep them from stepping foot in his house. That's probably why they're a little standoffish to you—they don't understand your courage to actually live with him.

"Anyway," Art continued, "I think Amos has had a hard time being away from his animals. He's never gone a day without caring for them, and he misses them. Being confined to the house hasn't helped his disposition."

Frieda added, "Ruth, maybe this is a chance to have your sweetness rub off on him. Your good influence could make him more pleasant."

Ruth snorted, "Me, sweet? Maybe years ago, it would have been possible to think that. Not now."

Frieda's words caused Ruth to stop and think. Had she ever influenced anyone? It had always been too easy to let others influence her. She had been the pampered recipient of Daddy's and Ben's indulgent love. She was not a giver.

"One more thing, Ruth," Art interrupted her thoughts. "Don't ever feel guilty when Amos complains about paying you 'big money.' He doesn't drink, smoke or gamble, and he's a good farmer, so I think he must have a stash of cash piled up somewhere—but probably not in a bank."

"It's probably filling a sock under his bed," Frieda ventured.

Ruth shuddered. "Another reason for me to wash my hands when he gives me cash each month."

The ride and conversation ended when they arrived at the General Merchandise.

Frieda was going to visit the doctor with some questions she had about the pregnancy. Art would accompany her and ask about the doctor coming out to see Amos. Ruth had extra time at the general store. She tried to quell the uncomfortable feeling she had. She busied herself with filling the grocery list she had been compiling the last couple of weeks. The grocery bill was put on the ledger for Amos to pay. She paid for her personal items, including some yarn, out of her own money. It was nice to have money in her purse for what she needed for herself, even though she was very careful with every penny she spent. Ruth appreciated Art telling her that Amos probably was not short of money. His future earning power was questionable, and then he had her salary to pay. Art had told her not to feel guilty about taking his money. She hadn't felt guilty; in fact, she had not even wondered if he was doing okay financially or if it was a financial hardship to have hired her. *I'm still the self-centered naïve girl I have always been,* she thought.

Lord, help me to think of others before myself. Help Amos to get back to good health. With a rush of guilt, she realized it was the first time she had prayed for him. It would not be the last, she vowed.

There were few customers in the store. Ruth concluded her business without incident.

Art and Frieda soon came into the store and made their purchases. On the way home, Ruth wondered if they were a little less exuberant and talkative than earlier. *They're probably both tired*, Ruth reasoned.

"The doctor will be out to see Amos next Monday," Art told her. If everything seems good, he'll cut both casts off then.

Art carried Ruth's groceries into the house for her and then hurried home for chores. Amos had little to say about the doctor coming on Monday.

"Are you nervous about the casts?" Ruth finally asked him.

"Naw. I was going to cut off them casts myself if the doc didn't come out. I got to get the legs limbered up before spring planting. Are you nervous about how much them casts are going to stink? There's been lots of sweat inside them after all these months, and who knows what other little critters have lived in there. Course I don't sweat so much when you forget to bring in wood."

Ruth wondered what he really thought. What if he couldn't use his legs? Farming and cows were all he knew. How would he make a living? She had some praying to do before Monday.

On Sunday evening after supper dishes, Amos got out his cards, and Ruth opened her Bible. Besides the other Bible reading, Ruth read from the Psalms each evening. Every night the one she chose seemed to have something special to say to her. "Would you like me to read something out loud, maybe something from the Psalms?"

There was a long silence. "I can't stop you from reading out loud if you got a notion to. They ain't some magic words that will change anything anyway."

Ruth pondered for some time and then chose Psalm 86, verses one to seven. Amos's eyes remained on his cards as she slowly read the words. Surely, he could see how comforting they were.

When she finished, she quietly asked if he would like her to pray aloud for the doctor's visit. I'll pray for you either way," she said, "But I'll be glad to pray out loud."

"All this mumble-jumble about prayer words," Amos scoffed. "My ma made me say words from a book when I was a kid. They didn't mean nothing and didn't change nothing. I don't expect nothing to happen here. My legs are either good or they're bad—your words ain't goin' to change what's in the casts right now."

Ruth didn't know what to say. She had no answer for him. Hattie or Frieda would have just the right gentle, encouraging words. She had nothing. She bowed her head and prayed silently for him, for his legs, to prepare him for the results. *May God keep him from bitterness*, she prayed, *if the results are not good.*

She sat there praying for a long time before she realized that Amos had not made a move in his solitaire game. He finally broke the silence. "S'pose if you want, you can pray out loud. I can't stop you from praying. I might as well hear what you say."

Ruth suddenly felt timid. Never in her life had she prayed a prayer out loud that was not written or recited in a group. But this was her Friend she was talking to, a Friend who was only too glad to listen.

"Our dear Lord Jesus," she began slowly, "We pray for the doctor's visit tomorrow. We pray that Amos's legs have healed perfectly and that he can be healthy and strong again. We ask that you give Amos peace about the future. Help him to know that You love him and have good plans for him. In Jesus's name, we pray, amen."

They sat in silence for a few minutes. Then Amos began shuffling the cards.

"Perfect legs, my eye. Ain't had perfect legs since I was a baby. Perfect legs would be bee-you-ti-ful." He drew out the word sarcastically. "This should be great. We'll see if all them scars I've had for years are gone, too. When do I start feeling all this magic inside the casts while my legs are getting perfect?"

"Why did you ask me to pray out loud if you don't like how I pray?" Ruth answered angrily. Then she saw his eyes. They were eyes full of concern, eyes that stared at her wanting some reassurance. For the first time, she realized how scared he was, and she was sorry for her anger. His life and future depended on how things turned out the next day.

"No magic," she said softly. "Just Jesus. I don't know how He will answer, but He'll give you something that's good."

"I don't see all those great things in your life either," he countered. "Being nursemaid to cows and living in this stinking house ain't what you planned, I don't reckon."

Tears pricked Ruth's eyes. His words hurt, but she realized he probably didn't mean to be hurtful. He was right about her situation.

"Maybe we'll both see God's plans tomorrow. I'll bring in more wood and start some dough for bread so there's something fresh for when the doctor comes."

"Well, ain't you the one," he said, back to familiar ground. "Hope the doc's got strong teeth."

Chapter 28

Monday morning was sunny, but the temperature was back below zero. Ruth hurried through the early morning barn chores, so she could get the bread dough formed into loaves before the doctor came. There was some leftover stew from the day before that she could offer him if he was there at dinner time.

However, dinner time came and went, and the bread was baked without any sign of the doctor. Amos ate very little but made a second pot of thick black coffee. Ruth followed her usual habit of adding almost half a cup of hot water from the tea kettle to her coffee cup before she could drink it.

"Did ya mean that last night about God having good plans for us?" Amos asked as he stared out the window, drinking yet another cup of coffee.

"Amos, I'm a new Christian, so I don't know the right things to say. But I know the Bible is true, and that's what it says in there. I think sometimes we don't recognize what is good for us. I'm not an expert in that department."

Brute gave three loud barks.

"He's coming!" Amos almost shouted the words. "The doc's here."

The doctor was a small round man with rosy cheeks from his cold ride. He had very little hair, but he did have long bushy white sideburns that made his head look like the head of a snowman. His voice was piercing; he wouldn't be one to mince words with his patients.

"You must be the Gottlieb lady I hear about," he greeted Ruth. His eyes twinkled. "Too bad you didn't get that teaching job you came for last fall. Amos here is more trouble than a room full of rascals."

Ruth sighed. This community needed more news to occupy itself. It seems she must be the topic of many conversations. Everyone knew her business.

"Well," the doctor continued, "If his legs haven't healed right, you might have good job security for a long time." No one smiled at his blunt remark.

"Have you had dinner?" Ruth asked, knowing the question was expected of her. She was relieved when the doctor said he had. "But that fresh bread aroma smells delightful. I'll have a couple slices of that before we get started with our business here."

Amos mumbled something about aromas don't always tell the whole story, but he poured a cup of coffee for the doctor while Ruth cut two thick slices of bread and set it on the table with a chunk of butter.

"And, now my dear," he said as he quickly ate the bread, "If you will warm a large kettle of water on the stove and then make yourself scarce. I don't think you'll want to be present. Oh, but I do have a favor to ask of you…could you take my horse into the barn? He's had a busy morning, and I don't want him standing out in the cold. I don't usually ask a woman to do outside chores, but I know you're used to it."

Ruth was glad to be excused from the room. "I was going out anyway," she said quickly. "I'll take your horse into the barn and give him some hay. It's soon time to start the afternoon chores, so I'll just stay out there after I take care of your horse."

She put a large kettle of melted snow on the stove to heat and began putting on her outside wraps.

"Notice how generous she is with my hay?" Amos grumbled. "Won't last until spring, and she gives it away. Maybe I'll subtract it from the bill you're going to give me."

"I think you'll want me to take my time sawing off those casts," the doctor retorted. "You don't want me worrying about my horse being hungry out in the barn. Now let me lift your leg unto this chair."

Ruth couldn't leave the house fast enough. She unhitched the docile horse from the fancy cutter and got him settled in the horse stall, loosening his harness and supplying him with a good amount of hay. She dawdled with the chores, threw down extra hay from the hay barn—enough for three or four days. The doctor still didn't come to the barn, so she played with the cats. "That hay supply is really shrinking," she told the listening cats. "I suppose Amos has reason to worry, but the animals need more food now with this cold weather." Isn't that what Karl had told her? "He'll have to worry about it later."

Right now, the future depended on how things were going in the house.

The doctor finally bustled into the darkening barn. "Not the most pleasant way to spend an afternoon," he said as he began adjusting the harness on his horse. Ruth wondered if the news was bad.

"That man doesn't worry too much about keeping things clean. Course, he couldn't clean anything inside the casts, but he probably hasn't changed clothes since I put the casts on last August. Good thing I ate your bread before I started sawing. Not too appetizing after I got started. I cut his pants and underwear off and threw them away. Oh, and I threw the remains of the casts into my cutter. I don't think you'll want to keep those for any souvenirs. The house will probably smell better now."

Ruth understood the doctor's complaints about cleanliness, but she was impatient to hear about the results.

"How about his legs, Doctor? Have they healed? Will he be able to walk and work again?"

"Well, those muscles have atrophied pretty badly. It's going to take a while before he has any strength. But he's ornery enough that I expect he'll do anything he wants to in a month or so. Actually, those legs came out as close to perfect as I could hope for."

The house was quiet and dark and cold when Ruth entered. *I need to build up the fire and light the lamp. I wonder why Amos isn't sitting at the table waiting for supper. He has surely heard the good news. After not eating much of anything all day, he's got to be starving.*

Ruth heard a sound from the closed door to Amos's bedroom—a squeaking or whimpering sound. Brute was quietly napping under the table, so the sound didn't come from him. What was it? She put her ear to the bedroom door to hear better. She realized what she was hearing. Amos was sobbing.

Chapter 29

Ruth had made herself some supper and was about to climb the ladder to bed when Amos came out of his bedroom. Ruth looked at him and then looked again before realizing it was the same man. He was dressed in clean clothes. His pants legs were no longer slit to fit over his casts. Presumably, with the help of the doctor, he had taken a bath of sorts. His face was clean-shaven. He sent a self-conscious look in Ruth's direction and walked slowly to his place at the table. He was using a cane, but reaching the table took all his strength.

"Can't a fellow get something to eat around here?" he asked. He tried to speak loudly, but he was clearly out of breath from the short walk.

"I'll scramble some eggs for you," Ruth said quickly. "It will just take a few minutes. I have some ham chunks to put in it. Oh, and I'll toast some bread on the hot stove top. I think there's a boiled potato in the pantry to fry."

"It sounds better than it'll probably taste."

Ruth found it easy to ignore the remark.

"I'm sure you're exhausted after your ordeal, but you look so much better without your casts. Was it terribly painful to take them off? The doctor said everything was a success. He used the word 'perfect' like in our prayer last night. God heard and answered the prayer with a 'yes.' I'm happy for you."

"And I'll be a lot happier when I get something to eat," Amos groused.

Ruth surprised even herself with how quickly she slid the food onto Amos's plate. She poured two cups of coffee and sat down across the table from him.

"Maybe you're too tired to talk, much less think about the future. But I'm so curious. Will you be able to take over the farm chores by springtime? Can you plant your crops?"

"What are ya talking about?" Amos answered between huge forkfuls of food. "Of course, I can take over the chores and do the planting. Do ya think I'm an invalid?"

"You have been an invalid," she reminded him. "I'm glad for you if you think you'll be able to do all your farming again."

A silence followed. The clock ticked loudly, and Brute sighed from the table, next to Amos's feet.

"How long do you think you'll be needing help?"

"What's your big hurry?" Amos replied. "Where are you off to?"

"I'm not in a big hurry to go…because I have no place to go. I just have to start making some plans."

"You do that. My plan now is to get some good sleep without them casts. Then my plan tomorrow is to get to the barn. I want to see what kind of job you've been doing with my cows. And, to see how much hay is left."

Ruth sighed. She could have repeated the last sentence with him, word for word.

Amos limped off to bed after finishing his meal.

Ruth sat at the table for a long time, no longer tired. What would happen when she was no longer needed here? *Lord, you said you have a plan for me, a plan to give me a future. Something to hope for. I'm happy for Amos's success, and I'll be happy to leave here, but where will I go? What is my future? Please, Lord, take care of my future—give me a plan. Give me something to hope for. Amen.*

Ruth brought down her writing tablet and pen from the attic and began writing.

Dear Mother,

I have not written for too long. I'm sorry. The cold weather makes for many extra chores.

Amos had his casts taken off today. The doctor said the broken bones healed well, and he should be able to take over his own farming by springtime. That's good news for him.

Please give my best to Anna, Kenneth, and the children. Have things slowed down at the parsonage now in cold weather? How is Anna feeling? It's good you are helping her. I send my love to all of you.

Ruth

Ruth blotted the ink and folded the letter into an envelope. She took out another sheet of paper and started the second letter.

Dear Karl and Hattie,

I hope this cold has not made the chores too hard for you. We will all be glad when warmer weather comes.

Ruth repeated the news about Amos's casts. She went on to write:

Hattie, your recipes and food suggestions have been very helpful. My bread might even be a little more edible—but only a little. Karl, I hope your arthritis has not been too bad. I want you both to know that I have been reading the Bible every evening lately. I read some parts out loud to Amos. I never know if he listens, but he must admit that God answered the prayer about his legs.

My time with you over Christmas was very special to me.

Ruth

Ruth propped up the letters against the sugar bowl on the cupboard. They would get mailed the next time someone stopped in before going to town. She climbed slowly to her attic bed.

Sleep was a long time coming. God always keeps His promises, she knew, but it was hard to have no plan and no future.

Chapter 30

Amos did not go to the barn the following morning. In fact, he kept his usual routine of making coffee and playing solitaire. Getting around the kitchen with the cane instead of the crutches seemed all he could manage for the present.

All that week, Ruth expected a visit from Art and Frieda. Ruth knew they would be eager to hear the results of the doctor's visit on Monday. She even made some cookies—rather flavorless and hard but dunking in Amos's coffee helped. Amos never commented on the cookies, but he ate enough that Ruth had to hide some in the cold box in the back room, so she would have some on hand.

It was the middle of the following week before Art's sleigh came crunching over the hard snow of the driveway. The bells on the horses' harnesses alerted Ruth to the arrival before she saw the sleigh. She was in the cow yard using the ax to chip away ice before pumping in more water. It was cold but a bright sunny day, and Ruth had let the cows out of the barn before starting this chore. She had already put out some hay, but they were more thirsty than hungry. Now they pushed around her, waiting for the water.

"Be patient, Black Face," she told a particularly pushy cow. "If I don't get the ice out, there's no room to put water in."

As Ruth worked, she kept an eye on the sleigh as it stopped in front of the house. She was disappointed when she saw Art was alone. He covered his team with warm blankets and then pulled a large wooden box out of the back of the sleigh. Ruth knew this would be baked items from Frieda. The box was always a part of their visit.

Ruth quickly pumped enough water into the tank to quench the cows' thirst, and then she hurried to the house. The barn cleaning could wait.

Art and Amos were at the table drinking coffee. They were discussing Amos's new appearance without his casts. Ruth saw they were eating some cookies that Frieda had sent. After greeting Art, she hurried to the cold box to get a few of her own to put on the table.

"I'm disappointed that Frieda did not come with you," Ruth told Art, sitting down with a cup of coffee. She took two of Frieda's cookies rather than her own.

"This is just a quick visit to drop off some baked goods for you and to check how Amos's doctor visit turned out. But I would like you to come to visit Frieda—maybe Friday? She'd like for you to come. Maybe you could have dinner with us that day if you find you have a little free time in the middle of the day. We'll send some dinner for Amos when I bring you back. He tells me he doesn't feel like going out yet, but we're really glad those casts came off and everything looks good."

"Friday dinner sounds good," Ruth answered quickly. "I'll be ready at noon. How is Frieda feeling?" She thought the pregnancy was probably the reason Frieda did not accompany Art on this visit.

"That's why we'd like you to come," Art answered slowly. After a pause, he continued, "Frieda lost the baby last week, and she's really feeling low. Having you come will help her, I'm sure."

Ruth was stunned. Pregnancies weren't talked about much until it was obvious that babies would soon be born. Anna was the only one that Ruth knew that talked about her unborn children (or rather her mother did). Ruth didn't know anyone who had had a miscarriage.

"What happened?" Ruth blurted out.

"Guess it just happens that way sometimes, the doctor says. But it's still hard to take. Well, I don't want to keep the horses standing out there in the cold. I'll tell Frieda we'll see you on Friday. She'll like that."

Art quickly left, taking the empty box to refill another time. Ruth hadn't even thought to thank him for the things he brought.

"What can I say to Frieda to make her feel better?" Ruth wondered aloud. She was already apprehensive about visiting her friend.

"You'll think of somethin' to gab about by then," Amos said shortly. "I ate enough of Frieda's cookies to last me a while. You can put yours back in the cold box. You might as well clean the barn before you make the dinner. I ain't hungry now anyways."

Ruth automatically bundled up in her outer clothes and went out to resume the barn chores. All through the next days, she prayed. "Why, Lord, would you take their baby? They are such good people and would have been such good parents. What am I going to say to Frieda? Help me to say something that will help, that will make a difference."

Ruth had finished the daytime chores early on Friday and was waiting for Art when he came. She left a sandwich for Amos on the table since his dinner would be late. As she walked out the door to Art's sleigh, she grabbed her Bible lying on the table.

The trip to the Weiler home was quiet. Ruth had never known Art to be without words and jovial words at that. It made Ruth more apprehensive than ever.

Frieda met Ruth at the door. The two friends looked at each other silently for a moment, and then Frieda threw her arms around Ruth and broke into sobs.

Dinner was forgotten for the time being. Art went out to take care of the horses. The women sat on the couch, and Frieda clutched Ruth's hands.

"I'm such a mess," Frieda began. "I thought I had such strong faith, a faith that nothing could shake. Yet here I am, grieving like one who has no hope. Art and I know our baby is in heaven right now, but we were so excited. I couldn't wait to hold him, to cuddle him, to love him. Now I won't see him until I get to heaven." Frieda wiped more tears.

Ruth was groping for words, but she was also puzzled. "Do you think your baby is in heaven? He (or she) wasn't even born."

"Oh, Ruth, of course, he is in heaven. He knew Jesus. He heard all about salvation from the Bible readings that Art and I had. I made sure I sang all the Gospel songs I know. I know he is in heaven. I just will miss having him here with me here on earth. We don't know if our baby was a boy or girl, but I always thought of him as a boy and referred to him in masculine terms."

"But was he a real baby already? You were only about three months along in your pregnancy. Was he completely formed? Do you think God knew him?"

Ruth felt so foolish for blurting all these questions. She had come here to comfort Frieda, and instead, she was trying to get answers for her own stupidity.

Frieda blew her nose and stood to get her Bible on the end table by the couch. "I can't tell you why I lost him, but I can answer those questions. God knows our baby. Here let me read these passages. I've pretty much memorized them these last few days." Frieda paged through her Bible to Jeremiah, chapter one, verse five. "God says, 'Before I formed thee in the belly, I knew thee; and before you camest forth out of the womb I sanctified thee.'"

All of this was new to Ruth. "Oh, Frieda, I'm such a foolish Christian. I don't know anything about these subjects. How could I be almost 20 years old and still be so naïve? I went to church every Sunday and apparently learned nothing. Since Christmas, I feel like I've awakened from a long sleep. I'm learning as fast as I can from my Bible reading each day, but I still know practically nothing. All I know is that I'm a terrible sinner—my thoughts are ugly, my actions are careless, and even though it might be getting a little better, I still hate Amos many days. I can only be eternally grateful that Jesus died to take away all those horrible sins.

"I came to try to help you feel better. I'm sorry, but I couldn't find anything in the Bible about a woman losing an unborn child. The last couple of nights, I've been reading in Philippians. The verse I planned to read to you today is Philippians 4, verse 19. 'But my God shall supply all your needs according to his riches in glory by Christ Jesus.' Jesus is all I know, but I know He will help you with this need. And I'm so glad to know your baby is in heaven. I'm the one who is learning."

Frieda smiled. "Thank you, Ruth. You chose a beautiful verse to share with me. It is very comforting. It's another one that I will memorize. While you couldn't find anything in the Bible about a woman losing her unborn child, we know that God lost His Son on the cross.

"Now, I must remember that this loss is God's will for me right now, although I don't know why."

"But you'll have more children, right? You and Art are young and strong, and God surely knows you would be good parents."

"Of course, that's our hope and prayer," Frieda answered. "But we've been married for almost four years, and we have no children yet. Would you pray for us, that God would give us children?"

"Oh, I will, I will," Ruth answered immediately. She felt honored to be asked to pray about a situation. It was the first time someone had requested prayer from her.

"I'm going to make a prayer list and put it in my Bible. You and Art will be at the top of my list. Oh, and I'm going to copy some verses down and try to memorize them each evening. If I try to memorize out loud, maybe even Amos can learn some."

They laughed at that. Somehow the idea of Amos quoting Scripture couldn't be imagined.

"God is a God of miracles," Frieda reminded Ruth. "And memorizing Scripture verses is a wonderful idea. If you're feeling like a baby Christian with a lot to learn, start with this verse in Psalm 32. Here it is, verse 8: 'I will instruct thee and teach thee in the way which thou shalt go: I will guide thee with mine eye.'"

"I will quote it to you the next time we are together," Ruth promised. "But I wish I had more comfort for you."

"Oh, Ruth, your whole visit has been a comfort. Thank you for reminding me that Jesus died to take away my sin. I admit I've not let Him—or Art, for that matter—into my grief. I've kept it too tight around me to let anyone get close to me.

"I've been feeling so guilty. When the cramping started, I was carrying some boards out to Art's workshop. I was impatient for Art to get started on shelves in the baby's room. The doctor said that since I'm strong and in good health, that probably had nothing to do with my miscarriage. I just wish I was sure I didn't bring it on myself. Life is so fragile; we lose it so quickly, and it changes everything."

Suddenly Ruth was reliving Ben's death again. It hadn't invaded her thoughts or dreams for some time, but now it came with such vengeance it took her breath away. She could hear Rex barking with a frenzy, her hurrying to the barnyard…and then seeing Ben's body being thrown into the air like a gunny sack…the bull standing over him when his body hit the ground with a sickening thud.

What did Frieda say about holding the grief so closely around you that no one could get close.... dealing with a guilty conscience as well as the sadness? Ruth realized she, too, had felt guilty in Ben's death. She accompanied him everywhere as he worked around the farm. In that instance, even though the new Holstein bull frightened her, or maybe because the bull frightened her, she had walked down the driveway to check on some lady slippers she had seen blossoming the day before. If she had been with him, perhaps she could have distracted the bull by waving her apron or shouting or throwing something....

For the first time, Ruth relived that terrible afternoon out loud to Frieda. Once again, she could see Ben's body being thrown in the air. It didn't matter whether her eyes were open or shut. Not even Karl and Hattie knew she had witnessed his death. Now looking at Frieda's compassionate eyes and hearing the words from her own voice, she found God's peace...He had supplied her needs.... the verse she hoped would comfort Frieda brought comfort to her own soul. Yes, God is a God of miracles.

The two women sat together holding hands and wiping tears, each feeling God's healing touch for their grief. Finally, they were aware of Art gently clearing his throat.

"I'm sorry, ladies, I can see that you are good for each other. But Ruth is going to have to get back for evening chores before too long, and I don't remember that we've had dinner yet."

"Oh, my goodness, Ruth, what kind of hostess am I? I invited you for dinner, and I forget to feed you. The stew is on the stove and done. I'll quickly cut some bread. Come to the table."

The meal was delicious, but they ate quickly. Frieda brought out pie for dessert. "We'll each have a piece, and then you take the rest of it for you and Amos. I'll put some stew in a kettle for you to take for him. His dinner is going to become his supper, I'm afraid. I have another loaf of bread to send, too. I've not felt like doing much since last week, but I still cook and bake. I told Art it's something I can do with my hands. Besides that, we do need to eat."

Art brought the horses and sleigh around to the door, and the women hugged in parting. "You've been a comfort to me," Frieda whispered. "Thank you."

"No, no, you have comforted me. I came, hoping I had something for you, and instead, you filled me. Thank you."

The ride home was as quiet as the previous trip, but Ruth felt peace in her heart. She prayed that Art and Frieda were feeling the same.

Chapter 31

Ruth had expected Amos to be impatient to get outside, to push his limits of physical ability. Instead, she was surprised that he seemed timid and afraid to do anything beyond his normal routine. The day after Ruth visited Frieda, she decided maybe he needed some encouragement. He was making his big pot of coffee as usual. He still leaned on his cane as he walked between the stove and the table, but he walked with much less effort.

"When do you want to try going outside?" Ruth asked Amos as they sat down to breakfast. It would soon be two weeks since the casts had been removed. "I can help you go down the steps."

Ruth had already been out to do the early chores and the morning milking. Some warmth could be felt from the sun as it shone in the east window.

"This would be a good day to try going out," she encouraged.

"That snow is gonna start melting…it's going to be slipperier than all get out on them steps," Amos answered harshly. "I ain't takin' no chances on rolling down them steps and breaking somethin' else."

"I'll go out when I finish the breakfast dishes and get the steps all cleaned off," Ruth offered. "Just standing outside and getting some fresh air will be good for you."

For several days, the steps were the extent of Amos's outside ventures. But he stood there many times a day, Brute at his side, staring off toward the barn. Spring was making a comeback. The sun continued to shine each day, and spring birds began to sing.

"I seen a robin," Amos stated one morning as he came back into the kitchen from the steps. His voice was sharp, almost grating, but underneath, Ruth heard the excitement of a small boy. She saw in Amos things she hadn't seen before.... maybe she hadn't been looking. "I think I'll walk out to the barn after dinner."

"Do you want me to hang onto your arm, and you can use the cane in your other hand?" Ruth asked.

"I'm goin' by myself—me and Brute. I want to see how them cows are gettin' along."

The food was hardly eaten before Amos was putting on his winter coat from his bedroom closet. Ruth watched from the window as he started out for the barn. He walked slowly, cautiously, putting one foot down carefully before taking another step. He pushed the cane into the snow beside him, yet it still seemed like he was walking on a tight rope. It took a long time, but finally, Ruth saw him stand by the fence, looking at the cows in the barnyard. He stood motionless, leaning heavily on his cane.

She busied herself around the kitchen, for the first time being there without Amos. She took advantage of the solitude by washing the kitchen floor and cleaning out the chamber pot. He still had not returned. She put on her own outside gear; it was time to do the afternoon chores. Glancing out the window one more time as she was about to leave the house, she saw the cows gathering around the empty water tank. Amos was at the pump beginning to pump water.

"I always chop away the ice before pumping more water," Ruth said as she hurried out to the tank

Amos stared at her for a full minute before replying. "Are you tellin' me how to do my own chores? Well, ain't you the one! Guess I'll pump water when I feel like it."

He had his usual derision in his voice, but he was breathing hard and pumped only a few times.

"You finish it," he panted. "I'm goin' to the house. And I'm gonna have to talk to the neighbors about buying some hay before the end of the month. You've been feeding way too much."

Ruth took the rebuke silently. She didn't disagree with him even in her own mind. She had been too generous in her feeding. Well, he would just have to buy some more hay. Or, pray for an early spring.

The next day Amos went out again. This time he went straight to the barn with Ruth following. He sat down heavily on a milking stool; his eyes swept over everything. The animals eyed him curiously.

"Where's the black cat?" he demanded. "He still around?"

"He's always the first one here for his food," Ruth replied. "Here he comes now."

Blackie came blinking and yawning from the hay pile in the corner of the barn. He stopped and stared at Amos. Amos held out his hand toward the cat and wiggled his fingers. Blackie seemed torn between visiting Amos and his food pan. Hunger won out, and he checked to see if any milk had been set out for him. Amos shrugged his shoulders and muttered something under his breath.

Ruth went about her chores. The chores were now a routine for her, but she felt uncomfortable with Amos carefully watching everything she did.

She stepped into the feed room to measure out the feed needed for each milk cow. She thought she heard soft talking in the main barn. Had a neighbor stopped in without her hearing the sleigh and horses come into the yard? She looked out of the feed room curiously. Amos was standing between two milk cows, his arms resting on each one's back.

"How've you been, ya big lout?" he asked the big brown shorthorn. He ran his hand along her back. "Ya remember me, don't cha?"

Turning his attention to the cow on the other side, he continued talking, "And, you, old Spots, you survived another winter. Just look at ya…fat and sassy like always."

Amos limped over and stood between another two cows. "Hey, hey, there, Knobby Knees, are you still my best milker?"

Ruth pulled her head back into the feed room before Amos could see her. His obvious affection for his cows touched her. Tears stung her eyes.

She coughed slightly before carrying the feed into the main barn. Amos sheepishly limped back to the stool and sat down heavily.

After his first couple trips to the barn, Amos seemed to quickly regain confidence. He often accompanied Ruth when she went out to do the chores. He sat on the milking stool and watched every detail of everything that happened. Ruth thought she had the chores down to a smooth operation, but now everything was scrutinized and criticized. She explained over and over why she did things as she did, why she did them in the order that she did.

"Why do you wash the cows' bags first before you give them their ground feed?"

"Because I bring warm water from the house. I'm sure they prefer their bags washed with warm water."

"They prefer to eat. Give them the ground feed first."

Similar conversation followed.

"The chickens don't need any of the skim milk. Give it all to the calves."

"I don't give the chickens much. I just give them a little after each milking. It's a nice treat for them."

"Chickens don't need treats. We have chickens to lay eggs, not to eat treats. Give the skim milk to the calves."

Resentment burned. She had been doing just fine all these months doing it her way. Why couldn't he wait until he took over to do it the way he wanted?

But then, there were the times when Amos would hold a cat on his lap, stroking it and mumbling words to it. Or, he would stand between two cows, rubbing their sides and reminding them that they would soon be eating green grass in the pasture.

The words were always said softly when he thought Ruth was out of sight or earshot. What she did overhear made her realize how much he had missed the animals. She should have told him more details about things in the barn. She had not thought enough about how he felt. She hadn't thought…how true those words were. "Lord, will I ever stop being so self-centered, thinking only of myself? Help me to see Amos's needs, to be aware of his feelings."

It gradually became easier to go along with Amos's demands with how things should be done. *It did work fine my way,* she thought. *But he's done it his way all his life…I must remember these are his animals. I am just his hired help. "God, help me from being so self-righteous and proud."*

***

Sam Bjork, a neighbor who was a regular visitor to Amos, stopped that afternoon on his way home from town. He had made a few purchases for Amos and had charged them at the store.

"He didn't even ask me what we needed here in the way of groceries. Guess he could have stopped on the way into town for a list first," Amos complained when he left.

Amos's lack of gratitude always amazed Ruth. She didn't remind him that this same neighbor had stopped faithfully through the winter, and Amos's list usually consisted of the same things. Besides that, he had often mailed letters for the two of them. And, today, he had brought Ruth a letter from Mother.

Both Amos and Ruth were in the barn when Sam had stopped. He gave the letter to Ruth personally, then he and Amos went to the house for coffee. Ruth hoped they wouldn't eat all the cookies. Finding time to bake was always a challenge. Art and Frieda hadn't been by since Frieda lost the baby.

Being alone in the barn gave Ruth the privacy to read her letter.

Dear Ruth,

I am so happy that you are soon done with that horrid job! I can't imagine how you kept at it all these months. Now please start looking for a school for next fall. This is when superintendents are looking for teachers.

Anna is feeling very well. Of course, it is good for her that I am here to help with the work. Now she can take a nap every afternoon. Andy and Alice are growing fast. Kenneth is a very popular preacher.

No, things have not slowed down much since Christmas. We seem to be the hub of the social events in the congregation. Kenneth and Anna have started a song fest every Sunday night at the church. Many people come if the weather is not too cold. I stay home with the little ones, of course. It is good that I am here to help them out.

Remember to start looking for a school right away.

Love,

Mother

It was a week later when Ruth received another letter; this one from Hattie.

Dear Ruth,

We were so happy to hear that you have been reading the Bible each evening.

Don't be discouraged if Amos doesn't seem to be hearing what you read. God's word has great power.

It is good that Amos's legs are healing well and that he can soon take over his own work. What a joy that must be for him. Your life will change, too.

Since you were here at Christmas time, Karl and I have been talking some things over. First of all, we owe you a huge apology. I can only say that our grief over losing Ben kept us from thinking straight. It was our agreement with Ben—although nothing was put into writing—that he would have the southeast forty acres for his work on the farm all those years. Since you are his wife, that should now belong to you.

Also, Karl's arthritis is becoming so painful that he will not be able to continue to milk the cows. Having a woman doing barn work is not what we think is ideal; but if you would like to do the milking, it would be a great help. At this time, Karl can still do the other chores.

There are two schools within a close area. If you are interested in teaching, that could be done in addition to the milking if and when these schools need teachers.

We would like to offer our home to be your home. The income from the southeast forty would be yours. You could build there as was your plan when Ben was alive, or you could continue to live with us as part of our family. It would give us joy to have you live here as our daughter; you would be most welcome.

We have prayed about this situation and ask you to do the same. We await your answer.

Love,

Hattie

Chapter 32

Ruth's head bobbed in rhythm with the chugging of the train. Everything had a dream-like quality. Once again, she was on the train to Karl and Hattie's farm. So much had happened since she had made this trip at Christmas time.

Her job with Amos was finished. She had seen it through to completion. The cows were out in the pasture now. The barn chores were down to milking, caring for the chickens, and feeding a couple baby calves kept in the barn. How wonderful it was to have warm weather—no ice to chop from the water tank, no bitter cold to seep into her bones as she worked in the barnyard, no chapped hands so rough that they bled.

She relaxed now in her train seat, thinking about the last few days. Amos had done the chores almost single-handedly. Ruth helped only because there was not much for her to do.

***

Paul Thompson had brought back Amos's team of horses. Ruth

shuddered when she thought of how they threw their heads and pawed the ground, eager to get to work. What a blessing she did not have to take care of them through the winter. When Paul Thompson had taken them to his home in October, Ruth had not considered that it was God's intervention that kept her from having that responsibility. Back then, she had not considered God's intervention in anything she did. Now she repeated Romans 8:38: "'All things work together for good to them that love God.' I do love you, Lord," she whispered. "Every day, I'm finding out how much I love You."

Neighbors were still offering to help Amos with some of the spring field work, but he turned down most of the offers. "Gotta get these legs in good order. Guess I can take care of my own fields."

Ruth thought it would have been nice to thank the neighbors for their attempts to help. That was not Amos's way.

Leaving Amos was… awkward. They stood in front of the house. The small, battered trunk was on the steps, ready to go. Art and Frieda would be arriving in their wagon any minute to take her to the train station. Ruth held out a Bible. She had had Frieda special order it some weeks before. She felt shy about giving it to Amos.

"I hope you will read it every day."

"With them big words? Newspapers is easier."

"But reading the Bible will give you lasting benefits. I hope you will try to read it."

Amos turned the Bible over in his hands. "Ain't never had a book before. Would be something to brag about if I read through that thing during my lifetime."

"And, when you finish reading it once, you can go back and read it again. That's what Frieda told me. Jesus wants to talk to you through the Bible. You can talk to him by praying."

"If everybody prayed as much as you, God would get a sore ear. If I pray, I'm gonna get right to the point."

Ruth hoped that meant he would try to pray.

"Thank you, Amos, for giving me a job and letting me stay here when I had no place to go," Ruth said hesitantly. Pleasantries with Amos were never easy.

"Well, ain't you the…" Amos began, but stopped. The words threatened to choke him, but he continued, "Except for feeding them cows way too much hay, spoiling the chickens with skim milk, and usin' up all the eggs for meals, you did okay. I woulda had to have sold everything if you hadn't done them chores for me. Guess it worked out both ways."

"God does nice things like that."

"Wasn't so nice to get my legs broke."

"But He fixed them. And maybe you learned some things from all you went through. I know I did."

"Hah," Amos snorted and then became quiet. They heard Art's horses and wagon turning in at the driveway.

"Guess I learned that not all women know how to cook." A pause. "Anyway…uh…thanks."

Ruth smiled to herself as she remembered the embarrassed look on his face as he turned quickly to meet Art and Frieda.

The trip to town was bittersweet. She realized how much she would miss these dear friends. "You can come back to visit us, you know," Frieda said more than once. "Anyway, I have the perfect reason for you to come."

She looked at Art, who gave her a smile and a nod. "We're expecting another baby," Frieda confided. "If it's God's will that this baby goes full term and is born alive and well, we'd like you to come to the baby's baptism and be the sponsor."

"Oh, Frieda, of course I would!" Ruth replied joyously. "But how can you want me when I'm such a baby Christian myself?"

"I don't think you can accurately call yourself a baby Christian anymore," Art joined in. "You've grown up fast. Trials do that sometimes."

"Write to us as soon as you get settled there. I know God will use you to be a blessing to your in-laws," Frieda said as they pulled up at the train station. Art carried her trunk that held everything she had in the world.

"Here's some lunch to eat on the train," Frieda said, pushing a box of food into Ruth's arms. "And a sunbonnet that I made for you. This is for relaxing out in the sunshine. I don't think you've done much relaxing the last months."

Ruth's eyes blurred with tears as she hugged them both. "I have no gift for you, but I'll pray for you both every day," she whispered.

"That's the best gift you can give us," Art assured her. Frieda could only nod through her tears.

***

Saying the good-byes were the worst part, Ruth thought as the train sped through the countryside. Now she felt refreshed as she saw the pastures green with new grass and cows frolicking after spending the winter months in barns. The black soil of the worked fields waited for the seeds that would burst into new plants. New beginnings were all around her. *In me, too,* she thought. *I feel this new life in Christ, this joy of knowing Jesus and His love.*

Her eyes were closed in reverie when she heard an outburst of laughter from the back of the train car. It was so full of joy that it made her smile, and she turned in her seat. A young man was laughing as he visited with several people. He made his way through the swerving aisle and caught her eye.

"I'm sorry if I startled you," he told her, "I know I laugh too much and too loud. But life is good, isn't it?"

"Oh, I totally agree," Ruth smiled. "And your laughter is good to hear."

"Where are you heading for?" he asked her.

"I'm going to Twin Oaks. I am making my home there with my dead husband's parents." The words came easily; there was no longer a sting to them.

"Hey, I'm going there, too. And, I am going to make my home, temporarily, with my uncle and aunt. I hope to buy a farm around there as soon as I can afford to. I grew up to be a farmer, but I have four older brothers, and my dad's farm can only support so many. Uncle said there were farming opportunities around Twin Oaks, and he and Auntie said I was welcome to stay with them—providing I work for my keep. I'm glad to do that.

"Maybe you know my uncle? He's the preacher at the German Lutheran church—Rev. Schwartz."

Ruth caught her breath. Now she realized why his eyes looked so familiar.

"Oh, yes, I do know him. He's a wonderful pastor. My in-laws—and I—belong to his church."

"Well, then, I'll see you next Sunday. I'll look forward to it. Now I better get back to my little sister sitting up ahead. She's going to visit for a few days before going back home. This is her first train ride, and she likes an explanation of everything she sees."

Ruth smiled as she watched him sit down with a young girl at the front of the train car. She soon heard that joyous outburst of laughter as he talked with his sister.

She settled back in her seat and saw a farmer in a passing field, working with his horses and plow. Suddenly she couldn't wait to arrive at the Gottlieb farm. She wanted to be part of the soil, of new life. "Let me be the daughter they never had," she prayed. "Let me be the help they need. Let me bring them joy."

***

Karl dragged her trunk up to the back of the wagon while Hattie gave her a quick hug.

"Oh, Ruth, thank you for coming to us. Karl is thrilled to have you here. We have so much to show you," Hattie said warmly. Her eyes had regained some of the sparkle lost in the grief of the past year.

"The garden is just beginning to come up, the cat has had her kittens, and the cows are doing so well now that they are in the pasture. We want to share all of this with you. Your coming has given us new life and new hope. Welcome home, Daughter."

About the Author

Delores Kading is a retired Christian Day School teacher who lives with her husband on a small farm in northwestern Minnesota. They have three adult children, a daughter-in-law, two sons-in-law, and four granddaughters. Delores enjoys all aspects of homemaking—gardening, cooking, baking, and entertaining guests. She loves the farm life and caring for their animals. Her family is her greatest earthly blessing.

www.ingramcontent.com/pod-product-compliance
Lightning Source LLC
Chambersburg PA
CBHW030359310726
48979CB00001B/364

* 9 7 8 1 7 3 7 5 1 7 7 9 5 *